# CAPE MENACE

## A CAPE MAY HISTORICAL MYSTERY

## AMY M. READE

PAU HANA PUBLISHING

Publisher's Note: This is a work of fiction. Names, characters, places, and incidents are a product of the author's imagination. Locales and public names are sometimes used for atmospheric purposes. Any resemblance to actual people, living or dead, or to businesses, companies, events, institutions, or locales is completely coincidental.

Pau Hana Publishing

Print ISBN: 978-1-7326907-8-3

Ebook ISBN: 978-1-7326907-9-0

Printed in the United States of America

# BOOKS BY AMY M. READE

## STANDALONE BOOKS

*Secrets of Hallstead House*

*The Ghosts of Peppernell Manor*

*House of the Hanging Jade*

## THE MALICE SERIES

*The House on Candlewick Lane*

*Highland Peril*

*Murder in Thistlecross*

## THE JUNIPER JUNCTION HOLIDAY MYSTERY SERIES

*The Worst Noel*

*Dead, White, and Blue*

*Be My Valencrime*

*Ghouls' Night Out (coming soon!)*

## THE LIBRARIES OF THE WORLD MYSTERY SERIES

*Trudy's Diary*

*Dutch Treat (coming soon!)*

*For Jason and Adam*

# ACKNOWLEDGMENTS

I would like to thank Kate Wyatt of the Greater Cape May Historical Society for her invaluable assistance in meeting with me, answering my questions, helping with my research, showing me the secrets of the Colonial House Museum, and providing my imagination with fodder for future stories. I look forward to learning more from her. With that being said, any errors in this book are mine and mine alone.

I would also like to thank my editor, Jeni Chappelle, whose advice is always spot-on. If you're looking for an editor, I highly recommend Jeni. You can find her at https://www.jenichappelleeditorial.com/.

I would also like to thank my husband, John, who is always my first reader, and two other special people whose help with my manuscript was invaluable: Holly Bolicki and Patti Linder. Many thanks for all your assistance, ladies.

# GLOSSARY

ague: a fever marked by fits of chills and sweating

apothecary: a person who prepares and sells medicinal remedies. Such remedies were often made from herbs and spices. The apothecary was often considered a physician. "Apothecary" can also refer to the shop where the medicinal remedies were mixed and sold.

counterpane: quilt

Goodman: the husband of a Goodwife.

Goodwife: a title denoting a married woman. The social status of the woman would have been lower than that of a woman referred to as "Mistress."

Goody: a shortened form of Goodwife.

hang in chains: a vile, desperate person

homespun: coarse, handwoven cloth

hyssop: a member of the mint family, often used in medicinal preparations for digestive and intestinal issues.

kid shoes: shoes made from soft, thin leather

laudanum: a strong opioid tincture with a bitter taste, used for pain relief

lawn: a fine, plain-weave textile

physick book: a reference book of the human body, including maladies, diseases, and remedies

trencher: dinner plate

# PREFACE

It was a humid summer day in the year 1623 when Captain Cornelius Jacobsen Mey, sailing under the auspices of the Dutch West India Company on the ship *Blyde Broodschap* ("Good Tidings"), first laid eyes on the peninsula of land separating the Atlantic Ocean from the Delaware Bay. He immediately christened the land "Cape Mey" and that name has persisted through the ages, albeit with a slight change in spelling.

At the time of Captain Mey's "discovery," this part of North America had been home to Native Americans for centuries. In particular, the Kechemeches tribe, part of the Lenni-Lenape, a peace-loving branch of the mighty Algonquins, fished and hunted on these shores long before the arrival of the Europeans. Although Native Americans are not featured in this story, their long-ago presence can still be felt in this area, especially in place names and roadways, which were often constructed along ancient Lenni-Lenape footpaths.

Upon the arrival of the Europeans and with the introduction of never-before-encountered European diseases, the population of Native Americans in this area slowly began to decline. Within a hundred years of Captain Mey's first glimpse of the cape, the population of Cape May County, which had been incorporated in 1695, was less than seven hundred people of European descent and far fewer Native Americans.

There was only one settlement on the cape at that time in history, and it was known by a variety of names: Portsmouth, Falmouth, Cape May Town, Town Bank, and New England Town (or simply, "Town"). It was a tiny settlement, with less than twenty houses and few comforts. Many items, such as saddles, sugar, and cooking utensils, had to be purchased and brought from Philadelphia, which was an arduous two-day journey distant.

It was topography that dictated where this first settlement would be located on the cape. The town, about four miles north of Cape Island, where sits the present City of Cape May, overlooked the Delaware Bay from a high embankment. Fishermen and whalers found it easier to moor their boats in the calmer waters and protected coves of the bay than to be at the mercy of the open ocean in all its moods.

Though whaling was one of the original lures that brought men and their families to Cape May, the industry did not last for many years. Farming, shipbuilding, and the production and sale of building materials (in particular, cedar shingles) became more stable and profitable pursuits. Farming, especially, was a common undertaking, since the sandy, loamy soil along this part of the Atlantic seaboard was perfect for many crops, from maize to vegetables.

Pirates were also known to frequent the waters of the Delaware Bay because it presented a multitude of good hiding places. Captain Kidd and Blackbeard were among the more famous pirates who allegedly visited these shores. Pirates, though outlaws, were often welcomed by the settlers because they brought goods and coin into the economy. There were always those, however, who wished to curry favor with the crown and the provincial governors and these people presented great challenges to the pirates.

Alas, the original settlement in Cape May County was lost to the pounding waves of the Delaware Bay and the erosion of the banks below the village. The original Town Bank is now located underwater about three hundred feet from the current shoreline.

It is in and near this settlement of Town Bank, long years before it disappeared into its watery grave, that *Cape Menace* takes place.

# CHAPTER 1

## 08 JANUARY 1711

*I* was afraid of wolves even before I journeyed to America. Stories of the creatures abounded in England, where no wolf had trod for two hundred years. Stories of their vicious appetites, of their stealth and speed, of their nighttime prowling through forests and dales.

Just stories, but I believed them, nonetheless.

So when I saw my first wolf in the woods near our new home in New Jersey, I was given quite a fright. It was getting dark and my mother and I were hurrying through the woods to get home from delivering a packet of herbs to a family nearby. The husband had cut his leg and was suffering greatly from the pain.

I stopped short when we came upon the wolf. I knew straightaway what it was, for I had seen the pictures that accompanied all the stories I had been told. Mamma told me in a low voice to remain still and it would go away, but she did not remain still. She moved toward me ever so slowly until she was standing directly in front of me. The wolf watched us with its haunting eyes, its huge paws motionless in the snow and its nostrils widening and narrowing as it sniffed the air.

I did not realize I had been holding my breath until the wolf turned away and padded farther into the woods. Mamma unclenched her fists, which she had been holding tight against her legs, and turned to me.

"We shall not come through the woods again at dusk. We must respect the animals that hunt in the nighttime. We are the intruders."

Even then, she had known how dangerous wolves could be.

## CHAPTER 2

## 04 DECEMBER 1712

*T*he day Mamma disappeared she had been feeling unwell. After harvesting the remainder of the root vegetables from the garden before the ground was frozen solid for the winter, we wrote a letter to Grandmamma, Mamma's mother, in England. We told her of the rapidly-approaching winter weather, but I forgot long ago what else was in the letter.

Mamma asked me to go to the tavern in Town, where letters from people in the village were held for mailing. She would have gone with me, but she was needed in the apothecary since Pappa was busy preparing the fields for the winter fallow. Mamma had heard that Captain Winslow was in the village, en route to Philadelphia from his home further south, and that he would be crossing to England soon. He had been the captain of our ship when we sailed from England to Philadelphia, and he had been the one who told Pappa about the fertile farmland farther to the south in New Jersey. He and Pappa had become good friends during the crossing. Since that time, he had taken our letters back to England for us and returned with letters from Grandmamma and others. We always waited anxiously for news of his return to Town.

Going into Town was exciting because there were always people about, but more than that, it was exciting because it was so close to the water. Looking down over the bay from the twenty-foot-tall bank at the end of the main street of Town, I could often see fishing boats, whaling boats, and vessels from the north and the south laden with goods like sugar, soap, and tea. I loved the smell drifting up from the harbor, too—the tangy scent of the salt water mingled with the smell of fish and the scent of wet ropes coiled on the sand. When a whale had been killed, the odor wafting from the beach was never pleasant, but there was no such odor that particular day.

Down the road, at the house closest to mine, I stopped to ask my friend Patience if she would go with me to the village. She agreed to go with me not only because she was my best friend, but also because it gave her some time away from her own heavy responsibilities at home. With four younger sisters, she was often called upon to help with the cooking, the cleaning, and even some of the farm work.

Upon arriving in Town, we watched the activity among the fishermen and sailors for a bit. I was happy to see Captain Winslow down among the other men. He was standing on the ground not far from where his boat, the *Hope*, was moored. He was gesturing toward *Hope*'s hull and talking to one of his crew nearby. Patience and I clambered down the embankment and ran over to where he stood. When he saw us, his face broke into a broad smile. He was so dapper in his uniform of the trading company. He wore a dark blue waistcoat with shiny gold buttons and a dandy pair of white breeches. They were true white, too, not the dingy white of our homespun and wool. He told us of his upcoming trip to England and talked to us, just as if we were grown women, of some of the work that had to be done before he could leave.

"I'm glad you've brought this letter today, Sarah," he told me. "We are hoping to leave by tomorrow or the next day. The voyage promises to be a long one. I'll put your letter with the others you've given me. What special thing would you like me to bring back for you this time?" He winked then because my answer was always the same.

I didn't hesitate. "I would love a bit of tea," I told him with a smile.

"I knew it," he chuckled. "You miss your tea, don't you? Well, you shall have tea upon my return."

"Thank you, Captain." We took our leave after wishing him and his crew safe travels.

Patience and I climbed back up the steep slope and wandered a bit along the main street, but since it was cold outside and Patience hated the cold, we left and parted ways at her house.

When I arrived back at our house Mamma wasn't there. I didn't worry at the time because there were many reasons she could have been gone: often she would leave to attend a sick neighbor, or help Widow Beall with her chores. Goodman Beall, a fisherman, had recently been lost at sea, leaving his poor wife with eight children and few means. Or Mamma could have gone out to pick herbs, which she often did. Though Pappa was the apothecary, Mamma was a skilled herbalist in her own right and she spent a great deal of her time preparing remedies and tinctures for those who needed medicines.

I set about preparing the dinner we usually had at midday. Pappa would be in soon and would be very hungry. I was surprised that Mamma hadn't prepared the potatoes in the hearth ashes before she had left the house.

Mamma still wasn't home when Pappa came in a short time later. He had to get back to work, he said, so he couldn't wait for her to eat his meal. I decided to wait for Mamma to return before eating. After Pappa left, I cleared off the table and stacked his trencher away. I sat down to begin the mending in the basket near the hearth. I worked for several hours, as the light outside began to wane and shadows shifted inside the house. Still no word from Mamma. I was hungry.

But I wasn't worried yet.

Early in the evening, after darkness had fallen, Pappa came back into the house. I had fixed supper and we ate together. It would be the first of countless meals we would eat without Mamma. But we didn't know that yet.

"I'm not worried," Pappa assured me, but his eyes belied his words. Mamma had never simply gone away and not told Pappa or me where she was going. And she certainly had never stayed away after dark.

Pappa pushed himself away from the table after our silent, listless meal and took his hat and cloak from the hook near the door. "I'm going to Widow Beall's to see if Mamma is there."

I nodded, turning away from him so he couldn't see the fear in my eyes, couldn't hear my breathing becoming shallower, faster. I didn't want him to think I was being silly.

After an hour, Pappa came home. He opened the door slowly. I looked up from where I sat by the fire, expecting to see Mamma follow him through the door, but he was alone. He looked at me solemnly, his eyes strained and worried. "She hasn't been at Widow Beall's at all today."

"Do you think she went into Town for some reason?"

Pappa stroked his beard. "Not without telling one of us." He was silent for a few moments, then seemed to come to a decision.

"I'm going to see Daniel Ames. He'll help me look for her." Patience's father was a kind man, always willing to help a neighbor. "We'll gather a few more men and spread out."

"What should I do?" I didn't want to be idle while Pappa was out looking.

He looked around searchingly, as if Mamma would appear at any moment from behind the bedchamber curtain. He closed his eyes and rubbed his beard again. "Wait for her here. I don't want her to find us both gone when she comes back."

I didn't know what to do while I waited, so I sat, staring at the flames, straining my ears for the sound of a footfall outside. But I heard nothing except faraway shouts, shouts I knew were from the men helping Pappa look for my mother.

"Ruth! Ruth!" they called over and over. I finally put my hands over my ears. I couldn't bear the thought of Mamma lying somewhere, hurt or sick, unable to answer their cries.

Where had she gone? My stomach was twisted into knots. I stood and paced the room, peering uselessly into the darkness each time I passed the window, hoping I would see her running lightly up the path to the door, her cloak billowing behind her, a lantern swinging gently in her hand.

But I saw nothing. Nothing but darkness.

It was hours before Pappa came home again. This time Goodwife Ames came with him. I raised my eyebrows in question.

"Eliza Ames is going to stay with you tonight, Sarah. I'm going back out with Daniel and some of the other men from the village and we're going to keep looking for your mother. You need to get some sleep." He took another lantern and two candles from the shelf above the fireplace and was out the door again before I could ask any questions. I looked at Goodwife Ames, not knowing what to say.

She obviously didn't know what to say, either, but she tried. "I'm sure Ruth just became lost looking for herbs. They're bound to find her."

I didn't tell her what I was thinking: Mamma never got lost. She knew her way around the forest with her eyes closed.

"Or maybe she's helping a neighbor," Goody Ames suggested feebly. She knew as well as I that my mother could have heard the men shouting for her from any of the neighbors' houses.

There was only one explanation: she was gone.

Suddenly I was struggling to take a breath. Everything faded into a brief darkness as a buzzing sound grew louder in my ears. I tried to catch my own fall, but ended up in a heap on the floor. Goody Ames let out a cry and rushed to my side. She knelt and cradled my head in her lap, smoothing my hair as it tumbled in an unruly mass from my cap.

"There, there," she cooed. "The men'll find your mother, do not worry." Everything went black again and the last thing I remember is seeing Goody Ames's face, her concerned eyes searching the room wildly for something that would help me.

When I woke up I was alone in the bedchamber, covered to my chin with a counterpane. I was simultaneously perspiring and freezing. As it all came rushing back to me, I thrust back the counterpane and ran out into the main room, my feet cold on the wooden floor. Goody Ames sat in the chair next to the fire, and another woman stood by the window with her back to me, peering out into the darkness as I had done.

"How long have I been sleeping?" I asked in a tremulous voice.

Goody Ames's head came up with a jerk. Perhaps she had been sleeping, too. She stood quickly and crossed the room to me, her hands held out. "You were in a fit, so once your breathing became normal again I let you sleep." She motioned to the other woman, who was still looking out the window. "The pastor's wife came over to see if we needed anything. She helped me get you into the bed."

Mistress Reeves turned around from her post at the window, her long face solemn. "It's the middle of the night, Sarah. I came to see if you and your father needed anything and I decided to stay and keep Goodwife Ames company while we wait for the men to return."

I looked from one woman to the other, trying to read their thoughts on their faces. "Where's Pappa?"

"He's still out looking for your mother, my dear," Goody

Ames replied.

"I'm going to help them," I declared suddenly. Goody Ames looked at me with something akin to horror in her eyes.

"You cannot go out there alone!" she cried. "We don't know what happened to your mother. It's not safe for you to be out there alone. What about the wolves?" She had apparently forgotten her earlier assurances that my mother was simply delayed with a neighbor or had become lost searching for herbs.

"I am going," I told her quietly. Mistress Reeves watched us with wide eyes.

"I agree with Goodwife Ames," she said firmly. "The forest is not a safe place for a young lady to be alone, especially in the middle of the night."

"I won't be alone. There are lots of men out there looking for Mamma. I want to help. I can't stay inside any longer and do nothing. Surely you can understand that?" I asked them in a pleading voice.

They looked at each other. Neither woman suggested going with me. Patience's mother was afraid of the dark, so I knew what she was thinking. She was weighing the terror she would feel going into the forest in the middle of the night against the responsibility she felt for me. Exasperated, I gave her an excuse to stay in the house.

"Goodwife Ames, would you please stay here in case Mamma returns? I know Pappa doesn't want her to come back to an empty house."

I could see the relief on her face, even in the flickering firelight.

"Of course I will, dear."

"And Mistress Reeves, could you perhaps get some cider ready for the men to have when they come in from their search? I'm sure they'll want for drink."

She nodded. I suspected she didn't want to be in the woods at night, either.

Before the two women could think of any more protests, I pulled on my shoes and cloak and hurried outside, shutting the door firmly behind me. I headed northwest, directly into the forest where Mamma often looked for herbs and plants. She *had* to be in the forest. She hadn't said anything about going out to pick herbs that morning, but there was no other explanation.

There were animals in the forest, wild animals, and I hoped she hadn't run into any of them. There were coyotes. There were raccoons and bears.

There were wolves.

If she had stumbled upon a hungry animal … I couldn't stand to think about it. I tried to focus on finding her favorite spots in the near-darkness, with just a feeble lantern to guide my steps. I walked slowly, since the light from the candle only illuminated a few feet in front of me. I had to step carefully to avoid running into a tree or a rock.

I called for Mamma many times, until my throat became hoarse and it was hard to speak. I called even though I was afraid for myself. But there was no reply. My breath quickening, my mind conjured up images of Mamma lying on the cold, unforgiving ground. Was it possible she had become too ill to get home? After several paralyzing moments I was able to force myself to be calm and move forward through the trees. The lantern swung gently in my hand, the light from the candle dipping and swaying as I moved. Then I stopped.

Straight ahead of me were two small, bright circles, reflecting the candlelight from my lantern.

"Mamma?" I asked breathlessly. There was no answer.

"Mamma, are you all right? It's me." I took a cautious step toward the circles. A low, guttural growl greeted me as realization dawned. It wasn't Mamma. It was an animal, and I was in its home, its hunting space. I took a slow step backward, then another, keeping the lantern as still as possible. The bright circles grew larger as the animal approached.

I was terrified. The possibilities sped through my mind as I considered what to do next. I couldn't remember what Mamma had told me the time we saw the wolf in the forest. Should I turn around and run toward home? Should I try to climb the nearest tree? Should I dash past the animal, whatever it was, and run farther into the woods? But fear rooted me to the spot where I stood. Another menacing growl escaped the throat of the beast, this time much closer. I closed my eyes, wondering in a flood of panic if this was how my mother went missing. Then, in an instant, I made my decision. I couldn't stand here and wait to be attacked by the animal, so I spun around and ran.

But the animal was more nimble than I. It set off after me as I crashed through the thick forest, its long howl splitting the air. And I knew with sudden clarity that the monster behind me was a wolf. I could practically see its teeth, its foaming mouth, its hungry eyes, the hairs on its strong back standing in a long, straight line.

I dashed headlong through the trees, the lantern swinging wildly, the wolf panting behind me. I ran straight into a tree, banging my head hard and falling to the ground. A searing pain shot through my ankle. I was dizzy and sick to my stomach, but I picked myself up and continued hobbling along as fast as I could. The wolf did not slow its pursuit.

It seemed I had been running for miles, though I suspect the chase only lasted a few minutes. My lungs were burning, my legs had become jelly, and my head and ankle screamed for relief. As I raced through the dark maze of trees, I spied two spots of uneven light just a bit farther ahead. I recognized the light as lanterns, likely held by men from the village looking for Mamma. I tried yelling, but my throat was closed from fear and exertion. A choked sob escaped my lips and I heard raised voices coming from the direction of the lights.

"Ruth? Is that you?" a man's voice shouted.

I didn't know the voice, but I could have cried in relief when the wolf, apparently sensing danger from the voices ahead, stopped abruptly and turned, running away in the direction from which we had come. I stumbled to a stop, falling on the ground, my chest heaving and my ankle and head throbbing.

Footsteps rushed toward me as I struggled to sit up. "Ruth?"

"No, it's Sarah," I answered hoarsely.

"Sarah! What are you doing out here?" One of the men held a lantern close to his face so I could see him. It was Pastor Reeves. Without waiting for an answer, he asked, "Have you seen your mother?"

"I came out here looking for her, but I surprised a wolf and it's been chasing me," I explained in a rush. "I wasn't able to find her." My feeble voice trailed off.

Pastor Reeves bent down so the lantern was close to me. "Are you hurt, my child?"

"I've hit my head and turned my ankle." Pastor Reeves and the man with him bent over me and decided between themselves that the other man would hold all three lanterns while Pastor Reeves helped me walk home. I wanted to curse myself for taking them away from the desperate search for Mamma.

When I limped slowly through the door, Goody Ames roused herself again from the chair next to the dwindling fire and Mistress Reeves hurried forward to help me into the room, where I sat down at the table. The men didn't stay long, explaining that they were still searching for my mother, and left after I thanked them several times for being in the forest just when I needed them. I shuddered to think what would have become of me if that wolf hadn't been scared off.

I prayed Mamma hadn't met with a similar fate.

Goody Ames found some clean linens in Pappa's shed and worked quickly to bandage my swollen, purple ankle. The pain was overwhelming. There was little to do for my head, where a large bump had formed. Mistress Reeves looked on as Patience's mother worked.

"It was the will of God that you were hurt," Mistress told me severely. "He did not want you to go looking for Ruth because young women should not be in the forest at night. Goodwife Ames and I told you as much."

Goody Ames looked up at her and I could see the surprise and dismay on her face. I remained silent. Though Mistress Reeves surely knew God's ways better than I, I didn't think God wanted to punish me—after all, hadn't He put the men in the forest to help find me?

"I know there are tonics in the apothecary," Goody Ames told me. "I'm going to find something to relieve some of your pain."

I listened to tinkling glass as she rummaged through Pappa's carefully arranged bottles and jars in the apothecary shop. Eventually she returned with a brown bottle. I recognized it as one we had brought with us from England.

"I found the birch bark tonic," Goody Ames said. "You just need a good sip of it and the pain in your ankle shan't be as bad."

I grimaced and took a swig from the bottle. I swallowed the foul liquid and squirmed uncomfortably. I was thankful Goody Ames didn't know about the bottle of laudanum Mamma always kept under her bed or I would have been drinking that, I was sure. Mamma had brought it from England, too, but seldom had occasion to use it.

Goody Ames helped me to my feet and led me over to the chair next to the hearth. "Sit here," she insisted, turning to stoke the fire. "You can't go out looking for your mother again in this condition. We shall have to wait for news from the men. I found lavender in the shop. I am going to make you a lavender tisane to ease the pain in your head."

I sipped the hot tea Goody made for me and the three of us sat in the darkened room, the only light and sound coming from the low, crackling fire.

Before daybreak several men from the village trudged

through the front door. I only needed to look at their faces to know they had not found Mamma. Pappa was not among their number. They were tired, hungry, and thirsty. Goody Ames and Mistress Reeves bustled about, ladling cider for the men and serving them the porridge that had been hanging in a kettle over the fire. Most of these men would spend the entire day working or helping Pappa search before being able to return to their beds for sleep.

There was little talk among the people in the house. The men chewed their food silently and quickly before heading back out again to continue searching until the break of day. None of them met my eyes before leaving. I couldn't blame them.

Pappa came home much later, long after sunrise. Goody Ames had returned home to rouse her family and Mistress Reeves had left, too, after stoking the fire for me and milking both cows. Thankful for her help, I sent her home with a measure of molasses for the pastor's morning meal.

When Pappa came into the house, I hastened to fix him a hearty meal, despite the pain in my ankle. He sat at the table, alternately staring straight ahead and cradling his head in his hands, his fingers raking through his hair. I longed to assure him that Mamma would come home to us, but the words wouldn't come.

I put the porridge in front of him and he looked at it blankly. He lifted the spoon to his mouth and put it down again without touching the food.

"Pappa, you must eat," I said gently.

He pushed himself back from the table. "I can't."

"Would you like some salt pork?"

He shook his head. "I don't want anything to eat."

"Please? You must eat something."

He sighed. "All right, Sarah. If it will make you happy I will eat a bit of salt pork. I will not be going into the fields today. I'm going out again to look for her. If anyone comes needing any remedies from the apothecary, will you help them?"

"Of course."

He left shortly and came back again after nightfall. Some of the men from nearby farms were able to help him search during the day since they didn't have as many chores to do now that winter was coming. None of the men saw so much as a single sign of her.

Pappa looked at me with arched eyebrows when I served him supper. "Are you limping?"

I nodded. "It's nothing. I turned my ankle." Because of my skirts, he couldn't see the bandage still wrapped tightly around the lower part of my leg. I was glad—I didn't want him worrying about me, too.

That night, under the counterpanes Mamma and Grand-mamma had made, I tried to sleep but tossed and turned most of the night. I could hear Pappa moving around the main room, too. I stayed as silent as I could, listening for Mamma's step, but it never came.

Over the next several days, Pappa searched for Mamma from before dawn until after dark. Men from Town and other farms helped every day, but their numbers dwindled as the time dragged by. Goody Ames and Mistress Reeves, along with other women from the village, visited me every day. I didn't want them there. They thought I needed help with chores, but I wanted to do the work by myself.

Finally one evening Pappa sat down heavily in his chair after a long, cold day spent searching outdoors in vain.

"Sarah, she's not coming home."

We never found a trace of Mamma's body, and Pappa and I were convinced that she had been killed by a wolf, perhaps by the very same one that had chased me that first night she went missing.

I've hated wolves ever since.

# CHAPTER 3

## 04 DECEMBER 1714

*I* pulled the long cloak around my shoulders more snugly and hurried along the muddy road beside the dark wood. I dared not glance behind me, but I knew something was there. I could hear it—its swishing footsteps, the sound of its breath reaching my ears. I never went into the woods at night anymore, but even on the road I was afraid of encountering a wolf. This was his hunting time and I was the intruder. I quickened my steps.

Peering ahead through the dense blackness, I caught a glimpse of warm firelight, a scent of acrid smoke that I couldn't see but knew was curling up from the chimney of my house.

By the time I reached the house I was running, afraid to stop and listen again for the thing behind me—whatever it was. Yanking on the leather door handle, I swept into the room and slammed the door behind me. My father, dressed in a woolen great coat, looked up from where he had been putting on his boots.

"Where have you been? I was just about to go looking for you. Why are you breathing so heavily?" His eyes were worried, his brow creased with concern.

I leaned against the door for several moments, catching my breath, waiting until the pounding in my chest calmed. I held up my hand, not yet ready to speak. He waited in silence. Finally I answered him. "I was running. I think there was a wolf outside."

"I've heard talk of a pack nearby. Did you see one?" he asked, glancing toward the window. I shook my head. "I do not want you to be outside in the dark. I've told you that many times before. What if ..." He stopped and I knew what he was thinking. I gazed at him with sadness. He looked older than his thirty-seven years, having never regained the weight he lost after Mamma disappeared.

"I am sorry, Pappa. While you were in the barn I went to Patience's house to give her the tincture you mixed for her mother. Goodwife Ames was in dire need of it." I hung up my cloak on the peg and was startled to hear a muffled knock at the door. I jerked around to face my father.

"Who is that?" I whispered.

He stood up and crossed the small room to the door. "I have a feeling it's someone for me. I'll take care of it. You go to bed, Sarah."

He watched as I ducked under the old coverlet that hung between the main room and the bedchamber. When he opened the door, I peered around the side of the makeshift curtain.

He stepped outside, leaving the door slightly ajar, and spoke in low tones to the person who stood in the cold darkness. I couldn't hear what he was saying. After a short time, he came back in and closed the door firmly. I waited, listening. I expected him to go to the opposite side of the room and open the door to the apothecary, but he didn't. The chair creaked as he sat down again by the fire.

I slid under the coverlet, the cold taking my breath away. Though it was kind of my father to let me use the bedchamber while he slept in the main room, it did get awfully cold in there and sometimes I wished I could sleep next to the fireplace.

I fell asleep wondering who had been at the door. It had not been a wolf hunting me, after all. It had been a person.

As happened every night at this time of year, I was warm soon enough and I was not ready to leave the comfort of the bed when the cock crowed the next morning. Dressed in several layers, I made my way out into the late fall dawn, in the almost-darkness, to the cow pen. I chose the cow I would milk first, then pressed my cold face against her body as I filled my small bucket with the warm, frothy white liquid. My father was in his shed preparing for the day. After his farm chores, if no one came to the apothecary needing his assistance he would head eastward across our fields to Widow Beall's house, where he had promised to fix her front door.

I took the milk indoors and set it aside to make butter later in the day, then ladled cornmeal mush onto our trenchers. From our small jug, I drizzled molasses over the mush and set the jug on the table along with two mugs of cider. While I waited for Pappa to come in, I swept the floor and tidied the hearth.

He came indoors just a short time later. "The sky looks like snow. I'll patch the cracks in the cow pen after I return from Widow Beall's house."

I nodded, waiting for just the right time to ask him who had come to the door in the darkness the previous night.

He sat down to his meal. I sat down opposite him, my chair scraping across the rough pine floor, disturbing the silence. He glanced at me over the rim of his mug. A smile flickered in his eyes.

"You are just bursting to ask me something, I can tell. What is it?"

I fumbled with the handle on my mug, gently sloshing the cider inside. "It's nothing, really. I just wondered who was at the door last night."

It was as if a veil descended over his face. His look of amusement disappeared, replaced by a look I couldn't decipher. Was it anxiety? Consternation? "I told you I would take care of it, did I not?"

I nodded. "Yes, Pappa."

"And I did. That is all you need to know."

I would get nothing further from him, that much I knew. It would be useless to try. He pushed back from the table, wiping his mouth with his sleeve. Mamma would never have let him get away with that.

"I'll be off, then," he said.

I tidied the bedchamber and made my way back outside to the garden. There was still time to pull the last few potatoes out of the ground before the snow came. I gathered the dirty brown vegetables in my apron and took them into the house quickly, stamping my feet to keep warm. I put the potatoes on the table and took up the two pails I used to carry water. Grabbing a scarf as I left the house, I ventured out again into the biting wind. I walked briskly to the well at the far end of the main street in Town. It would have been quicker to take the path through the woods, but I chose to take the road instead. Even walking quickly to stay warm, it took many minutes to get to Town. I waited in line at the well behind two other women, both of whom were bundled up against the wind and cold. One blew into her hands, looking skyward and scowling as she waited to draw water for the day. We had a well on our farm, but it had been low for over a month. With all the work of harvesting the crops, Pappa had not yet found the time to dig another well, and with the coming of winter, the ground was sure to be frozen before long. I would have to get water from the village well for several months.

When it was my turn, I filled my buckets while several other women arrived at the well and waited in line. I was acquainted with all of them and we spoke briefly, commenting about the weather, about the early onset of winter. One of them was a young woman I had met only briefly. As I recalled, her name was Ada and she had a braying laugh that quite grated on my ears. I tried to ignore that and draw her into the conversation, but she seemed more interested in looking around at the men who occasionally strode past in small groups. Finally I gave up and directed my conversation to the other women whom I knew better.

I was leaving the well to return home when I saw Patience hurrying toward me breathlessly, her skirts rustling. She held two pails.

"Will you wait for me?" Patience called in greeting. I nodded and set my buckets on the ground, rubbing my hands together. It didn't take long for Patience to join me. I fell into step with her and we struck off to the north, walking slowly along the road, not wanting to hurry and risk sloshing the water on our cold hands or wasting it on the ground.

"Looks like it's going to snow today," she said.

"I hope so. I love the snow," I answered with a wide smile.

She smirked and shook her head. "I'll never understand how you can like winter."

"It's better to be too cold than too hot." I smiled fondly at her. We walked for some distance in companionable silence, each lost in our own thoughts, before we reached her house. Sighing with relief, I set the two buckets down on the hard ground to rest my hands.

"What are you doing today?" she asked.

"Mending and making butter. And you?"

"I'll be mending, too. Mother's not feeling well again today, so I'll also need to do the heavier chores."

Patience's mother was with child and expected to deliver very soon. Though Patience normally performed quite a number of chores around the house, she had been taking on most of her mother's chores during her expectancy. Her mother had been quite ill from the beginning. Patience's younger sisters helped, too, but they were not as skilled as Patience at many housekeeping duties.

Patience gave me a long look. "I can't believe it's been two years," she said quietly.

I looked up at the gray sky. "I know. I miss her." I swallowed hard, not trusting myself to say anything else.

She wrapped me in a big hug, one that filled my cold body with warmth. I smiled at her through hot, stinging tears. I sniffled and wiped my eyes with the back of my hand.

"I shouldn't be long helping Mother with the mending and doing my housework," she said. "Shall we go for a walk later?"

I nodded, smiling gratefully at her. Patience, more than anyone, knew my heart, and I hers. She knew that what I needed today was to get out in the fresh air, to spend time talking of girl things and, if I felt like it, about Mamma.

"I will be waiting for you." I squeezed her hand.

She gave me another quick hug and turned around, hurrying toward her house. I picked up my two buckets and headed for home.

Inside the house, I washed the dusty dirt from the potatoes and put them in the fireplace ashes to cook for our midday dinner. They would be ready by the time Pappa returned from Widow Beall's house. Next I churned the butter we would need for the next two days. Then I dug out the supplies I would need for the mending, noting the room becoming darker. Heavy clouds scudded across the sky, holding the promise of snow before nightfall. I sat down in a chair next to the window and began the tedious task of mending the clothes and linens.

I wish it had been baking day or even the dreaded laundry day, because as long as my brain and muscles were occupied, I didn't have time to think. But since it was mending day, I had no choice but to sit in silence with my thoughts and my needle and thread, wishing Mamma was with me. Not a day went by that I didn't hope to hear her voice, her footsteps outside the door, or some news of her.

But none ever came.

Patience came for me later that afternoon and we went for the walk she had promised. It was a welcome diversion, since my eyes ached from mending in the dim house and my fingers needed a rest.

We walked in silence for a short time, watching tiny snowflakes swirl through the sky, then Patience asked, "Do you and your Pappa talk about her?"

"Sometimes. But I'm always the one who mentions her first. He rarely brings up her name unless I do."

"Why do you think that is?"

"Because he misses her so much. Perhaps he thinks if he talks about her it will hurt him more. But I don't think it can hurt more." Patience was silent.

"I see reminders of her everywhere," I said, my voice quiet. "She is all through the house, by the hearth, in the bedchamber, in the cow pen, at the table, in the apothecary. Her memory is in every corner."

"I have fond memories of her, too. She was the reason I'm able to read." Patience smiled. "Well, your mother and you."

"She was the reason quite a few women and girls in the county can read." I couldn't help the hint of pride in my voice. Mistress Reeves always said that pride goeth before a fall, but this kind of pride was acceptable because it was pride in Mamma, not in myself.

"I'll always remember the day she offered to teach me to read." Patience's eyes had a faraway look. "It was like a dream come true."

Patience's family did not have enough money to buy the

primer and the chalk and slate she would have needed to go to school, and the school was far away, so my mother offered to teach her to read and write. Patience's own mother and father couldn't read, so they weren't able to teach her themselves. Some weeks after Mamma disappeared I took it upon myself to continue teaching Patience to read and write. We had since finished one of the books my family had brought from England.

We hadn't gone far when we spied a familiar figure walking toward us. It was Arthur Reeves, the pastor's son. Tall and lanky, he walked with his head down, as if lost in his thoughts.

"There's Arthur," Patience whispered, squeezing my arm.

"I see him."

Arthur chanced to look up just then and we waved to him. He smiled and waved back. I had been friends with Arthur for almost as long as I had been friends with Patience. "Good afternoon, Sarah, Patience," he said when he had nearly reached us.

"Good afternoon," Patience said.

"Hello, Arthur. Where are you coming from?"

"I had an errand in Town for my father. I was just going home. And where are you two headed?"

"We're just out for a walk," I said. "Patience doesn't like the cold as much as I do, so we shan't walk for long."

Arthur looked skyward. "It looks like there's going to be snow soon."

"I hope not," Patience said.

"I hope so," I said with a laugh. Arthur and Patience joined in.

"Well, I'll leave you two to get along on your walk. Will I see you at service on Sunday?" Arthur looked directly at me, though I assumed he was speaking to both of us.

"I shall be there."

"I shall be there, too, unless Mother needs me at home," Patience said.

"Goodbye, then." Arthur waved again and headed past us toward his own house, which was not far from Patience's house.

Patience and I continued along the edge of the forest, our heads bent against the chilly wind. She tucked her arm under mine and gave me a sly look. "Fancy meeting him," she said with a grin.

I rolled my eyes. Patience was convinced that he and I were destined to be man and wife, but I did not want any such thing. She giggled. "Will I see you at service?" she repeated in a low voice. Then she laughed aloud. "I'll bet he asks for your hand before summer!"

I let out an impatient sigh. "Patience, Arthur is just a nice young man. That's all."

"Ha!" she laughed. "A nice young man who is quite smitten with you!"

"I hardly think so."

"I think the name Mrs. Arthur Reeves suits you very well." Her eyes twinkled. "Another Mistress Reeves."

"You are insufferable," I said, laughing in spite of myself. "Besides, Arthur has never so much as come closer to me than an arm's length."

"He will in time."

"Can we please speak of something else?"

"Of course, but your face is turning red," Patience said, giggling again.

"It's the cold."

We had skirted the woods near my house; it was getting darker and the snow was falling a bit more thickly. "Let me walk you home," I suggested.

"No," she answered quickly. "I'm walking *you* home." She held my arm tighter under hers and we headed briskly for my house. When we got to the front door, I turned to thank her.

"This walk was exactly what I needed today. Thank you," I told her.

"I'm glad we could talk." She squeezed my hand in hers. "Perhaps I'll see you tomorrow." She waved, then turned and hurried back toward the road leading to her house. It was quickly disappearing under a light blanket of snow.

I closed the door behind me, savoring the warmth inside the house. I busied myself making dinner for Pappa and me, mentally making a list of the ingredients I would need to gather for the following day's baking.

Pappa was not in the house, nor was he in the shed or the apothecary. I went outside to look in the barn; he wasn't there, either. Darkness enveloped the house as I waited for him to return home. The fire threw long shadows on the dark walls and I debated whether to use any of our whale oil to light the lamp. I decided not to, since I didn't want to waste it. It smelled bad, too. As the time passed and Pappa didn't return home, I became more and more worried. My thoughts traveled back to the night Mamma disappeared and I began to feel panic rising in my throat. *Please come home, Pappa.*

I finally lit the lamp to dispel some of the darkness, and with the lamp burning I somehow felt less alone. The bread, hard and stale from last week's baking, sat on the table waiting far more patiently than I for Pappa's return. The cup of cider I had set out to drink with the bread was getting warm from the heat of the fire.

Finally I could stand the waiting no longer. Sweeping on my cloak, I set out into the snowy darkness toward Town. I tried not to think about wolves or other nighttime hunters.

The temperature had fallen since my walk with Patience. I shivered in my cloak as I hurried past the homes of our neighbors and down toward the main street of the village and the tavern and workshops. The street was dark and deserted. It was a bit unsettling to be on the street alone, so I quickened my pace. I didn't even have a destination in mind—I was just hoping to see Pappa somewhere.

But he was nowhere to be found. I had no choice but to go back home and hope he had returned in my absence. As I approached our house, I went around to the side to see if he was in the apothecary, which had an outside entrance in addition to the entrance through our main room. I thought perhaps he was preparing a remedy for a patient or doing an inventory; it had been several days since he had gone into the shop.

I peered through the window. The room was dark and appeared to be empty, so I didn't go inside. I wondered what to do next. *Should I eat supper? Should I go to a neighbor's house to see if anyone has had word of him? Where could he be?* I peered through the glass in the door once more.

That's when I saw two small points of light toward the back reaches of the large room. *He must be working in there,* I thought. I put my ear to the heavy wooden door and listened for a moment. No sound. I knocked softly and, without waiting for a response, pushed on the heavy door. To my surprise, it wasn't locked. It creaked as it swung inward and I stepped indoors as the smell of herbs and various tinctures, as well as pipe tobacco, reached my nose. The room smelt of my father, but the sweet, dried scents of the room also reminded me of Mamma. I closed my eyes to dispel a sudden, bittersweet image of her and noticed that the candles I had seen from the window had been extinguished.

"Pappa?" I asked tentatively into the gloom.

A shuffling noise, then Pappa's voice. "Sarah, what are you doing here?"

"I was worried about you when you didn't come home to supper, so I went out to look for you. Are you all right, Pappa?"

"Yes, my dear. I'm fine. Go into the house and I'll join you in a moment."

"Why are you working in the dark?"

I heard another shuffling noise, this time from a direction different from whence Pappa's voice had come.

"Pappa?"

I heard him sigh. "Sarah, there is a customer in here with me. We have a few things to discuss, then I will join you for supper."

*What is happening here?* I could not fathom what Pappa and his customer were discussing in near-darkness. I pulled the door closed behind me, but instead of going into the house I waited around the back of the apothecary in the cold. I would tell Pappa that I heard a strange sound coming from the cow pen in order to explain why I didn't go right into the house as he instructed me. I hated to lie, but I had to know what was happening. Presently the door opened again. I peeked around the corner and saw two figures emerge. One quickly turned away and almost ran in the direction of the village, heavy boots thumping on the frosty ground. I could barely make out the person's form. It was a man, that much I could tell. Long dark hair grew down his wide back. A short cloak hung around his shoulders, fluttering as he moved away.

The other figure was my father. He looked around and ducked quickly back into the apothecary. I took the opportunity to run lightly around the other side of the house to the front door so Pappa wouldn't see me. I had just hung up my cloak when I heard his footsteps coming closer to the door. He opened it slowly and took his hat off while I stood by the table watching him. I didn't mean to, but I blurted out my questions before he had a chance to sit down to his meal.

"Pappa, why were you conducting business by candlelight in the apothecary? Why did you blow out the candles when I came in?"

He turned to me and spoke in a low voice, as if someone else might hear him. "Sarah, I am not at liberty to discuss the matter. For now, you must be content with that and you must also promise you will keep it to yourself. Don't even tell Patience. Do you understand me?"

I was taken aback. I didn't know Pappa kept secrets from me, secrets that required him to conduct business in the dark. "Yes, Pappa."

"Good girl," he said, and he sat down to eat. The subject was apparently closed. "I'm starving. I need a big supper tonight," he said.

After supper Pappa sat in front of the fire smoking his pipe while I put away the trenchers and mugs. "Would you like to read?" he asked me suddenly.

I turned toward him in surprise. "Really?"

He laughed. "Yes, really."

"That would be wonderful!" He hadn't read with me in two years, not since Mamma disappeared. "But isn't it too dark?"

"We'll light a lamp," he said simply. It wasn't my place to remind him that whale oil was expensive and that we should save the scant amount we had, so I picked his favorite book from the shelf above the front door and opened it to the first page while he adjusted the flame of the oil lamp and set it on the table he had dragged near the fire.

We spent the next lovely hour visiting old friends in the book, old places in England, old gardens and houses that we used to read about regularly. Pappa read aloud. I sat on the floor before the fire and listened as his voice lilted over the beautiful words, wishing we could read the entire book in one sitting.

But presently he closed the book with a sigh. "It's been a long time since I read aloud like that." He looked into the fire wistfully. "We should do it more often."

"We should!" I said quickly. "Thank you, Pappa."

"Your Mamma would be angry at me if she knew it had been two years since we read aloud." He was right, though I didn't reply.

Pappa seemed to be in a pleasant mood. I was still concerned about the man who had hurried away from the apothecary in the dark and I wanted to ask about him again, but I thought it best to wait. I put the book away and blew out the lamp before going into the bedchamber. "Goodnight, Pappa."

"Goodnight, Sarah, and don't worry about anything we discussed earlier."

He seemed to know what I was thinking. I ducked under the coverlet separating the two rooms. As I got into bed I could hear him moving around in the main room. I listened as he made up his bed on the floor next to the hearth, then as he settled down for the night. I couldn't sleep yet, so I lay staring into the dark recesses over my head. Before long I heard hearty snores coming from the other room. I smiled to myself, knowing that Pappa was not worried about anything—if he could fall asleep that quickly, all must be well.

# CHAPTER 4

*I* was up before the sun rose the next morning. Baking day. Pappa was moving around in the main room, stoking the fire. I dressed quickly and went out to prepare his breakfast. We ate hurriedly, then I put a piece of burning wood from the fireplace into the oven and the kindling inside slowly flickered to life. I shut the door to the oven to let it get very hot.

Pappa informed me that he had to go to the tannery in town for a piece of hide. After he left I tidied the house and went outdoors to muck out the cow pen. I had finished the filthy job and was scrubbing my hands in a bucket of soapy water by the fireplace when there was a knock at the door. Wiping my hands on my apron, I answered the door and was surprised to see Mistress Reeves standing outside, bundled up against the cold, a long scarf covering most of her face.

"Come in, Mistress Reeves," I said, stepping aside so she could come through the doorway. "How can I be of service this morning?"

"I fear my husband is feeling poorly today. I've come to see if your father has a remedy that could help him. Is he in the apothecary?"

"No. He went to the tannery. Perhaps I can be of service?"

She looked at me doubtfully. "I do not think so." she answered. "I will return when he is at home. When do you expect him?"

"I'm sorry, but I don't know."

"Very well. I will be back later today." She nodded her thanks, turned, and left without another word.

I was eager to start the baking and was already several minutes behind schedule. I mixed and kneaded, punched and shaped, until there were several loaves of bread ready to go into the oven. I also prepared a pumpkin pudding and a bean porridge. Then I threw a handful of cornmeal into the oven to see if it was hot enough; the cornmeal started to burn.

"It's ready," I announced to myself. I hastily and carefully withdrew the smoldering wood from the oven and put it in the fireplace. Then, working very quickly, I put the loaves and the pudding into the oven and closed the door.

Baking, as usual, took most of the day, but I enjoyed it because it reminded me of Mamma. She had taught me to bake and she had taught me well. She had been a wonderful baker herself.

Mistress Reeves returned during the afternoon. I had been thinking about her visit while I baked, and I had decided what to do if she came back before Pappa did.

I would lie to her. I didn't see any need for the pastor to suffer needlessly when I knew exactly how to help him. He was such a nice man, and I felt sorry for him.

When I opened the door to her, I invited her into our main room. "Your father is home?" she asked.

"He did return, but I'm afraid he had to leave again. When he was here I told him about the pastor's malady and he told me exactly what to give you to treat it. Come along and I'll get it for you." I beckoned her to follow me through the room to the apothecary door. I unlocked the door and stepped inside. It smelled of something strange in the shop—the outdoors, Pappa's pipe smoke, and a tangy scent I couldn't place. It wasn't unpleasant, just different. For the first time since Mamma's disappearance, the scent in the apothecary did not remind me of her.

I went to one of the shelves containing numerous small brown bottles. Though some of the older bottles were labeled in Mamma'a dainty script, most were labeled in Pappa's hand. Mamma had known as much about herbs and apothecary as Pappa, and I had spent innumerable hours at their sides learning about medicines and remedies. Once Mamma disappeared I had taken her place by helping Pappa, so I knew well my way around the apothecary.

"Here is some dandelion." I poured a good amount of crushed dandelion into a paper packet and handed it to Mistress Reeves. "If you make a tea with it, that should bring some relief to the pastor. I will also send you home with some dried spearmint, too, which is helpful in cases of stomach ache."

"Please tell your father I said thank you." Mistress Reeves paid for her remedies and left.

By evening I had enough brown bread and pudding for the two of us for the upcoming week and the house smelled wonderful. I hurried to prepare supper, wondering where Pappa was and why he wasn't in the apothecary. He couldn't still be at the tannery. Several times I opened the door separating the house from the apothecary shop, hoping he had come back and returned to work. But the shop was empty.

Eventually he came home, his cheeks bright with color, a smile on his face, his hair sticking out in all directions, and smelling of seawater. "How was baking day, Sarah?" he asked cheerfully.

"All was well," I replied, turning to retrieve a potato for his supper from the ashes in the fireplace. "Have you been out in the cold for a long while?"

"That I have," he responded. "After I visited the tannery I had to meet a fellow down at the bay. It is quite windy down there today."

"Oh?" I tried to affect a casual interest. "Why did you have to go all the way down there?" *Why couldn't he conduct business in the shop, as he normally did?*

"I was conducting a bit of business," Pappa said. Then he changed the subject. "I chanced to meet old Captain Eli this afternoon. I'm afraid he becomes more odious every time I see him." Pappa shook his head.

Captain Eli Barnett wasn't a captain any longer—he had retired from a life spent on the sea and lived in Town. He had attempted to maintain a rescue station along the shore to watch for ships in distress, but his love of drink had made it impossible to maintain the station dependably. A well-known teller of tales, he took much pleasure in sharing his more ribald stories in polite company, embarrassing the women and angering their husbands. I was a bit afraid of him, with his grizzled face and his lewd, toothy grin.

If I had hoped to learn more about the business Pappa had been conducting in the darkened apothecary shop the previous night, I was to be disappointed. He did not address it at all, nor did he explain further what business had necessitated a trip to the bay. He dug into his supper with gusto, remarking on how good the food tasted when one was very hungry. It was clear he would entertain no questions from me regarding his unusual activities of the day and the previous evening. I told him about Mistress Reeves' visit, and he told me sternly that I should not have lied to her. But the corners of his mouth twitched up when he spoke and I knew he was not angry with me.

After supper Pappa went into the shop and returned a moment later with his large ledger, a quill, a bottle of ink, and the slate he used for calculations. He opened the book on the table and began making notes in chalk on the slate. I tried to peer over his shoulder to see what he was writing, but he hunched over the table, his back preventing me from seeing anything.

*What secrets was he keeping?*

"Pappa, can I get you anything before I retire?" I asked.

He glanced up at me with a startled look, almost as if he had forgotten my presence. "Oh. No, my dear. Goodnight."

I went into the bedchamber and lay down, listening for him to return the ledger to the shop, but all I could hear was the continued scratching of chalk on slate and eventually I drifted off to sleep.

I awoke earlier than usual the next morning and slipped quietly into the main room where the embers of the fire glowed dull scarlet in the darkness. Pappa slept on his mat facing the fireplace, breathing deeply. I felt an overwhelming urge to see if the ledger was still on the table. Stealing quietly across the floor, I crept to the table and felt for the big book.

It was there. I was faced with a dilemma: should I light a candle and try to see what was written on the pages? Or should I return to bed and wait for Pappa to tell me about his business dealings when he was ready?

I chose to return to bed. There was no way to light a candle without reaching it into the fireplace embers. That would surely wake Pappa and I didn't want him to catch me at something I shouldn't be doing.

I lay in bed for as long as I could, then dressed quickly in the cold room. Peering around the coverlet separating the bedchamber from the main room, I could see dusky gray light filtering through the window. The sun would soon be up, and Pappa with it. I wondered if I could see any of the writing on the ledger in the dim light of predawn. I determined to try.

I crept lightly and silently toward the table, checking several times to make sure Pappa was still breathing deeply in slumber. I bent over the ledger until my nose was practically touching the rough paper. I could barely make out his heavy handwriting on the hand-drawn line, but a little frisson of shock went through me when I saw the number under the "total" column, the right-most column on the page. It was quite a large number. Not a number an apothecary should be showing on a business ledger. A merchant, yes. But a herbalist, no.

*What is going on?* I wondered.

Pappa stirred suddenly, moving to face away from the fire-place. I stepped back hurriedly, my heart beating faster. I knew I shouldn't have looked, but I couldn't resist. And now I was left with more questions than answers. I smiled ruefully, knowing Mistress Reeves would scold me for sinning against God and against my earthly father. I soundlessly prayed for forgiveness and slipped out the door to milk the cows.

When I returned Pappa was awake. He had taken up his straw sleeping mat from the floor and placed it under the bench where it resided during the day. I noticed the ledger was gone.

"I need you to mend an apron for me today, Sarah," Pappa said while he ate his morning meal.

"I'll do it first thing," I told him with a smile. I began to worry that my face or voice might somehow arouse Pappa's suspicion, that it might in some way convey to him that I had knowledge of the ledger which I should not have had.

But Pappa didn't say anything else other than to thank me for working on his apron and to bid me goodbye when he went to work in the apothecary.

There were several customers that morning. When Pappa came into the main room for his noonday meal, he explained why.

"Sarah, I have spoken to quite a few people this morning, all suffering from a similar illness. I do not want you going into the village right now. I want you to stay in the house where you'll be safe."

"What kind of illness?" I asked.

"An ague that produces cough, chills, and difficulty breathing. It has taken hold in a few homes in Town and promises to spread to affect others." He gave me a stern look and I knew I wouldn't be seeing Patience that day.

While I was in the apothecary that afternoon helping Pappa with his orders, Mistress Reeves returned to purchase another tincture for her husband. He was still suffering from stomach troubles, she told Pappa, and needed something to give him strength so he could work on his sermon for that week. I was glad I had told Pappa about her visit the previous day.

"I'm quite worried about him," Mistress Reeves said, her voice quavery. Her eyes looked tired and her mouth was drawn at the corners. Her usual pinched look was made even more severe by the worry etched on her face.

"Do not worry, Mistress Reeves," Pappa assured her. He reached for a jar of dried chamomile and placed a large pinch of it inside a paper packet. He handed the packet to Mistress. "If he continues to take this with his drink, he should start feeling better soon. How is young Arthur?" he asked, his eyes twinkling as he glanced in my direction. I'm quite sure I blushed at the question.

Mistress Reeves appeared to take no notice. "He is doing quite well, thank you." she answered. Then she leaned in closer and spoke in a low voice, as if there were people all around who could overhear her. "He is planning to follow in his father's footsteps in service to God, so we are sending him to England to continue his studies."

*England?*

I must have betrayed my surprise, because I looked up and noticed both Pappa and Mistress Reeves staring at me. "I'm sorry," I mumbled. "If you'll excuse me, I'll be getting back into the house." I almost tripped in my haste to get to the door leading out of the apothecary, but I caught myself and held my head up as I disappeared from view of my father and Mistress Reeves.

I don't know why I was surprised to learn about Arthur's upcoming trip to the land where I was born. I knew what Patience would have said: *Ooh! You'll be returning to England as Mrs. Arthur Reeves! I will miss you so!*

But Patience was mistaken. And though I would never be Mistress Arthur Reeves, he was a good person and my friend. I would be sorry to see him leave. I knew from experience what a long and arduous trip it would be across the sea, and I didn't envy him for it.

Mistress Reeves returned the following day to tell Pappa that her husband was, indeed, feeling better. She asked if there was anything he should be taking to keep the stomach pains at bay. Since I was busy helping Pappa in the apothecary, he instructed me to give Mistress Reeves a small bottle of mint syrup and asked her to give it to him every few hours until the syrup was gone. When she tried to pay Pappa, he refused to take the money.

"You tell Pastor Reeves that I look forward to hearing his sermon this week," Pappa told her with a smile. "A powerful sermon will be more than enough for my payment."

Just then the apothecary door opened and Arthur poked his head into the shop.

"Mother? I'm glad I've found you." He came in and closed the door behind him. "Father is asking for you."

A worried look crossed Mistress Reeves' face. "Is there something wrong?"

"Nothing of which I am aware," Arthur answered. Then he looked toward Pappa and me. "Good afternoon, sir. Hello, Sarah."

"Hello, Arthur," I said, then turned back to my work. Pappa reached to shake Arthur's hand. "How are you doing, young man?" he asked.

Arthur smiled. "I am quite well, sir. I wonder if my mother has told you that I shall be going to England to study at seminary?"

"Indeed, she has," Pappa answered. He turned to me. "What do you think of that, Sarah? Our own Arthur is going to England!"

Pappa was always interested in hearing of people going to England. Not that he wanted to return—he loved living on this wild, unforgiving cape.

"Congratulations, Arthur," I said, smiling at him. He smiled at me in return, his eyes dancing, but I noticed a frown crease his mother's forehead.

"Perhaps you can tell me all about England before I am to leave," Arthur suggested. Was he talking to my father or to me?

I didn't respond, in case he meant for my father to answer, but then I noticed it had grown silent in the room and I looked up to find three pairs of eyes on me.

"Oh, yes," I stammered. "I shall certainly be happy to tell you about England."

"Shall we go see what your father needs, Arthur?" Mistress Reeves tucked her hand under her son's arm and gave me an indecipherable look before nodding toward my father and saying, "Thank you for the mint syrup. I shall pass your message along to my husband." She opened the door and put up her hood, waiting for Arthur to follow her. He smiled at me and Pappa as he joined her. I grinned and waved as he glanced toward us one last time.

"Mistress Reeves doesn't like me," I said to Pappa as we worked side-by-side in the cold apothecary.

"What makes you say that?"

I shrugged. "It's just a feeling I get, I suppose."

"I think she doesn't want to lose her son to an apothecary's daughter." Pappa's eyes were smiling.

I must have blushed to my very toes. "Pappa!" I scolded. "I

am sure neither Arthur nor Mistress Reeves has any such thing on their minds!"

Pappa merely raised his eyebrows and shrugged, then turned back to his work. "We shall see," he finally said.

I changed the subject. "Have you heard of anyone else who has come down with the fever?" I asked.

"I believe it is slowing down," Pappa said. "Only two new people have come in today looking for something that will provide some relief."

"Are we running low on any supplies?" I asked.

"We are running out of a few things. Several days ago I sent a message to the apothecary in Philadelphia who supplies me with some of my remedies and I hope he sends along replacements soon."

"It's strange how quickly you've begun to run out of some remedies." I turned back to pick the leaves from a stem of basil.

My father turned quickly to look at me, but didn't say anything. Had I said something wrong?

I left him working in the apothecary when it began to get dark. I had late afternoon chores to complete outside and I wanted to get them done before it got too much colder.

Snow swirled in the air as I made my way to the cow pen. I milked the cows with fingers that were growing colder with every pull, then placed the pails by the pen door. I went to the chicken coop and gathered two eggs for Pappa and me to have with our supper. I was going inside with the eggs in my apron pocket and the pails of milk in my hands when I heard a voice whispering my name.

I whirled round, trying to figure out the source of the sound. "Patience?" I spoke into the air.

"No, it's me. Arthur." The sky had become the color of a stormy sea. I squinted my eyes to see Arthur.

"Arthur! You scared me! Where are you?" I asked.

"Over here, behind the chicken coop. Sorry, I didn't mean to scare you."

I set the milk pails down again and walked over to the chicken coop, where Arthur was standing, hidden in the shadows.

"What are you doing back there?" I asked. I faced my friend with my hands on my hips.

"I wanted to talk with you, but not with your father around." My senses were immediately alert.

"You know you can speak in front of my father."

"I think you misunderstand," Arthur hastened to say.

I didn't say anything, but lifted my chin higher and raised my eyebrows at him. He probably couldn't even see me in the gathering darkness.

"I only thought you might like to take a walk with me tomorrow. I would like to talk to you about my trip to England."

So that was it. He wanted to know about England.

"That would be fine. I can tell you everything I remember. I can go with you early in the afternoon."

I sensed rather than saw his grin. "I'll come for you tomorrow in the afternoon, then," he said, and I heard him turn around. He was gone in an instant.

The next day brought even fewer visitors to the apothecary, and it was a good thing because Pappa had run out of several bottles and medicines he used to make his remedies. I was surprised at the amount that had been used over the days when the ague ran rampant through the village and surrounding farms. I asked him about it during our noonday meal.

"Pappa, you must have treated more people than I realized," I began. "I had no idea our medicine supply had run so low."

He seemed not to hear me at first, for he just nodded his head and stared out the window.

"Pappa?" I asked.

He gave himself a little shake and faced me. "Hmm?"

"I was saying that I had no idea we had run so low on medicines."

"Yes. Well, I'm hoping to get a delivery from Philadelphia tomorrow," he said. Then he hurriedly finished his meal and left the table.

I had just finished cleaning up from our meal when there came a knock at the door. Casting a quick glance toward the apothecary, I went to the window to look outside. Arthur was standing in front of the door, blowing into his hands. I opened the door for him.

"Good afternoon, Sarah. Do you still care to go for a walk with me? It's quite cold outside, but we can make it a short walk if you'd like."

"You know I like the cold. Let me get my cloak." I removed my cloak from the peg by the door and tied it under my chin. I also added a hat and a pair of gloves Mamma had made for me years ago. They were worn and a bit too small for me, but they brought back happy memories and I refused to stop wearing them.

I stepped lightly across the room and opened the apothecary door. "Pappa, I'm going for a walk," I said.

"Are you going alone?" he asked.

"No." I hesitated. "Arthur is going with me."

Pappa gave me a look I couldn't read, but I'm quite sure I saw a hint of a smile prod the corners of his lips upward. I shook my head in exasperation. He was as bad as Patience.

"Be back before long. It's getting dark earlier and earlier."

"Yes, Pappa."

Arthur and I walked out into the bracing wind and flying snowflakes. I was glad to be bundled up so well, and wondered when we might get a good snowfall.

As I walked with Arthur, I found he had more questions about me and my life in England than questions about things he might see on his own trip.

"Did you live your entire life in England before coming to New Jersey?" he asked.

"Yes."

"Where did you live in England?"

"Oxfordshire," I said.

"What was it like there?"

"It was a gentle place to live, with soft rains and easy winters, not like you have here. The houses were small, smaller than they are here, and there were far more hills and valleys than I've ever seen around this area."

"Do you miss living there?"

I had to think for a moment before answering. "Sometimes. I miss my grandmother and the other family we left behind. I miss my old friends, though I'm sure they've changed as much as I have in the past four years. I think Mamma might still be with us if we had stayed in England, so I suppose there are times I wish we had never come here."

Arthur was silent for a few minutes, perhaps not knowing what to say. Finally he spoke again.

"Maybe I shall meet your grandmother when I move to England."

I thought it quite unlikely that he would meet one particular woman in the whole of England, but I nodded.

"Wouldn't it be nice if you could see her again?" he asked.

"Of course it would. But I'm not returning to England and she will not be coming here to New Jersey. We will have to make do with sending letters to one another," I answered him, in a voice which I'm sure sounded harsh to his ears. In truth, I was becoming annoyed by his questions. Was he *trying* to make me melancholy?

We walked almost to the end of the street in Town before I told him that Pappa wanted me home long before dark. I didn't want to spend any more time walking with Arthur. His questions had unnerved me and made me peevish and irritable.

We had just turned around to start our walk back to my house when I spotted a man standing behind the tanner's shop. He was tall with hair the color of jet, long and flowing down the back of his short cape. He wore heavy boots. I got the sense he was younger than his appearance indicated. He happened to turn around to face the street as Arthur and I were walking past him, and my eyes met his.

It was as if a bolt of lightning coursed through my body when I saw his eyes. I had no idea who he was, but I had a feeling I had known him forever. His dark gaze followed me for just a moment before the tanner came out the back door of the shop and called for the man's attention.

Arthur noticed my sudden interest in the stranger. "Who is that?" he asked.

"I don't know."

"I thought perhaps you were acquainted with him somehow, though I can't think how. It would be unseemly for someone like you to be in the acquaintance of someone like him."

"What do you mean by that?" I asked.

"He has rather a dangerous look about him, don't you think? With those flashing eyes and that long black hair. I half expected to see a wooden leg under those breeches!" Arthur laughed as if he had made a humorous comment. I found no humor in it, though, and when he noticed I wasn't smiling, he stopped smiling, too.

I couldn't shake the thought of that man from the tanner's shop all the way back to my house, and I'm sure Arthur noticed. I was sorry I couldn't be more engaging, but my mind was back in Town, wondering why the sight of that man had produced such an effect on me.

At my door, Arthur bowed slightly and thanked me for walking with him. "I hope the cold didn't bother you," he said in a solicitous tone.

"Oh, not at all. I love the cold and the snow—that's one of the things I like best about living here," I answered.

"Perhaps you'd like to do it again sometime?" he asked.

I didn't know what to say. Normally I would have accepted immediately, since I enjoyed spending time with my friend, but all the talk from both Patience and my father had flustered me. Now, I thought, what would Pappa think, what would everyone think, if they saw me walking with Arthur again?

I didn't answer him. Instead, I waved goodbye to him and ducked through the door. Pappa came into the house from the apothecary shortly thereafter and did not ask me about my walk with Arthur.

Later on, Pappa and I ate our evening meal together before Pappa suggested that we read together again. As I listened to his voice telling an old English story, my thoughts began to wander back to the country of my birth. I smiled remembering the gardens, the voices of the people who lived around us, and my old house. It, too, had been next to Pappa's apothecary shop and I loved to go in there to watch him work, measuring and mixing and, on the rare occasion, tasting his mixtures to see if they were too bitter for patients to swallow.

I missed England and my family and friends, yes, but I belonged in New Jersey now.

## CHAPTER 5

*W*hen Pappa finished reading, he told me that he had a patient coming to the apothecary that night and that he wanted me to stay in the house.

"Is it someone with the fever?" I asked.

"No. It is someone who is very busy during the day. He is only able to come to our shop at nighttime."

"Do you know what he wants?" I asked.

"Yes."

"Do you have enough medicines to help him?"

"Yes. Don't worry about anything, Sarah. Our delivery of medicines should be here in another day or two, and as long as the ague continues to abate, we should have sufficient supplies to get us through."

"But ..." I began.

"I have to go now, Sarah. Do not leave this house." He chucked me under my chin the way he had done when I was a child and my shoulders relaxed. I couldn't understand why we suddenly had visitors in the night when we never had before.

He left the house and closed the door to the apothecary behind him. I heard him slide the rod across the door. I felt a pang of hurt because I knew why he did that—so I couldn't go into the shop while his patient was in there.

What was going on? I felt a stab of sorrow that he didn't trust me.

I cleaned up from our meal slowly, trying not to make any noise, while I waited to hear some sound either from the shop or outdoors. For a long time I heard nothing. I had given up on learning who Pappa's patient was when I saw a faint light flicker outside. I extinguished the only candle that was burning in the house and crept to the window, hoping to see the person standing out there. I couldn't see anyone.

But moments later I heard Pappa unlock the outside door to the apothecary and two sets of soft footfalls made their way to the rear of the shop.

I strained to hear their voices through the wooden door that separated our house from the shop. They were speaking in very low tones, as if they didn't want to be overheard.

Who could possibly overhear them but me?

No one.

Why would Pappa be taking such care not to let his daughter hear his conversation with a patient?

There was no explanation.

I continued listening at the door to the apothecary until I heard the stranger leave. I hurried to our front door and, as silently as I could, opened the door a hand's width to see who was leaving. I would hear Pappa sliding the rod to come back into the house, so as soon as I heard him I could close the door quickly and be in the bedchamber doorway before he could come into the house.

The moon shone brightly on the dusting of snow outside. There was no other light save for the low orange glow coming from the embers in the fireplace behind me, so I didn't worry that the person could see me.

I covered my mouth with my hand to keep myself from

gasping aloud when I saw the man coming around the corner of the house from the shop.

It was the stranger from behind the tannery in Town.

The same boots, the same cloak, the same long hair.

And then a sudden recognition dawned on me like a shaft of sunlight through a heavy cloud—he had been the person leaving the apothecary the night Pappa was doing business by candlelight. The same boots, the same cloak, the same long hair.

Who was he? And what did he want with my father?

I knew better than to ask Pappa about the man the following morning, and later that day we became very busy as a wagon bearing a delivery arrived from Philadelphia with all kinds of supplies, medical implements, and medicines. Between patients who came into the apothecary, we sorted and catalogued the items in the delivery.

Gray light was seeping across the sky from east to west when I told Pappa I would leave to prepare our supper. He nodded, noting something in his ledger, and I left the shop quietly.

After supper Pappa and I read for a short time by the fire, then I went to bed. I hadn't been asleep long when I heard a soft scraping sound coming from the main room. Creeping to the coverlet that hung in the door frame, I watched as Pappa disappeared into the apothecary. Was he worried about our inventory? Did he forget something in there? Was he conducting further business in there under the blanket of darkness?

I only hesitated a moment before stepping across the main room in my bare feet. The floor was still warm from the fire, but as soon as I opened the apothecary door a crack, I could feel the cold from the room envelope me.

"Pappa?" I called out in a hoarse whisper. Why was I whispering?

"Yes, Sarah, I'm over here."

"Are you all right, Pappa? I heard the shop door open and I thought you might need help in here. Are you alone?"

"Yes, I'm alone. I, uh, merely forgot to make a notation in the ledger before eating supper. I came in to do it in case I forget before morning."

"All right, then. Good night, Pappa."

"Good night, my dear."

Pappa wasn't telling me the truth.

The next day Widow Beall sent for Pappa because she needed a poultice for one of her children. Pappa went to examine the child to know exactly what was required in the poultice and, though I knew better, I sneaked into the apothecary and opened the ledger to the pages where he had noted the contents of the delivery.

Something wasn't quite right. Not everything was listed. I remembered having seen a pair of small forceps and those were not noted in the thick book on the page marked "Supplies." Nor were the pliers I had seen, nor the small saw, nor the tins that would normally be used to catch blood and store tablets and other small medicines.

I wondered why those items had been left off the list, and how many other items that I couldn't remember had been left off, too.

I turned quickly to the shelf where Pappa kept his liquid medicines and remedies. With bottles tinkling and bumping each other, I hurriedly looked for items we had received the previous day. Pappa would label them in Latin in his strong hand later in the day, after he returned from Widow Beall's house, but I felt sure I could remember at least some of the remedies we had received. I wanted to know if they were missing, too.

And as surely as day turns to night, I realized several bottles were not among their brethren on the long wooden shelf. I did not know how much time I would have before Pappa returned from the Widow's house, so I did not dare dawdle in the apothecary to look for the things I knew I had seen the previous day.

While I waited for Pappa to come home, I sat in the main room and wondered what he could have done with the missing supplies and remedies. There were boxes and crates on the floor of the apothecary—items from Philadelphia often came in wooden boxes because they had to be protected—so it was possible he had hidden the items in one of those.

But why? Why would Pappa have to hide his inventory?

As the days passed, the fever returned to Town and it seemed everyone in the village had caught it except for a very few people. We were lucky to have escaped it. It caused fits of coughing, flushed and hot skin, and labored breathing. Pappa did not let me leave the house, though he left on several occasions without explanation.

"I rely on you for too many things now that Mamma is gone," he said one morning. He had a wistful look in his eyes as he stared out the window. "I know you want to see Patience, but I'm afraid I just can't let you go anywhere until this fever has exhausted itself. God willing, it will go away and never return to these shores."

"I don't mind, Pappa. I want to help in the apothecary and I don't mind staying home. I am content doing my chores and watching the snow fall outdoors." I wondered how Patience's mother was faring in the snow. She disliked snow as much as Patience did and with a new baby about to arrive, she must have been feeling trapped in the house. I prayed that the fever hadn't visited their family. I prayed for Arthur and his family, too, asking God to keep them all well.

It had been snowing for four days. A deep blanket of white covered the ground in graceful hillocks and curves. It made fascinating shapes where the wind blew it into corners and around obstacles. A little bit of snow came in under our door, but I was quick to sweep it into a small pile and put it outside whenever I noticed it. There were times I forgot about my chores in my enchantment when the snow was falling. The ground around our house was perfectly smooth and white—I remembered how Mama had disliked the snow. She had missed the milder winters in England.

When my thoughts turned to Mamma, I often got right back to work to keep my mind and my hands busy. I would bake, mend, clean, and even wash our clothes in snow that I melted over the fire.

I was tidying the hearth one evening long after the sun had gone down. Pappa was in the apothecary and there came an urgent thumping noise at the door. I hurried to open it.

I was shocked when the stranger from behind the tanner's shop stumbled through the door, holding his arm. By the light of the moon I could see a jagged line of blood droplets trailing behind him in the snow. Blood seeped between his fingers and he looked at me, surprise evident in his eyes.

"Is William here? I am in need of his services." He spoke through clenched teeth.

I helped him to sit down on the stool near the fire. His legs appeared a bit shaky and his pallor had turned a ghastly gray. I turned and ran to the apothecary door.

"Pappa! Come quickly. There's a man in here who's hurt." I turned back to the man sitting by the fire with his eyes closed. He was taking big gulps of air.

It only took a moment for Pappa to reach the man's side.

"What happened?" he asked grimly as he gently peeled off the man's cloak.

"Wolf," was all the man could utter.

The man's answer shocked me into paralysis. I could only stare at him, my mouth open, as Pappa worked to free the man's arm from his shirt sleeve so he could examine the wound more closely.

"Sarah, are you listening? I need your help," Pappa said in a sharp voice. I looked at him in confusion, obviously having missed something he had said. His words pushed me into action.

"What do you need?" I stepped closer to him.

"Get me a pair of snippers, a roll of lint, and a jar of honey. You know where they are in the shop." I fled to the apothecary and rifled through Pappa's supplies until I spied the thin box containing rolls of lint. I grabbed a roll, then took a jar of honey and a pair of snippers from the counter and returned to Pappa, who was telling the man to close his eyes and look away from the wound.

He took the snippers from me and carefully cut the skin from around the gaping gash. The skin was craggy, its edges rough. Pappa, I knew, wanted to make the edges of the skin smooth and straight so he could see the wound more closely. He examined it while I held the lamp aloft near the man's shoulder. I tried not to look as the man inhaled sharply every time Pappa touched the skin to cut it.

Finally Pappa seemed satisfied with his work. He took the honey I held out to him and applied a thick coating to the wound. Then he took the lint and wrapped it carefully around the man's arm. "I'll need to replace this every day until you're healed, Richard," he told the man.

Richard. It seemed a refined name for someone who went about after dark, conducting business in the backs of unlit rooms. He was far younger than Pappa—so how had Pappa come to know him?

"Thank you, William," Richard said. He winced and swallowed hard.

"Sarah, please get a piece of willow bark from the shop and bring it here," Pappa said. For the second time, I hastened to the apothecary and, holding a candle so I could see the writing on the bottles and jars, found the willow bark. I removed the cap from the jar and took one rather large piece back to Pappa. He handed it to Richard with the instruction to chew on it for the relief of pain caused by the wolf's bite.

"Was there only one wolf?" asked Pappa. "And where did you come upon it?"

Richard swallowed hard again, then tilted his head back and let out a short burst of breath. "I was coming through the woods to see you when I was attacked. I know not how many wolves there were. There seemed to be two or three, but I could be mistaken. One wolf could have just as easily done this damage." Pappa nodded gravely.

I was intrigued by Richard's voice. I knew from the way he spoke that he was from England. Now I was even more curious to learn how he was acquainted with Pappa. Had he known Mamma, too?

"Can I get you a drink of cider?" I asked, standing before the young man. He looked up at me and nodded, chewing furiously on his willow bark.

"The bark will lessen the pain from the bite, but it will take some time," Pappa cautioned. "Perhaps you should sleep here tonight. You should not be going back to town with a wolf out there, and you already hurt."

Richard touched his bandaged arm gingerly. "It would not be proper, William."

"Bah. Who cares about propriety right now? Would you rather be eaten alive by a wolf?"

Richard grimaced. "Of course not."

"Then you'll stay here. You'll use my bed in front of the fire.

That way I can keep watch on your wound and treat it again if the need arises."

"You're very kind, William. Thank you."

"Pappa, if you would prefer to let him sleep in the bed, that would be fine," I said.

"I think he should stay in front of the fire, where he will be warmer," Pappa said, glancing at me. His pointed look told me I had said enough.

When I had poured cider for Richard and a measure for Pappa, too, I retired to the bedchamber, pulling the coverlet across the doorway after me. I lay in bed for a time before going to sleep, listening to the low voices of Pappa and Richard in the main room. I could not hear what they were saying, but it was evident from Richard's weakening voice that he was in pain and needed to sleep.

Pappa must have known it, too, because very soon their talking ceased. I could hear Pappa dragging the sleeping mat in front of the fireplace. I could hear soft scuffling sounds and knew Pappa was helping Richard down onto the mat. A groan of pain from Richard confirmed this. Then I heard the *creak* of the rocking chair and I knew that Pappa was settling into it for a long night of watching Richard.

The hideous, angry look of the wolf bite weighed heavily on my mind. I kept returning to the same horrifying thought: had something like that, only worse, befallen Mamma the day she disappeared?

When I woke up the next morning Pappa and Richard were still sleeping. Pappa looked uncomfortable, slumped in the rocking chair, his chin resting on his chest. I wondered about Richard's ability to sleep through the pain of a wolf bite—he must have been exhausted. I shivered from the cold in the room as I bustled about quietly, fixing the morning meal for the two men. The fire needed wood, but I dared not add wood because it would make so much noise. Pappa always rose early, but I was sure he hadn't enjoyed much sleep. Both men needed to rest.

I returned to the bedchamber and tidied the tiny room while I waited for them to stir. I wished I had something to read, but it was so dark in there that I probably would have had to strain my eyes to see even the largest print. I sat on the edge of the bed wondering again about the wolf that had bitten Richard. Could that very same wolf have been prowling about the day Mamma disappeared?

My thoughts were interrupted by sounds of movement from the main room. I pulled aside the coverlet and peered into the gloom. Richard was attempting to raise himself from his position in front of the fire. He winced as he tried to rest on one elbow, then he lay back down and exhaled heavily. My father stirred in his chair, but only shifted slightly and gave a loud snort before going back to sleep.

I must have made an involuntary noise, because Richard looked in my direction. I looked down, embarrassed that he had seen me behind the coverlet. He probably thought I had been watching him sleep. I stepped into the room, determined to prove that hadn't been the case.

"I was tidying the bedchamber when I heard a sound. Can I help you?" I asked in a whisper.

Richard grimaced in pain, still lying on the floor. He tried lifting his injured arm, but was only able to get it a few short inches from the floor.

"Can you help me to sit?" he asked.

I stepped toward him just as Pappa looked up with a start.

"What? Hmm?" he asked. He realized then what was happening and stood up to help Richard himself.

"I'll take care of Richard, Sarah. Is there food ready?"

"Yes, Pappa, there is porridge. I thought you both might like eggs, too, but I haven't been outside yet because I didn't want to wake you."

"Thank you," he said, nodding. "If you'll gather the eggs, I'll help Richard to sit up and then get some wood on the fire."

I reached for my cloak, then for the basket that we kept on a shelf near the door. As soon as I opened the door, I was beset by a shock of air so cold it made me sneeze. I hurriedly pulled the door closed behind me, not wishing to let any more cold air into the house, and strode to the coop where the hens were abed. I unlatched the henhouse door with fingers that fumbled from the cold, then stepped inside, wrinkling my nose from the odor. But it was warm in there, and I was grateful for its brief respite while I gathered several eggs. I promised the hens I would return shortly with their food, then ran back to the house.

"It's cold out there today!" I exclaimed when I was inside. The fire was beginning to roar again with wood Pappa had added, and the room was growing a bit warmer.

"I'm sorry to make you go outside," said Richard from where he sat on the stool next to the table. He looked worn and haggard. The apothecary door was closed, and I assumed Pappa was in there.

"Don't apologize," I said, setting the basket on the table and taking off my cloak. "I have to go back outdoors to feed the animals. I'll do that as soon as I've prepared your eggs."

"It is very kind of you."

I am sure I blushed, but I didn't say anything.

Pappa came into the room from the shop just a few moments later, rubbing his hands together. "Sarah, we may need to open the door between the house and the shop today so I can get some heat in there. I don't want my medicines to freeze."

I was cracking eggs into the pan hanging over the fire. "That's fine, Pappa. It will still be warmer in here than it is outside," I said with a smile. "I'll be grateful for any heat from the fire when I get in from feeding the hens and cows."

I put the eggs on our trenchers, along with a scoop of porridge for both men, and took them to the table.

"Thank you." Richard looked up at me with his arresting eyes as he spoke, and for the first time I noticed what I had missed before.

A white scar ran from the outer corner of his right eye diagonally down to the corner of his mouth. I was so startled when I saw it that I almost dropped his trencher before him on the table.

"I haven't had eggs in a long time. These look good," he said. He had surely noticed my rudeness on seeing his scar and was no doubt ignoring my reaction to be polite.

I knew the color was rising in my cheeks and I hastened to retrieve the cider from the shelf where it sat. I poured three mugs of cider while the men ate their eggs.

"How is your arm feeling now that you're moving around a bit?" Pappa asked as he took a bite of porridge.

Richard looked at his arm and tried lifting it as he had when he first woke up. "It's quite lame from sleeping."

"I'll redress it before you leave this morning," Pappa said. "Will you be able to get back to the village by yourself, or will you need my help?"

"I'll be fine getting back by myself. I must thank you again for your hospitality and your speed in binding my arm last night."

"Do you need more willow bark?"

"No, thank you. I have some in Town."

I watched the exchange with interest, wondering why I had only seen Richard in the village one time. I wondered where he lived and what his occupation was.

As soon as the men had finished eating, I cleared away their trenchers and they went into the apothecary. I wondered if Pappa would bring the rolled lint into the house to dress Richard's arm, but I knew it was unlikely. Last night had been an emergency; Pappa had had no choice but to remove Richard's shirt while I watched, but I knew it had been improper and an action Pappa would not willingly repeat in the light of daytime. I could hear their low voices in the shop as I cleaned up from our meal and readied to go outside to the cow pen.

"Sarah, I will accompany Richard as far as Daniel Ames's house to make sure he is strong enough to continue on to town, then I will stop in at Widow Beall's house to make sure she doesn't need anything. I'll be back before long."

"All right, Pappa."

"Thank you again for your assistance last night," Richard said as Pappa helped him pull his cloak on. I noticed, as I hadn't before, that the cloak was too small for Richard's frame. I glanced at his boots, which had seemed heavy and sturdy from a distance in town, but upon closer examination were torn and stained.

"You are welcome," I said, then ducked out the door in front of them. While I fed the animals I wondered about Richard. He carried himself with a decided air of refinement, but the scar on his face and the shabby cut of his clothes...

"Hullo!" came a voice from beyond the henhouse.

I glanced up to see Arthur standing there.

"Good morning," I answered. "Is everyone at your house well? Have you come for medicine?"

"No, thanks be to God," he answered with a smile. "Everyone is well. I came to see if you would like to walk again with me today."

I decided I didn't care what people might think if they saw us out walking again. "I might be able to walk for a short while later this afternoon. I have mending to do today and I must do that while the light is strongest."

"Very well. I'll come for you later today," he answered. With a short wave he turned around and disappeared from view.

# CHAPTER 6

*A*fter I had fed the animals I went into the house to begin mending. I hadn't completed the first of Pappa's two shirts when there was a knock at the door. Patience was standing there in the cold, blowing on her fingers to keep them warm. I smiled when I saw her.

"How is everyone feeling at your house?" I asked.

"Fine, thank God. Did you and your father get sick?"

"No," I said. "We've been staying in our house as much as possible."

"That was wise," Patience said. "Are you mending today?"

"Yes. How about you?" I replied.

"I was, but Mother sent me over to pick up some basil for one of her headaches. We've used up our entire supply because of all the headaches she gets."

"Pappa's not here, but I can fetch you some from the shop," I said, beckoning for her to follow me into the apothecary.

Patience watched as I rummaged around on Pappa's shelf, looking for the jar containing the basil. Dried, it could be used as a snuff for relief of headaches. Patience's mother had used a great deal of it trying to rid herself of headaches; they had been getting steadily worse since the end of summer.

When I finally located the jar of basil, I was surprised to find that it only contained a small amount. I knew we had a large store of it somewhere, so I set the jar aside and bent down to look through some of the wooden boxes under the shelf. Glancing quickly through the closest boxes, I didn't see any basil. Patience watched me, shivering.

"Do you need some help?" she asked.

"No, thank you," I grunted, reaching far under the shelf to pull out one of the boxes. I pulled it toward me and sat back on my heels to pry off the lid.

I didn't see any basil at first, but what I did find was surprising. Many of the items we had received in the delivery from Philadelphia were in there—the jars and boxes and containers I hadn't been able to find earlier to catalogue.

I must have looked shocked, because Patience came to stand next to me. "What did you find?" she asked.

Something told me not to tell her about the medicines that had been missing, so I made up an answer.

"Oh, nothing of importance. I just didn't expect to find so many things in this box. I didn't realize what a large inventory we had!" I laughed lightly, hoping she didn't realize I was telling an untruth.

"Any basil?" she asked, moving back toward the door to the main room of the house, where it was warmer.

I had noticed some basil in the box, but just as I had felt I shouldn't reveal anything about the missing medicines, I had a hunch I should not tell Patience I had found basil in the box. For some reason, Pappa had put this basil away and not set it out.

But we had harvested a huge amount of basil from our summer garden, and I knew there had to be some more of the comforting and fragrant herb somewhere else in the shop. After replacing the box with the missing medicines, I pulled out three other boxes and rifled through them before I found the basil I had dried early in the fall. I refilled the jar on the shelf, inhaling the dusty, pungent scent, then poured some into a small sack for Patience to take to her mother.

"I'll put this on your father's account," I told her as we went back into the main room. "Would you like to stay for a bit?"

"I can only stay for a few minutes," she replied. "I am worried about Mother's headache. It seems she's in pain more often, but also that the pain is getting worse each time. I worry about the new babe, too. I hope it arrives soon and that Mother and the babe are healthy."

The furrow in Patience's brow told me more than her words. She was in a constant state of worry and I was concerned that her fretting might result in headaches of her own. Her father needed her to help around the house and farm when her mother was confined to her bed.

"Let me make you some tea," I said. "We have some peppermint left and it makes a wonderful, refreshing tea. When Captain Winslow returns from his trip to England, he shall bring me more English tea, but for now we have our own mixture." I took two mugs from the shelf near the fireplace and set them on the table. I crumbled a goodly portion of mint leaves into a strainer and placed it over one of the mugs. When I had poured hot water into each mug and the scent of warm mint was wafting through the room, I gave one of the mugs to Patience as she sat by the fire.

"Are you able to go for a walk this afternoon?" she asked. "I know it's cold outside, but we wouldn't have to walk for long. I feel I'll need a few minutes away from the house."

I looked into the fire while I answered my friend. "I'm so sorry, Patience. I can't go out walking today because I have promised to walk with Arthur."

"Arthur?" she exclaimed. I looked at her to find her eyes dancing, her mouth set in a wide grin. "I told you Arthur fancies you! This is wonderful news. I would rather you spend your time walking with him than with me—just think, it won't be long now before he asks you to marry him!" Her feet were tapping on the floor with excitement.

"Slow down, Patience," I said with a laugh. "Arthur wants nothing of the sort, and neither do I. He will be moving to England shortly to continue his studies to be a pastor, just like his father. He likes to talk to me because I came from England just four years ago and I can tell him about the land and the people."

"I'll just bet that's all he wants," Patience said, a sly smile on her face. "Never mind. We'll see who's right and who's wrong soon enough. I heard the news that he is going to England. When does he leave?" She had ignored my protestation about marrying Arthur.

"He hasn't said, but I imagine it won't be too long now because his mother was talking about it, too, when she was in here a few days ago."

"I wonder if he's nervous about leaving Town. He's never been away from here, you know." Sometimes I forgot Patience had grown up in New Jersey, back when it was called West Jersey, and knew far more about the area and the people than I did.

"He doesn't give the impression of being nervous, but he's a man. Men don't often show how they're really feeling," I said in what I hoped was a wise voice.

Patience stood up and took her mug to the shelf near the fireplace. "I should be getting back so Mother can use the basil. Thank you for the tea, Sarah. Remember all the things you and Arthur talk about on your walk today, because I want to hear everything next time I see you!" She winked, then pulled her cloak over her shoulders.

I opened the door for her and just as she was leaving I had a thought. "Patience, you've lived here all your life. Do you know of a young man named Richard—" I stopped as I realized I didn't know Richard's surname.

"Richard who? I have known two or three people named Richard," she said.

"I don't know his surname. When I know, I'll ask you again."

She seemed content with my answer and didn't ask any questions about Richard, for which I was grateful.

I returned to my mending and worked until it was time to prepare the noonday meal. I knew Pappa would be home soon and he would be hungry.

When he returned he stamped the snow from his shoes as he came into the house. "It's a goodly cold day!" he exclaimed.

I hurried to lay another log on the fire, then placed the trenchers on the table as Pappa sat down. We both ate in silence for several minutes before I broached the subject that lay on my mind.

"Pappa, do you think Richard's arm will heal properly?"

He nodded, still chewing, then swallowed and set his knife down. "As long as he continues to change the dressing every day and doesn't develop a fever, I think he will be fine. It may take some time before he can return to his full work."

Pappa had unwittingly invited more questions from me about our mysterious visitor.

"And what does he do for a job?" I asked.

Pappa narrowed his eyes for just a moment, then picked up his knife and speared a piece of pork with it. He put it in his mouth and chewed slowly, almost as if he was trying to avoid my question.

"He is skilled. Do not worry yourself about Richard. He will recover the full use of his arm." With those words, Pappa implied that there would be no further discussion of Richard or the condition of his injury.

After our meal Pappa left to work in the apothecary while I continued the mending until the sun was much lower in the sky.

I was startled when there was a knock on the door, and suddenly I remembered having promised Arthur I would walk with him. I had forgotten about it in the mindless drudgery of mending clothes and linens.

I opened the door to find Arthur smiling. I invited him to come indoors while I put away the mending and donned my cloak, but he chose to wait outside, as propriety dictated. I hurried to put away the mending, then opened the door as I was pulling the hood of my cloak over my head.

"It's chilly out today!" I exclaimed as we set off toward the village.

"I'm sure it will snow before morning," Arthur answered, looking up toward the sky. "I hope you don't mind being outside for a short while."

"Mind? I love it," I assured him. "It's invigorating!"

"Mother and Father say the snow is God's way of reminding us that He watches over us by providing us with warm homes and food to eat during winter," Arthur said.

I thought about it for a minute as we continued to walk in silence. Then I spoke. "I'm not sure I agree with that, but it's an interesting way of looking at the changes of season. What do your mother and father say about summer? It's very warm and there are few places to cool off."

"I don't know. I've never asked them about summer. I will ask them this evening."

I groaned inwardly. When would I learn to keep my mouth closed and my opinions to myself? The last thing I wanted was to have Pastor and Mistress Reeves think I was contradicting the pastor's teachings.

"You don't need to ask them," I hastened to assure Arthur. "I think they would say that summer is God's way of making us grateful for the cool of spring and autumn."

Arthur looked at me with bright eyes. "I think you are absolutely right. That is highly insightful."

"Thank you." I changed the subject quickly. "How is your father feeling? Has the ache in his stomach improved?"

"It is much improved. Thank you for asking. He is still not taking much food, but he is feeling better. I will tell him you were asking after him."

I didn't mind that, so I merely smiled at Arthur.

"Say, Sarah, would you like to join my family for the Sunday meal this week?"

I almost tripped over something on the ground. Or perhaps there was nothing there at all. I didn't know what to say. It was such an unusual request. Had Patience been right all along? Did Arthur have something in mind other than simply friendship? The thought frayed my nerves.

"I will ask my father if he thinks that would be acceptable," I answered. I couldn't think of anything else to say. I didn't know if I wanted to eat a meal with the Reeves family.

We hadn't gone far when there was a shout behind us. We turned around to see Arthur's young brother running after us.

"Wait, Arthur!" he cried out.

"Peter, is there trouble at home?" Arthur asked. His voice was edged with a touch of anxiety I hadn't detected until that moment.

"No, none at all. I just wanted to join you on your way to the village. It gets so boring when one walks by oneself."

Arthur sighed and turned to me. "Do you mind if Peter comes along?"

I smiled, secretly relieved to have another companion, in case Arthur wished to discuss matters I didn't want to talk about.

"I don't mind at all," I said in my most charitable voice. Arthur looked at once relieved and frustrated, but I pretended not to notice.

"Peter, it's nice to see you," I said to the boy, who was about ten years old.

"Thank you, Miss. It is a pleasure to see you, too." I again pretended not to notice when Peter nudged Arthur with his elbow and winked at his older brother. What was going on here?

Our trio had only walked past two houses when Arthur said to Peter, "You go along to the village. It's getting colder outside and I think Miss Sarah should return home. I will accompany her and meet you at home later."

Peter nodded and waved as he began running toward the village.

"I must apologize for Peter," Arthur said as we turned around and headed back in the direction of my house. "He could use some lessons in discretion."

"I think he's delightful," I answered. Arthur smiled and his shoulders seemed to relax. He offered me his arm and suddenly I was again filled with such indecision as to not know how to respond. Should I take his arm because it was the polite thing to do and he expected me to do so? Or should I refrain, unsure as I was now about Arthur's intentions and my readiness to discuss certain matters regarding the two of us?

I decided to take his arm for just a moment, then I pulled away, breathing into both hands to keep them warm. It seemed a good compromise.

When we arrived at my house, Arthur lingered at the door to chat about meaningless things. I reached for the door handle several times, trying to hint to him that I was ready to go inside, but he seemed not to notice. My fingers were becoming more numb from the cold with every passing moment, and I was eager to get inside to warm them.

I had just reached for the door handle for what I hoped would be the last time when, quite unexpectedly, I heard voices coming from the side of the house. I whirled 'round, startled, as Richard and Pappa came around the corner of the house from, I assumed, the apothecary.

They were talking in low, earnest tones, but stopped immediately upon seeing me and Arthur standing in front of them.

"Ah, Sarah. I'm glad you're home," Pappa said. He turned to Richard with a blank expression which gave me no clue as to the tenor of their conversation. "Thank you for stopping by, Richard. Your arm is healing nicely."

Whatever Pappa and Richard had been talking about, Richard gave no indication as he took his leave and lifted his worn, dirty hat with his good arm. "Thank you, William. Miss Sarah." He bowed ever so slightly, his eyes catching and holding mine for an instant. I looked away.

"Good day," I mumbled.

Pappa thanked Arthur for seeing me home, then we went inside and Arthur went on his way. As I hung up my cloak near the door, I could feel Pappa's eyes on me in the swiftly-darkening room.

"Did you and Arthur enjoy your walk?" he finally asked.

"I suppose so," I answered. I glanced quickly at Pappa out of the corner of my eye.

"He is a fine young man," he said, nodding.

I could feel my eyes narrowing. "I suppose so," I repeated.

"Has he told you any more about going to England to continue his studies?"

"No, his younger brother accompanied us for much of our walk, so Peter did most of the talking. He is a most precocious boy."

"Hmm," Pappa said.

"Why do you say that?" I asked. I had a feeling I knew the answer; it seemed to me that Pappa was happy with Arthur's attentions toward me and he did not want Peter interrupting our time together. I was not as happy as Pappa about Arthur's attentions.

His next words confirmed my suspicions. "I do believe he may be planning to ask for your hand." I could feel my stomach begin to ache and my hands became clammy. I wiped them on my skirt.

Then I closed my eyes and said a silent prayer for the wisdom to answer my father without upsetting him.

"Pappa, I am not sure I want to be married. I like living here, with you, taking care of the house and helping in the apothecary." I didn't add, *and I do not love Arthur Reeves.*

Pappa looked at me kindly, with a faraway look of sadness in his eyes. "Sarah, your help around the house and the apothecary have been invaluable since your mother—" He paused for just a moment. "—since your mother disappeared, but if you were to marry Arthur I would simply hire a girl from the village to help me. I do not want you to remain unmarried because you desire to help your old father."

I suppressed a groan. I should have known Pappa would not simply accept my explanation and suddenly decide I needn't marry.

I was spared from having to respond to him by a heavy knock on the door. Pappa rose and opened it.

The village magistrate, Josiah Browne, was standing in the doorway. "William, I'm glad you're here. I'd like to talk to you, if you have a moment," Mister Browne said.

"Of course, Josiah. Come in." Pappa stood behind the door as he held it open, waiting for Mister Browne to enter the house.

Mister Browne stood in the center of the room, twisting his hat in his hands. He glanced toward me with lowered eyes. "Do you suppose we could talk in your shop, William?" The implication was clear—he didn't want me to hear whatever he had to say.

My father looked at Mister Browne, then at me, then back at Mister Browne. He was clearly surprised by the request.

"Of course, Josiah," he answered. "Come with me." Mister Browne followed him through the door that led to the apothecary, then Pappa closed the door softly.

Knowing that Mister Browne didn't want me to overhear their conversation, I was naturally seized with a blazing desire to hear what he had to say to my father. Was it about Arthur? I supposed not. Why would Josiah Browne want to discuss Arthur with my father? Was it about village business? I doubted it, since Pappa had never shown much inclination to involve himself in the business affairs of Town Bank. And if it were village business, why would Mister Browne wish to discuss such a thing out of my hearing?

I inched closer to the shop, wondering if I could hear their conversation through the wooden door. I pressed my ear to the door, trying to block out the low hissing and crackling from the fireplace, but I could only make out a few words, spoken in a low rumble.

The words I heard chilled me.

"Ruth..."

"Her disappearance..."

"Captain Eli..."

Now I knew why Mister Browne hadn't wanted me to hear him talking, and I wished I hadn't heard a single word. I chided myself for eavesdropping. I knew better than to do such a thing, and God had punished me for committing a sin.

I shrank back toward the fireplace where, just a few minutes earlier, Pappa and I had been discussing a possible betrothal to Arthur. Suddenly the unease of that conversation seemed preferable to the torment in my mind.

What did Josiah Browne know about my mother's disappearance? And what did Captain Eli have to do with it?

I buried my face in my hands as tears sprang to my eyes. It was as if Mamma had disappeared again. The memories of the days after she went missing roared around inside my head like one of the violent thunderstorms I remembered from England.

I could hear my father's voice coming from the apothecary, raised now in response to whatever Mister Browne was telling him. But this time I didn't want to know what he was saying. I ran into the bedchamber, put my hands over my ears, and closed my eyes.

I sat there for several long minutes before I opened my eyes and noticed a sliver of light on the floor, coming from the main room. I looked up and saw my father holding back the coverlet which separated the two rooms.

"What are you doing?" he asked.

I folded my hands and put them in my lap. I couldn't look at him. "I didn't want to hear what you and Mister Browne were saying."

"Sarah, look at me," he said. Head down, I lifted my eyes toward his.

"Did you hear anything Mister Browne said in the shop?" he asked. I couldn't lie to my father and make my sin even worse. I nodded.

"I'm sorry," I said in a quiet voice. "Temptation got the better of me."

"And what did you hear?"

"Only a few words. Mamma's name, and Captain Eli's name." I paused. "And the word 'disappearance.'"

Pappa said nothing, so I continued to talk.

"Does Captain Eli know something about Mamma's disappearance? Does Mister Browne know?" I asked. I knew I should leave the subject to Pappa, but I couldn't help myself.

"Mister Browne was merely here to repeat something he thought I should know," Pappa said. "The truth is, I don't know whether Captain Eli knows anything about Mamma's disappearance."

"So why did Mister Browne mention the captain's name?"

Pappa sighed, running his hand along the length of his beard. "I'm afraid that's not something I can discuss with you, Daughter. Let us eat supper so we can get some sleep." He seemed suddenly tired, as if all the cares of the world were weighing on his mind.

I set out our evening meal and we ate in silence. Even the sounds from the fire, normally comforting and warm, sounded harsh in the quiet of the room. Pappa's thoughts were far away —I could tell from the blank expression in his eyes as he ate dinner without seeming to taste the food. I had added extra butter to his potatoes, just the way he liked them, and he didn't even mention it.

That night while my body adjusted to the frigid temperature in the bedchamber, I could hear Pappa readying for bed. But the longer I listened, the longer he stayed awake, tossing and moving about on the floor in front of the fireplace. I wanted to talk to him, to have him answer all my questions, but I knew he would not. So he didn't sleep, and I didn't sleep.

What had they been saying about Mamma?

When I got out of the bed the next morning I was cross from not getting enough sleep and from not being privy to the information about Mamma that Mister Browne and Pappa, and perhaps Captain Eli, seemed to share.

I decided that if they weren't going to tell me, I was going to figure it out for myself.

# CHAPTER 7

*W*hen Pappa was in the apothecary later that afternoon, I went to visit Patience. I took a loaf of bread and some fresh butter for the family to enjoy; Patience's mother always praised my bread.

I nodded toward the door when I saw Patience to let her know there was something I needed to talk to her about in private. After I had visited with her mother and sisters for several minutes, Patience asked for permission to go on a short walk with me.

Once we were out of earshot of the house, she turned to me eagerly.

"Well, what is it? What do you have to tell me?"

I knew she thought it was about Arthur, and I wasn't wrong. When I told her it was about something I had overheard Mister Browne saying, her face fell.

"I thought you were going to tell me that Arthur asked for your hand," she groaned. "And it's just about Mister Browne?"

"Yes, but listen. He came to the door and wanted to discuss something with Pappa. But he would not talk until he and

Pappa had gone into the apothecary and closed the door behind them."

"And?" she prompted, clearly not understanding my urgency in wanting to talk to her.

"And he mentioned the words 'Ruth,' 'disappearance,' and 'Captain Eli.'"

"How do you know that, if the door to the shop was closed?"

"Because I was trying to listen to them."

Patience gave me an arch look. "You shouldn't have done that," she scolded.

"But then I wouldn't know what they were talking about." I raised my eyebrows at her.

She could not possibly argue with such logic, so even though she disapproved of my eavesdropping, she nodded. "So now what are you going to do?" she asked.

"I'm going to find out for myself what they were talking about."

"What?" Patience cried. "However are you going to do that?"

"I need your help."

"How can I be of help to you?" Patience asked, stopping to stand still and stare at me. "I don't know Mister Browne and I only know Captain Eli through the stories I've heard about him."

"Those are probably the same stories I've heard. We don't really know anything about him, do we? We need to figure out a way to find out more. Does your father know him?"

Patience thought for a moment, then she shook her head slowly. "Not well," she said.

We started walking again, this time more slowly, both of us lost in thought. "I am going to go into Town and down to the bay," I said at last.

"Why?" Patience asked.

"Maybe I can overhear a snippet of conversation, a bit of information about Captain Eli. I have a hunch there is more to

him than we understand. Perhaps if I can learn more about him
…"

"I think you should be very careful with such a plan,"
Patience said, turning toward me with worried eyes. "I do not
think it is safe for a young woman to go down there alone." She
did not offer to accompany me, so I didn't ask her to.

"I will be careful," I answered. "I shall write a letter and take
it to the bay under the pretense of giving it to Captain
Winslow to take back to England. Of course, I know that
Captain Winslow is at sea right now, but no one else has to
know that."

"I wish I could offer to go with you, but Mother has asked
me not to stray too far from our house. The baby is coming any
day now and she needs me close by."

"Of course you must stay near your mother. In fact, you
should probably get back there now." We turned around and
walked back toward Patience's house as we continued talking.
"May I ask a favor?" I asked.

"Certainly," Patience said. "I'll do anything I can to help you."

"I only ask that you listen for anything your father may say
about Captain Eli. We don't even know where he lives. Does he
live in Town Bank? Does he have a wife? Any information
would be helpful."

Patience nodded, her face grave. "I will listen for anything
my father says, but I'm afraid it likely won't be much."

We had arrived at Patience's house. "Thank you, Patience," I
reached out to squeeze her hand. "Thank you for helping me to
find out what happened to my mother."

Patience ran lightly toward the door of her house and turned
to wave at me before going inside.

When I returned to my house Pappa was waiting for me by
the fire.

"Where have you been?" he asked.

"I went to see Patience and to take her mother a loaf of bread and some butter. She is growing more uncomfortable by the day."

"I expect the babe will be here very soon," Pappa said. He probably assumed I had gone to Patience's house *only* to deliver the bread and butter, for he asked no more questions. I was relieved, since I did not want to deceive him about my conversation with Patience. But I certainly couldn't tell him the truth about it, either.

As night drew near the snow began falling in earnest, blanketing the ground and drifting against the door. The wind picked up, lashing our house with strong gusts and howling sounds. Pappa and I went outdoors together to finish the chores quickly, to feed the cows and chickens, and to make sure the pens were secure. When we returned to the house, Pappa suggested that we sit in front of the fire to read together. I was elated.

He read from a book that was set during the summertime of England. For an hour we were transported to our old garden, with its delphiniums, roses, and foxglove. The snowstorm raging outside seemed to quell while Pappa's voice danced lightly over the words written many years before. When he finally closed the book I found myself thinking wistfully of England.

"Do you miss living in England?" Pappa asked, gazing into the fire.

"Sometimes," I admitted. "Especially when you read from the books we brought with us. I miss Grandmamma and my old friends."

"Maybe you can go back there sometime."

"What?" I turned to him with a look of surprise. "How could we ever return to England? The voyage was so long and so difficult."

"I did not say *we* could return to England—I said perhaps *you* could return."

"But why would I ever go back without you?" I asked, my voice rising just a bit.

"Sarah, we talked about this. If you and Arthur are married, you may be going back to England so he can finish his studies."

I bit the inside of my cheek to stop myself from saying anything. Why couldn't Pappa understand that I didn't want to marry Arthur? Why did he and Patience insist on trying to get me to marry him? Besides, he hadn't even asked me! He was merely my friend. It was all too premature.

"Sarah?" Pappa prodded.

"Yes, Pappa?"

"What would you think of going back to England?"

*I'd love to visit someday, but not as Arthur's wife.* Aloud, I answered, "I'm not sure about that, Pappa. I believe I'm getting a headache. I'd like to go to bed a bit early."

Pappa looked concerned. "Let me get you some basil from the shop." He rose and walked toward the shop door.

"No, Pappa. I'm all right. I would rather save the basil for Goodwife Ames. She has had so many headaches that I fear for her. I will feel better if I lie down. Goodnight, Pappa."

"Goodnight, Sarah." I could feel him watching me as I ducked under the coverlet separating the bedchamber from the main room. I knew he didn't understand my reluctance to go back to England. I was afraid to tell him I didn't want to marry Arthur.

I didn't love Arthur. Was there anything wrong with that? I knew from stories Mamma had told me when I was younger that she and Pappa loved each other when they were married. I only wanted the same thing for myself.

But Pappa wouldn't understand.

I hadn't been lying about my headache, but it wasn't so bad that I needed basil or extra sleep. I just wanted the conversation about Arthur to stop. Besides, I needed to think about the letter I would write the next morning and what my next steps would be to figure out what Mister Browne and Captain Eli knew about Mamma's disappearance.

When I had finished my chores the next day, I sat down near our window to write a letter to Grandmamma. Paper was precious, so I only wrote two pages. I used my smallest handwriting and hoped that Grandmamma would be able to see the words or at least find someone who would be able to see the words and read them to her. I told her about the upcoming winter and the preparations we had made for the bad weather. I told her about Patience and her mother's ills during her expectancy. I told her about Pappa and how the apothecary had been busy lately with different fevers and illnesses abounding in the village. When I finished the letter, there was still bright sunlight shining through the window, reflecting off the snow that covered the ground in drifts, sparkling like a million gems. I pulled on my heavy winter shoes and tucked Grandmamma's letter into a pocket of my cloak and slipped out the door, glancing behind me to make sure the door to the apothecary was still closed. I hoped not to be gone long.

I should have known better. The snow was too high and I floundered up to my knees in the bitterly cold stuff until I admitted to myself that I would have to wait until the snow had been tamped down a bit before venturing into the village and down by the water, near to the place where all the boats were moored.

I returned to the house and took up the broom from its spot in the corner, then I went outside again and began sweeping the snow back and forth into higher and higher drifts on each side of the path leading to our front door. I did this until I reached the frozen track of road running past our house under the snow, then realized how hot I had become while I worked. I took off my cloak and hung it up inside, then went out and got back to work. This time I swept snow off the track in the general direction of the village. I hadn't gone far, though, when I heard Pappa calling my name.

"Sarah!"

I turned to look behind me. "Yes, Pappa?"

"What are you doing? You'll catch your death of illness out here in the cold without your cloak! Come inside!"

Dragging the broom behind me, I returned to the house, where Pappa waited for me in front of the door. It was closed to keep the warmth inside.

"Why are you doing this?" he asked.

"I wrote a letter to Grandmamma today and I wanted to go down to the harbor to give it to someone." Pappa opened the door for me and followed me inside.

"Captain Winslow is abroad right now. He can't take the letter to your grandmamma," he said.

"I know, but I thought maybe I could find someone else leaving soon to sail to England. Or perhaps at least going to Philadelphia."

"Very well, if you can get to the bay without having to sweep away the snow the entire way, I will allow you to go. As long as Patience goes with you, or Arthur."

It took great effort not to huff in frustration, but I managed to remain quiet. He mistook my quiet for acquiescence.

"And for the sake of your health, please don't go outside again without your cloak," Pappa finished.

"Yes, Pappa."

A knock sounded at the door and Pappa, who was still standing near it, opened it to find Arthur standing in the snow, a wide smile on his face.

"Hullo, Arthur. How can I help you?" Pappa asked. "Please come in. I hope your family is well?"

"Yes, sir. Thank you, sir. I, uh, I wondered if perhaps I could have a word with you in private."

"Certainly, Arthur. Come into the apothecary." Pappa moved

toward the apothecary door with nary a glance in my direction. Arthur cast a shy look at me. My knees went weak as I suddenly realized why Arthur was here, wanting to speak to my father in private.

He was going to ask for my hand in marriage.

This was dreadful.

The sun had peaked in the sky and was descending toward the west when Pappa and Arthur came into the house from the apothecary. Pappa was grinning and Arthur still wore a look of apprehension. My heart sank because I knew with sudden and ruthless clarity what was coming. I had been foolish to deny the possibility for so long.

Pappa found an excuse to go outside into the cold and snow —he mumbled something about checking on one of the cows— and Arthur remained inside with me.

I didn't know what else to say, so I offered him a drink of cider.

"No, thank you," he replied, intertwining his fingers and then disengaging them again. "Sarah, I would like to talk to you about something."

I had been facing away from him; I turned around slowly, with reluctance. "Yes, Arthur? How can I help you?" I asked, feeling silly.

"Sarah, will you come and sit with me by the fire?" he asked. I nodded and sat down abruptly in the rocking chair in front of the hearth.

He took a deep breath. "You and I have known each other these past four years," he began.

"Yes," I said. "We're good friends."

He gave me a look I couldn't read. "Yes. And in that time, I feel we've come to know a great deal about each other," he continued. I had the feeling that, although we knew a great deal about each other, we did not know a great many *important* things about each other. But I remained silent.

"Sarah, would you consider becoming my wife? I promise to be a good and faithful husband to you. Your father has graciously granted his permission for me to ask you."

I looked into his face, hoping the panic and dismay I felt did not show on my own. The expression in his eyes was anxious, pleading. I couldn't decline without embarrassing him, but I certainly couldn't accept.

I drew a long breath and blew it out slowly. "Arthur, I do not know what to say. This is quite unexpected. Do you suppose I could think about it for a while?"

He was clearly surprised by my response. Had he expected me to accept his proposal immediately? Was that how these things worked? I knew I had disappointed him, but I felt I had answered him in the most honest way I could without humiliating him further.

"Uh, of course not. I mean to say, of course. Take whatever time you need to think about it, discuss it with your father, whatever you need," he repeated. He stood up hastily and looked down. "I'll be going now, Sarah. I hope to talk to you again very soon."

He strode toward the door, pulled it open, and let it close behind him. I sat down again in front of the fireplace, gazing into the flames and wishing more than anything that Mamma were sitting next to me, telling me I had done the right thing and assuring me that waiting for love was the only way to begin a marriage.

Pappa came inside shortly. As he stamped the snow from his shoes he turned an expectant look upon me. When he saw my face, though, his expression became serious.

"You and Arthur talked?" he asked.

I nodded.

"I don't think I need to ask how you responded to his proposal of marriage." He sat in the chair Arthur had vacated only a few minutes earlier.

I shook my head.

"Sarah, why do you not want to marry Arthur? He is a kind young man with a solid future ahead of him as a preacher of God's word. I would think any young woman would be flattered by attention from such a person."

"I *am* flattered, Pappa. And I agree with all you've said about Arthur. It's just that I don't love him. You and Mamma loved each other when you were married, didn't you? Mamma told me you did. And I want that same thing." It felt unusual and rather uncomfortable to be speaking so freely of love to my father.

Pappa sighed. "Yes, Sarah. Your mother and I loved each other from the time we met. But that is not the usual way. The usual way is for love to develop slowly, as the marriage lengthens. We need to bear in mind that you don't want to end up a spinster, either."

I gave Pappa a sharp look and he held up his hands in protest.

"I'm not implying that you're going to be a spinster, Sarah. I am merely saying that spinsterhood is not something you should aspire to and if you wait for love to happen before you marry, it may take too long. It may be too late."

"I am willing to take that chance, Pappa," I said.

"What, precisely, did you say to Arthur?" Pappa asked.

"I told him I would like some time to think over his proposal."

He swallowed and his jaw worked noiselessly. I could tell he was suppressing his disapproval. I didn't blame him—he was worried about me, especially without a mother to offer encouragement.

"Are you simply going to wait a few days and then decline

his proposal?" Pappa asked. "It seems fruitless to wait, in that case."

"I need to do this my way, Pappa," I said. It was forward of me, but since I was being expected to make womanly choices, I would speak my mind to my father in a womanly manner.

He didn't seem taken aback at my audacity. "Very well. I won't speak of it again until you are ready."

We ate our evening meal in relative silence, not looking at each other. I was deep in thought and I suspected he was, too. He probably missed Mamma as much as I did in this circumstance, as any father would.

The sun had melted much of the snow the next day, so I took the opportunity to go to the bay under the pretense of looking for someone who could take my letter to Grandmamma on their next voyage. Before leaving the house I said a quick prayer, asking God to keep me from Arthur's sight when I was out. It was a sinful thing to pray for, I knew.

On my way to the village I knocked on the door of the Ames house to see if Patience would like to accompany me to the harbor. As I had suspected, though, she couldn't leave the house because her mother needed her.

I had promised Pappa I would not go down to the bay by myself, but I had no choice. I had asked Patience to go with me, but she couldn't go. And since I had talked to Pappa about going to the bay, things had changed between Arthur and me. I certainly couldn't go to him for company. I was, therefore, forced to go alone. I wasn't worried, but somehow I knew Pappa might not see things the same way as I.

It seemed my sins against Pappa were piling up.

Much of the previous day's snow had melted into a long, slippery, messy track of mud between our house and the bay at the bottom of the embankment in the village. My shoes were covered in mud by the time I had picked my way along the main street and scrambled down to the bay, close to the boats that were moored in the harbor. Even with the mud and the cold, throngs of men and even some women milled about on the packed sand and long boards that were used for walkways. I stopped for a moment to watch the activity, wondering, now that I was there, how best to go about finding people who might have information regarding Captain Eli.

I eventually decided to plunge myself into the thick of people and start listening to whatever they had to say. The ship that Captain Eli had sailed happened to be in port, so I moved in that direction first. I didn't want to run into the retired Captain because I knew I would stammer and fumble for words in front of him, thinking all the while about his possible involvement in my mother's disappearance.

I didn't see him, but I did see one of the mates I knew had sailed with him. The man was grizzled and dark, as though he had spent too much time in the sun. His hair, which was long and gray, was tied at the nape of his neck with a grimy black ribbon.

As soon as I saw him, I bent over and made a pretense of tying my shoes. I didn't want to draw his attention to myself.

After I had spent a ridiculous length of time pretending to tie my shoes, I straightened up to find that he had moved away into a crowd of men. I sidled over in their direction, thinking that perhaps someone would mention the old captain.

And I was mildly surprised when I did hear talk of Captain Eli. There was a barrel near the crowd and I sat down upon it, not facing the men, trying to look as if I needed a rest. I looked at the letter to Grandmamma which I held in my hand. And I listened, trying to make out strains of conversation. Some of the words I heard made me blush. They were words which Pappa would be angry to have spoken in my presence, but the men were paying me no heed and they didn't even seem to realize I was there.

I don't know how long I had been sitting on the upturned

barrel—probably not more than a few minutes, during which I heard nothing of interest about Captain Eli—when I heard my name called from someone nearby.

"Miss Sarah?"

I looked around in confusion, wondering who could recognize me and know my name down here by the harbor.

"Over here," the voice called.

# CHAPTER 8

*I* turned toward the voice and saw Richard striding toward me, his arm still bandaged and in a sling. There was a jaunty set to the hat he wore, and he looked cleaner than the last time I had seen him. I thought he looked quite handsome.

"Good afternoon, Richard," I said, inclining my head toward him. I hoped he wouldn't ask what I was doing by myself down by the water, but I should have known better.

"Miss Sarah, pray forgive me for being so forward, but are you down here alone?"

"Well," I stammered. "I, well, that is—"

Richard gave me a piercing look and said, "I thought as much. I shall escort you back to your house. This is a rough place, and certainly no place for an unaccompanied young lady."

I must have blushed to my toes, because he took back the hand he had offered to help me off the barrel.

I hastened to explain. "It's just that my father doesn't know I'm down here by myself. He told me to bring my friend, but she was not available and I wanted to get this letter to someone who would be sailing soon." I held up the letter to Grandmamma so he wouldn't think I was lying.

"And I presume you do not wish me to mention your presence here to your father?"

"I would be grateful if you didn't, sir," I said, looking him squarely in the eyes. Those eyes. I hadn't noticed how gray they were—almost like the color of an English sky before a hard rain. "I don't want him to worry about me."

"Then I shall make you an offer," Richard said. "I won't tell him as long as you don't call me 'sir' and as long as you don't come down here alone anymore." He smiled.

I wanted to smile back at him. There were two feelings at war within me. The first was gratefulness to Richard for finding me by the harbor and offering to accompany me home. The second was a smoldering frustration that he, who barely knew me, would have the effrontery to suggest that he would tell my father if he saw me again, unaccompanied, at the bay.

He held out his hand to me again and this time I took it lightly as he helped me hop down from the barrel. He let it go once I was standing next to him on the wet sand, but I noticed the rush of excitement that ran through me for just a moment. I coughed lightly.

Apparently our conversation had attracted the attention of some of the men to whom I had been listening, for they made some crude remarks as I walked away at Richard's side, my head held high and my chin lifted slightly.

But my knees were quaking. I think Richard suspected it, because he put out a hand in case I should need it for support. He ignored the remarks of the vulgar men as we passed them.

"Do you see why it's not a good idea for you to be down here by yourself?" he asked. "These ruffians would think nothing of embarrassing you with their ribald taunts and gestures."

My earlier frustration at him for his patronizing words had evaporated in my thankful relief at his presence, keeping those men from saying who-knew-what to me. I couldn't speak for fear I would break down in tears, so I merely nodded and kept walking.

I think Richard took my silence for peevishness, though. He turned a worried look on me. "Are you all right, Miss Sarah? I don't mean to sound like your father, but I couldn't bear the thought of you suffering taunts and ridicule from those barbarians."

By that time we had almost reached the steep slope leading up to the main street. I finally felt able to speak.

"Pay me no heed, Richard," I said with shake of my head. "I understand now why you said you would have to tell my father if you saw me down here again without a friend to accompany me. The words of those men were not what I expected to hear."

Richard tilted his head back and gave a short laugh. "What, pray, did you expect to hear?"

I shrugged, knowing my face was turning red again. "I expected to hear gossip, I suppose. Perhaps talk of upcoming voyages."

"You've been spending too much time reading those books of yours," he said with a smile. "The gentility you expect is not to be found near sailing vessels, but in a parlor."

"Are you from England?" I asked, surprising myself with the suddenness of the question.

Apparently I surprised him, too. He looked startled, raising his eyebrows at me and slowing his pace for just a moment.

"Yes," was his terse reply. His tone seemed to brook no further questions, so I changed the subject.

"How is your arm?" I asked. That seemed a safe enough topic.

He glanced down at his arm and lifted it a little, as if testing its strength. "It's much better, thank you. Your father probably saved my life the night I was attacked by the wolf. I wouldn't have been able to treat the wound myself because I had lost too much blood to be cognizant of what to do, but he did exactly what he should have done under the dire circumstances."

Richard's words puzzled me. Was he implying that he *approved* of my father's treatment of him? How dare he? My father was probably the best apothecary in the colonies. No one should have to approve of his methods.

I stiffened at his words, and Richard noticed immediately.

"Have I offended you?"

I didn't respond immediately. I had to think carefully about my words before saying them aloud.

After several moments of silence, I spoke. "Are you, perchance, surprised that my father knew exactly what to do?"

"Oh, no, not at all. I know your father by his solid and wide reputation as one of the finest apothecaries on these shores. I was rather clumsily trying to say that his method was exactly the same as what I've been taught."

"And by whom were you taught?" I asked in a rather haughty tone.

"By the excellent masters of the medical college in London."

I had to close my mouth tightly to keep from gasping at his words. "You are a physician?"

"I studied at the medical college, but I have not yet completed my studies. I hope to do so someday."

"Why did you not complete your studies?"

He was quiet for a moment. "There was not enough money for me to continue," he finally said, looking down at the ground. Or perhaps he was looking at his boots, which I noticed were now held together with string.

"I am sorry to hear it," I said. "How did you come to New Jersey if there was no money for you to finish at the medical college?"

"I am working aboard one of the ships," he said. Again, his tone seemed to invite no further questions.

By this time we were at the end of the main street in Town. I stopped walking and turned to him.

"Thank you for escorting me this far, Richard, but I do not wish to trouble you any longer. I will be fine walking the rest of the way to my house by myself." In truth, I would have liked nothing more than to continue walking and talking with him, for he intrigued me, but it would have been unthinkable to suggest such a thing.

The hint of a smile played around the corners of his mouth. He bowed slightly. "Very well, Miss Sarah. I will take my leave of you here and wish you a pleasant afternoon. And remember to bring someone with you the next time you want to venture down to the harbor."

I nodded and left off in the direction of my house, lost in thought. Richard had provided plenty of fodder for my imagination.

Who *was* he? And if he had started life in London—attended the medical college!—what was he doing here in Town Bank, wearing shoes that were tied together with twine? Why did he not wear a fine cloak, but instead a rough one, made of low quality wool?

I wanted to ask my father, but he would wonder where I had seen Richard and I would have to tell him the truth. I supposed Richard could tell Pappa next time they saw each other that he had seen me down by the water by myself, but something told me I didn't have to worry about him revealing my secret.

I quickened my steps when I walked past the lane leading to Arthur's house, not wishing to see him or anyone else in his family just then.

But I needn't have bothered. When I arrived home, I was startled to find Pastor Reeves sitting in front of the fireplace, in earnest conversation with Pappa. The pastor turned and gave me a weak smile when I came into the room, and Pappa closed his eyes, as if in weariness.

"I'll be going, then," Pastor Reeves said, standing up.

"Please, Pastor, do not leave on my account," I said.

"I have to be getting along home, child," he said. He nodded to me, then to Pappa, lifted his hat from the peg by the door, and left us.

After he had closed the door behind him I turned to look at Pappa, who was running his hand across his face.

"I apologize if I interrupted your conversation," I said.

"I daresay he was ready to leave," Pappa said. I wondered if he was going to reveal to me the topic of their discussion.

"We were talking about you, truth be told," Pappa said.

"Me? Whatever for?" But I had a feeling I already knew the answer.

"He came to see if I could explain why you didn't consent to marry Arthur," Pappa said with a short sigh.

"What did you tell him?"

"I told him that you were unsure about your readiness to marry, and especially to do so when it would mean moving back to England. I told him the truth. That is the truth, is it not?"

I nodded. "I'm sorry, Pappa."

"It was not proper of him to come here to seek my opinion," Pappa said. "He admitted as much when he arrived. He asked that I not mention his visit here to his wife, who wouldn't approve of it."

"It is a topic best discussed between Arthur and me, does he not agree?" I asked.

"I'm sure he agrees. I think he is worried that Arthur will not find a wife, that he'll have to travel to England alone without someone to take care of him. And I think there's no small part of him that is hurt that his son has been rejected in an offer of marriage." He gave me a pointed look.

"I should think he ought to speak to me about it, then, instead of you," I pointed out. "You are not the one who asked for time to think about the proposal."

"I reminded him of that, but he thinks I can persuade you to make up your mind quickly, and do so in the affirmative." Pappa chuckled. "He obviously does not know you very well."

I smiled. "I will decide by week's end, Pappa. I promise." But I had already decided.

He gave me a grave look, though his eyes shone. "I know you will do the thing that is right for your future, Sarah."

I busied myself preparing our meal and we ate in the darkening room. I had hoped Pappa would want to read a bit more, but he seemed tired, more tired than usual.

"Pappa, you look bone-weary. Would you like to sleep in the bedchamber tonight? I'm happy to sleep out here on the mat."

"No, Sarah, I'm fine out here. You go along to bed and do not worry about me."

I cleaned the trenchers and stacked them on the shelf near the fireplace, then tidied up the room, swept the hearth, and went to bed. Pappa would put more wood on the fire if he needed it. I heard him coughing as I readied for bed. I hoped he was not getting sick.

Pappa's cough worsened during the night. When I walked into the dim room early the next morning I could make out his form on the sleeping mat, his arm over his eyes, his chest making rasping noises.

I hurried outside to gather a bit of snow from the ground and returned to the hearth, where I set about making tea for him. He stirred and rose up on one arm. "Have the cows been fed yet?"

"No, Pappa. I'll feed them right now. I just wanted to set this water to heating so you can have some tea."

"Thank you, Sarah," he said, and sank back down onto the mat.

"Pappa, what else can I do for you?" I asked.

"Nothing. I'm fine, really. I just need to rest for a bit longer." He put his arm over his eyes again. I hurried outside to feed the cows and the water for Pappa's tea was ready by the time I went back indoors. I prepared the tea the way he preferred, then spoke to him quietly, in case he was sleeping again.

"Pappa, would you like your tea now?"

He struggled into a sitting position on the sleeping mat. "Yes, thank you." He accepted the tea and took a sip, wincing as the hot drink went down his throat.

"Blast. That hurts. Sarah, could you fetch me some honey and preserved lemon from the shop? I'll stir them into this tea and perhaps that will help the pain."

I hurried to get the honey and lemon, then was back in just a few moments. He stirred the ingredients into the tea and drank a long sip, then lay back down again with a stifled groan.

"I'll finish the tea later, if you don't mind, Sarah," he said. I set the cup on the shelf next to the fireplace and went into the bedchamber to tidy the small room. I wasn't surprised to find him sleeping when I returned to the main room.

His cough seemed to abate as the day wore on, but he would thrash about each time he fell asleep and that grew worse as the shadows lengthened. I woke him up several times to offer him small swallows of tea; his skin was hot to my touch. I dipped a square of cloth into water that had melted from snow earlier in the day and applied it to his forehead. He tried to form words with his dry lips, but all he could manage were croaks of sound. My alarm grew as night fell and he lapsed into a fitful slumber. He hadn't spoken a cogent word in hours—not since he had sipped his tea that morning. I watched over him all that night as he tossed about on the sleeping mat, calling out gibberish every so often in an anguished voice.

By morning his skin had grown even warmer and his face was red, his hair drenched with sweat. I tried waking him to help him drink, but he couldn't seem to arise from his stupor. I tried mixing some herbs and sugar in the apothecary to feed him, but he wouldn't open his mouth except to cry out. I tried every fever remedy I could think of, but nothing would work. I needed help.

And I knew where to find it.

For hours I had refrained from adding more wood to the fire because Pappa was so hot, but a small fire still flickered. I managed to tug Pappa and his sleeping mat a bit farther from the fireplace so he wouldn't become too hot while I was gone.

Leaving him asleep on the mat, I ran as fast as I could to Patience's house, where she answered my insistent knocking on her door in surprise.

"What's wrong, Sarah?" she asked.

"Pappa's sick. Please, can you stay with him for a little while so I can find someone to help?"

Patience looked behind her into the gloom of her house. "Mother's not doing well," she whispered. "Let me ask my father if he can look after her while I go to your house." She left me standing at the door while she spoke to her father.

Goodman Ames was with her when she returned.

"Sarah, what's the matter with your father?" he asked.

"He seems to have the fever, Goodman Ames," I said.

"I'll go to your house while Patience stays here with her mother," he said. "If your father needs to be moved, I'll be able to help."

"Thank you," I said, feeling a great sense of relief wash over me. "If you could go sit with him now, I'll run to the village for someone who can help."

"But who are you going to summon?" Goodman Ames called as I ran in the direction of Town Bank.

I didn't have time to answer him. I kept running until I spotted the harbor, then I slowed to a brisk walk. I knew Pappa wouldn't want me calling a great deal of attention to myself by dashing through the lanes of the village.

No one spoke to me as I approached the harbor, though a few people glanced at me askance. I made a beeline for the barrel where I had been sitting when Richard found me. I hoped he would see me again, wherever he was. I didn't know where else to look for him.

The rough men who had gathered near the barrel the previous day were not in attendance. Part of me was glad that I would not be subjected to their strong language and unpleasant odors, but part of me wished someone were nearby so I could ask about Richard's whereabouts.

I was pondering what to do if I couldn't find Richard when I heard heavy footfalls nearby. Glancing up quickly, I saw Richard approaching, his eyebrows knit together and his countenance glowering.

"Do you not listen?" he asked in exasperation when he reached me. He reached out to help me down from the barrel, but I hopped off without his help.

"Please, Richard, come with me to my house. Pappa is very sick and you're the only person I know who can help."

Richard's visage changed from disapproving to concerned in an instant. "What's the matter with him?" he asked, turning toward town and setting off with long strides. I struggled to keep up.

"He's got the fever," I panted, dashing along next to him.

"When did it start?"

"He began coughing last night during our meal. The coughing grew worse overnight but seemed to get better this morning. Now he's hot to the touch and restless." I took a deep breath and slowed down. "You go on ahead, please. I can't keep up with you."

Richard turned to me. "Do you want me to wait?" he asked, not unkindly.

I waved him on ahead. "No, please don't wait for me. I'll be along as quickly as I can." Richard nodded and began running in the direction of the house. I slowed down as much as I dared, but I wanted to get home to help. When I had caught my breath and my lungs had stopped burning, I hastened my pace toward home.

When I got there I swept in through the front door to find Richard kneeling on the floor next to Pappa's sleeping mat. Goodman Ames was in the corner, watching Richard as he spoke to Pappa.

"Can you hear me, William?" Richard was asking.

Pappa mumbled something; that was a good sign. At least we could suppose he had heard Richard speaking.

I went to stand next to Goodman Ames. "Did anything happen while I was gone?" I asked.

He shook his head. "Nothing but what you see now—mumbling, tossing about, that sort of thing. Who is that man you sent ahead of you?"

"His name is Richard and he's been to medical college." I realized I couldn't share any more information about Richard because I didn't know anything else.

Pappa moaned something that sounded like my name and I went to his side. Richard sat back on his knees and waited for Pappa to try to speak to me.

"Mamma," Pappa whispered.

"What about Mamma?" I asked.

"Find out ... find out what happened."

That sounded like a command one might make if one were dying. I gave Richard a wild look. "What is he saying?" I asked, my voice unnaturally loud in the quiet room.

Goodman Ames stepped forward. "Sarah." He reached for my arm.

"No!" I cried. "Leave me alone!"

The silence of the room deepened as I stared at my father,

unbelieving. For just a moment I took my eyes off Pappa's face. "Richard, is he dying?" I asked, my voice tremulous.

"I don't know," came the answer. "There is nothing more I can do for him. We have to wait to see what happens."

"Shave him!" I urged. "The fever stays in his hair and in his beard—surely that will help the fever to go away."

Richard gave me a sad look and stood up slowly. He went into the apothecary and returned with a blade and some oil. He deftly shaved my father's head and face while Goodman Ames and I watched. As the hanks of hair fell to the floor, I prayed to God to save my father from death, to heal the fever and make Pappa well again. As I prayed silently, tears ran down my face and onto the floor, mixing with Pappa's hair and the fragrant oil Richard had used to cut it off.

I saw Pappa's hand move out of the corner of my eye. I jerked my head toward him and he smiled faintly and opened his eyes wide. "Ruth!" he exclaimed.

And then he closed his eyes and was gone.

# CHAPTER 9

*P*appa's chest stopped its labored movements and his eyes closed as if in restful slumber. The years melted away from his face and I saw him as the young man he once had been, before we moved away from England, before Mamma's disappearance, before the worries and cares of his life had aged him.

The cry that escaped my lips was like that of a wounded animal. Richard was sitting with his eyes closed and Goodman Ames had sunk to the floor in a position of prayerful supplication, no doubt asking God to spare his family the fate that had met my father.

I sobbed until I couldn't breathe. I don't remember much of what happened after that, but I vaguely recall soft hands leading me into the bedchamber. I woke up in my bed the next morning, covered in sweat and tangled in the counterpane my mother had sewn so lovingly.

Then I remembered with a start what had happened the previous day. My father was gone. He had seen my mother again in his final moment of life and he had gone to meet her. My grief threatened to crush my chest. I sat on the edge of the bed and buried my face in my hands, sobbing as if my heart would break.

Hurried steps came into the bedchamber from the kitchen. I looked up and saw Patience standing in the doorway. Her father must have sent for her. She came and sat next to me, tears streaming down her face as she took my hands in hers.

"Sarah, I am so sorry," she said through the tears. "My father came to get me as soon as ... as soon as it happened yesterday. I came right away and I've been here through the night. I've been so worried about you." She held one of my limp hands to her face and squeezed, as if she could share her strength with me.

But her strength belonged only to her and she couldn't share it with me. I would have to find my own. And I already knew how hard that would be because it took me a long time to find it after Mamma disappeared. But Pappa helped me that time. He couldn't help me now. I started to cry again, leaning my head on Patience's shoulder.

"Mistress Reeves is going to come over to sit with you for a while so I can go home and check on Mother," Patience said after a little while.

"Oh, no, please—not Mistress Reeves," I said, looking wildly around the room as if I could find a place to hide.

"Why ever not?" Patience asked, her eyebrows knit together in confusion. "You really shouldn't be by yourself right now, Sarah."

Patience didn't know about Arthur's proposal, and this wasn't the time to tell her. Maybe she could get Mistress Reeves to stay home. It would be so uncomfortable having her with me.

"Please, Patience. I can't discuss it, but I really cannot face her right now. Will you please ask her not to come?"

Patience gave me a long, quizzical look. "Maybe she could just come and sit while you rest? You wouldn't even have to talk to her. You could pretend you don't even know she's here. I don't like the thought of you being here alone, Sarah." Patience put her arm around my shoulders, which were slumped and shivering.

"I don't want to pretend anything while she's here. I truly would not mind being by myself for a little while. I promise you I'll come by your house after I've had something to eat."

The look of doubt in Patience's eyes probably mirrored my own. She didn't believe any more than I did that I wanted to be alone. But she agreed to my wishes.

"Very well. I'll stop to speak to Mistress Reeves when I leave here and tell her not to come, that you want to be alone for a time. But I cannot promise that she won't come despite your wishes."

I nodded. "I know. Thank you, Patience. I need some time to think."

Patience gave my shoulders another hug and went back into the main room, leaving me in the bedchamber to dress for the day. I moved slowly, as though I walked through thick molasses, and when I finally went into the main room I found I wasn't the least bit hungry. Patience had set the table with porridge, a cup of still-warm milk, and freshly-made cheese that she must have brought from her house, but none of it tempted me. I sat in the rocking chair in front of the fire, which Patience had stoked to a low flame.

"Please eat something," she pleaded, standing before me. "You need to have food to keep up your strength."

Suddenly I realized Pappa's body was gone. I don't know why I thought I might be able to see him again this morning. The floor in front of the hearth, which the previous evening had been covered with a grotesque mixture of his hair and the oil Richard had used in an attempt to shave off the fever, had been cleaned. A faint scent of the oil hung in the air. "Where is Pappa?" My voice cracked and my chest heaved as Patience rushed to my side.

"It's all right, Sarah. My father and the man who was here

earlier took your father's body to the shed, where it's cold." She was, of course, referring to the shed attached to the side of the house. My feelings were at war with each other: part of me wanted desperately to see my father again, but part of me was scared. Too scared to even look in the direction of the shed.

"My father and Pastor Reeves will come and help lay out the body and—," Patience began, but I winced and she stopped.

"When will that happen?" I asked.

"In a day or two," she said. "Sarah, are you sure you're going to be all right without me? I need to go check on Mother. Would you like to come with me?"

Taking a deep breath to steady my nerves, I shook my head. "I need to be by myself for a time."

"I'll be back later on today, when Father and Pastor Reeves come," she said, reaching for her cloak. I went to open the door for her and she gave me a warm hug before she left.

"I'm so sorry," she whispered.

I swallowed hard and nodded, afraid that I might start crying and never stop if I opened my mouth. I watched her leave, then closed the door behind me and stood in the middle of the room.

How was I going to survive? How would I get through every day without my father? He was the only reason I survived the loss of Mamma, and without him I didn't think I could live. I wasn't even sure I wanted to live. I sat down again in the rocking chair and the tears started to fall. My whole body shook from the strength of my cries. I wept until I thought my heart would burst with pain and grief. I cried out loud, not caring how much noise I made. Who was there to hear it, anyway? I was thankful Mistress Reeves had not come.

I don't know how long I sat in the chair weeping, but eventually I could cry no more tears. They would return, I knew, but my body had rid itself of all of them for a time. My father's sleeping mat still lay on the floor; as much as I wanted to sleep, I could not bring myself to sleep where he had died. I went to my bed and slept, spent from sorrow and pain.

When I awoke, a feeling of dread enveloped me. I lay in bed for a very long while, listening to the incessant knocking on the door, no doubt people from Town and the nearby farms who were already coming to express their sorrow and condolences.

I couldn't answer their knocks. I knew my eyes were swollen from crying and I didn't want to face anyone, talk to anyone.

But eventually, when the knocking persisted, I couldn't hold them off any longer. I trudged through the house to the door, ready to fling it wide and demand that the person be off.

I was surprised to see Richard standing there. He held his hat in his hands and was twisting it round and round in his fingers.

"I came to see how you're doing, Miss Sarah," he said. "I'm … I'm so sorry about your father. I met quite a large number of people from the village as I walked here. They said no one was at home."

I swallowed hard, afraid I would start crying in front of him. He looked at me with concern. "Are you all right?" he asked.

I shook my head, then stood back so he could enter.

"No, thank you. It would be improper for me to come inside the house, now that—"

I winced as if in pain. I couldn't summon enough vigor to insist that he come in. But what did it matter that it was improper? There were no neighbors close enough to witness it. There was no one to scold me. Standing on propriety seemed silly.

I stood in the doorway, letting in all the cold air, while I waited for him to speak.

"I came by because I've been worried about you."

"My friend Patience has been here with me."

He looked beyond my shoulder and into the house. "Where is she now?"

"She had to go home. Her mother is with child," I said by way of explanation.

"Did you wish to be alone?"

I gave a slight nod. "I'm sorry if I'm disturbing you," he said, though he made no move to leave.

I took a deep breath, my shoulders shuddering at the effort. "You're not disturbing me."

"I, well, I didn't know if you needed help laying out ... well, laying out the body." He grimaced, as if it was a hard thing to say.

"Thank you," I said, lifting my eyes to meet his. "I'm sure Goodman Ames and the pastor would appreciate the help."

"Your father was a good friend to me when I needed someone to trust here on the cape," Richard blurted.

I was taken aback. Why should the people of Town Bank not be trusted? I didn't know what to say, so I merely nodded.

Richard had opened his mouth to say something else when I noticed a movement in the distance behind him. To my great consternation, it was Mistress Reeves—I recognized her black frock. Richard turned and followed my gaze, and we stood still, not talking, until Mistress Reeves had reached the house. I didn't know how she would react to seeing Richard at the house, even though he was outside.

"Hello, Mistress Reeves. Please come in." I stood aside for her to enter. She didn't go inside, but instead looked Richard up and down and turned to me with an unspoken question in her eyes.

Richard came to my rescue. He offered Mistress a short bow, saying, "My name is Richard Allerton, Madame. I am pleased to make your acquaintance, though I wish it were under happier circumstances."

So Richard's surname was Allerton.

Mistress Reeves cocked her head, as if she couldn't quite

understand the young man standing before her. Then she nodded toward him and murmured, "Thank you. Likewise."

She turned to me with a quizzical look and I felt compelled to explain Richard's presence in the house.

"Mistress Reeves, Mister Allerton was present when Pappa ..." I swallowed, giving myself a moment before continuing. "When Pappa passed from this life. He came to offer his assistance in laying out the body." It seemed so strange to my ears to refer to Pappa as a *body*.

"Ah, I understand," Mistress Reeves said. She turned to face me and handed me the basket she was carrying. "Sarah, I've come to express my condolences. I've brought you a loaf of bread and some cheese. I know you may not feel like cooking today, but you need to keep eating. I will also help with the laying out of the body."

"Thank you, ma'am."

"I will be getting back home," Mistress Reeves said. "I'm sure my husband will be along to see you very soon." She nodded to me, then turned to Richard.

"Mister Allerton, have you met my husband, the pastor?"

"No, Mistress. I have not had the pleasure of meeting him."

"Perhaps you would like to meet him now?" she asked. I knew what she was doing. She wanted Richard to go with her so my reputation would remain intact if anyone else should come by to visit. I knew she was horrified at the impropriety of Richard and me being alone at the house, even if he wasn't indoors. She did not know he hadn't come in.

Richard inclined his head toward the woman. "That would be very kind of you, as long as it does not require too much of your time."

Mistress Reeves gave a tight smile and nodded, then turned toward home. I was shocked when Richard winked at me once he knew Mistress wasn't looking. He realized what Mistress Reeves was doing, too, I thought with an inward grin. It was the first light thought I had had since Pappa had left me.

After my visitors had left I went inside to face the main room, feeling a stirring of desire to do *something*, anything that would help keep my mind and my memories occupied. I did not want to think about Pappa just then because I knew I would dissolve again in tears. Patience had already swept the room and the hearth, so I went into the bedchamber to tidy up in there. When that was done, I went outdoors into the bracing cold to milk the cows. I shared their warmth as I leaned into their soft flanks, my hands working to remain nimble in the frigid air. When that chore was done I cleaned out the chicken coop and collected a few eggs. I didn't know what I would do with all the eggs now that Pappa was gone—perhaps I should sell them. I didn't know if Pappa would want me to do that or not.

When I returned to the house I gazed into the fire, tears springing to my eyes again. It had done me good to get out into the cold and do some chores, for my mind had been occupied by rote movements. Now I was at sea again. The crushing weight of sadness and emptiness lay heavily on my chest and shoulders. What I needed was to get outside again.

I donned my cloak once more and walked briskly to Patience's house. When I arrived I was surprised to see several women waiting in attendance on Goody Ames. Patience pulled me aside.

"Mother says the baby is coming soon. I would have come to get you, but I couldn't leave her," she said in a low voice. "Father went to fetch all these ladies because he's worried and Mother is furious at him. She wants to be left alone."

"How can I help?" I asked.

"Sarah, Mother is afraid because the midwife isn't here yet. She says the baby is not in the correct position." Patience's voice went even lower.

The midwife lived in Town Bank. She had taken ill with the

same sickness that had taken Pappa, and everyone feared that she, too, would not survive the fever's course.

"Your father delivered a baby, did he not?" Patience asked.

Pappa had assisted at only one birth since coming to New Jersey, and even that had been practically scandalous. But his presence had been required since there was no midwife available and the women who had come to help had no idea how to assist in the particularly dangerous and difficult birth. Mamma and I had accompanied Pappa to the home where the baby was being delivered, and we had assisted him. Such appeared to be the case again.

"There was the one," I murmured. I dared not say more, because that baby, and her mother, had died in the process of delivery, despite my father's best efforts.

Patience was silent for a long moment, then she fixed me with an intense look. "Do you think you could help?" she asked.

"Me?" I was stupefied. "I don't know what to do!"

"But you watched your father that time, right?"

"Well, yes, but I don't know what to do. I only watched and waited for instructions in case he needed me."

"Mother needs you." Just then a cry emanated from the bedchamber.

"Patience!" her father called.

"Coming, Father." She hastened into the bedchamber. I followed her as far as the doorway where her sisters hovered, seemingly torn between a desire to know what was happening, to know their mother would be fine and healthy, and a desire to look away, to avoid having to look at what might turn out to be an unpleasant scene.

Looking at the frightened looks on the faces of Patience's sisters, I knew I couldn't stand idly by and wait for something to happen. I whirled around, fled out the door, and ran as fast as I could back to the apothecary. I gathered any supplies within easy reach that I had seen my father use during the other birth several years ago.

I found soft cloths, some tools I recalled my father using, and some remedies I knew might help the pain Patience's mother was feeling. I put everything into a basket and ran back to Patience's house.

After instructing Goodman Ames to go into the outer room to wait, though he needed no prodding, I joined Patience, her mother, and the other women in the bedchamber. There was nothing I could do until it was time to birth the baby, so I waited with the other women.

We took turns holding Goody Ames's hands, stroking her forehead, and clenching our teeth and murmuring words of encouragement when her pain was unbearable. We wiped her face with cool cloths, gave her hard sticks wrapped in cloth to chew on each time the pain renewed itself, and synchronized our breathing with hers even without thinking. I found myself thanking God many times that my mother only had to go through such an experience one time before she learned she would not be able to bear any more children.

As the pain became worse, Patience's mother would cry out with sounds almost too horrible to hear. I wondered what the children listening in the other room must be thinking. The women's soothing sounds became louder, too, during those long moments. I confess to being afraid, though I had witnessed the same thing when I had assisted my father. I wanted nothing more than to put my hands over my ears to shut out the sound of Goody's screams.

The ordeal in Goody Ames's bedchamber seemed to last for hours. The poor woman would scream with pain, then collapse with relief and exhaustion when the pain subsided for a blessed moment. The time for the baby to arrive grew imminent. When the child was finally ready to come into the world, I said a silent prayer for help.

Since this was something I had never done before, it was helpful to already know that the infant was not in the proper position. I closed my eyes and tried to remember everything my father had done at the previous birth when faced with similar circumstances. He had used a special tool to turn the baby to allow it to move more freely.

Thanks be to God, I had brought that tool with me. Gripping it carefully, I used it in the same way I remembered him using it, moving the tiny child's body little by little. Blood covered my hands and the sight of it, the metallic smell of it, made me nauseous. Every eye in the room was upon me, and I could feel droplets of sweat trickling down my face and back. I asked for someone to wipe the sweat from my eyes and several pairs of hands reached out to help. One woman, I didn't see which one, fanned me while another fanned Goody Ames. For all the cold that was outside the walls of the small house, the room was intolerably warm. I would have called for the door to be opened to the frigid outside air, but I didn't want Goody Ames or the babe to be chilled.

My arms were shaking from the strain of concentrating and my steady grip on Pappa's tool. I couldn't feel the baby moving, but I could feel the weight of the women's stares and, more importantly, of Goody's fear and worry. If the baby didn't move soon, I feared it would die. And if the child died…

I couldn't bring myself to think about it.

I had to let go of the grip, just for a moment. I needed to rest my arms. I asked one of the women to take my place briefly. I told her exactly how to hold the instrument and she did so, albeit with a look of grave concern and little confidence in her ability. I walked around the room, shaking my arms to get the feeling back. I looked up to see Patience watching me and I couldn't discern the look on her face. Was it fear? Was it a lack of faith in me? I confess I shared those feelings. As I moved closer to her, though, I could see the tears streaking down her cheeks, the haunted look in her eyes.

Seeing her face seemed to provide me with renewed strength and resolve. I *had* to bring the baby into the world without injury. I thanked the woman who had taken my place momentarily, then grasped the instrument in my hands again. The thoughts spinning through my head were dreadful and time was running out for the baby. If only I could remember exactly the steps Pappa had taken to deliver the other baby.

I closed my eyes again and forced myself to concentrate. I pictured the other birth. Pappa had talked through it, explaining what he was doing so the baby could be birthed properly. I remember he was able to reposition the baby just a tiny bit, then he told the mother to push, but not too hard.

I opened my eyes and swallowed hard. Moving very carefully, I felt a tiny movement and then another one. Gradually I could feel that the child was shifting. I hoped it was enough. I instructed Goody Ames to push, but not too hard. She cried out with the attempt, but it worked. The babe's shoulders turned just enough to give me a surge of hope. I asked her to do it again when she had taken a deep breath and blown it out, and she complied. Tiny bit by tiny bit, the babe was moving sideways, turning to allow me to withdraw the instrument I had been using. I could now see the top of the babe's head, and at that point I was able to get out of the way, sit back on my heels while I took deep breaths of air, and allow one of the other women to instruct Patience's mother for the rest of the birth.

I was worried for the health of the babe. Visions of the child my father had helped into the world swam before my eyes. That babe had been born with blue skin, without breath, without life. I swallowed hard and leaned back against the wall to prevent myself from fainting away at the thought of this baby being born with the same color skin. Patience came to help me stand when I was ready, and I held her hand while we waited.

When the babe finally arrived into the waiting arms of the women standing nearby, it was fully dark outside. Patience and I exchanged scared glances in the dim light of the candles in the room. I could not see the color of the baby's skin. No one spoke. We were all waiting, it seemed, for something.

And then it came. A loud wail, followed by a cry of exhaustion and relief from Goody Ames. I hadn't realized until then that I had been holding my breath, and I suspect Patience had been doing the same thing. She called for her father and rushed to her mother's side, holding her hand and whispering reassuring words to her.

Before Goodman Ames came into the room, the women had swaddled the babe in a soft cloth and handed him to Patience. I reached down for my basket of remedies and stepped over to where Goody lay on the bed, her tears slowing and her breathing becoming more regular. She was not yet strong enough to hold the child, but I knew that the herbs I had brought would strengthen her.

Patience leaned down to show the infant to her mother, then she and the other women stepped away from Goody while I mixed my herbs with a bit of cider and helped her to drink it. Her lips were cracked and dry and she gulped the remedy gratefully. She coughed, then looked at me, her eyes shining.

"Sarah, I will never be able to thank you enough for helping to deliver the babe. Without you we both would have died." She blinked quickly, to keep tears from falling.

I squeezed her hand. "I am just thankful to God that I knew the proper instrument to use and was here when you needed me."

Goodman Ames came into the room. Patience handed him the babe and he gazed at his son with a look of wonder. Tears sprang unbidden to my eyes and I wiped them away roughly with my sleeve.

The women were beginning to disperse so the family could

be alone, and I joined them. Outside they all chattered to me, thanking me for my work and praising God for the gift of a living child. They turned to go to Town and I turned in the other direction to return to my home. I hadn't gone far when I heard my name.

"Sarah!" It was Goodman Ames.

I turned around quickly. "Are Goody and the baby all right?" I asked. Dread and fear filled my body.

"They are, indeed," he said, running up to me and wearing a broad grin. "Patience is looking after the babe while my wife sleeps. She is too weak to hold the child right now. I will walk you home. It is late."

"Thank you," I replied. I wanted to insist that he stay with his family, but I had to admit to being scared to walk the distance to my house unescorted in the dark. We walked briskly, despite my exhaustion, because I knew he wanted to return to his home.

"I want to tell you that we intend to call the child William, after your father," Goodman Ames said as we walked. I stopped short, shocked by the kindness of his words.

"Thank you, Goodman Ames," I said. Tears began to gather in the corners of my eyes. I willed them not to fall, lest they freeze on my cheeks.

"Your father was a good and kind man, and everyone in Town and on the farms hereabout will miss him," Goodman Ames said. His voice caught a bit. "I will miss him. I was one of the first people he met when your family arrived in Town Bank."

I nodded, not trusting myself to speak. I had heard Pappa tell the story many times—how he and Mamma had been in the general store, inquiring about land to buy on the cape. Goodman Ames had been the one to walk them out to the property where our house now stood.

We walked in silence for many moments. When we arrived

at the house I let myself in and Goodman Ames wished me good night.

I stoked the flickering embers in the fireplace and added a piece of wood, waiting for the flames to begin licking higher. I went to the bedchamber and took the counterpane from the bed and wrapped it tightly around myself then went to sit in the rocking chair before the fire. My body was bone weary, but my mind was still racing, unsettled from my experience at the Ames's house. I bowed my head and prayed, beseeching God to allow the babe William to survive.

As the warmth from the fire began to envelop my senses, my mind slowed down and I became drowsy. I stared into the flames, marveling at how I had been able to help Goody Ames in the delivery of her child, and still amazed that the babe had been born alive. I smiled at the memory of his hearty cry and knew Pappa would have been very proud of me.

# CHAPTER 10

*I* missed Pappa with an aching emptiness, but that night I could not cry. I was simply too tired. I slipped into the bedchamber, the counterpane dragging behind me on the floor, and fell into a deep, restful sleep. The last thing I remembered before surrendering to beautiful slumber was the memory of my father's smile. I knew he smiled for me.

The next morning I woke up later than usual, but feeling restored, though nervous. This was the day Richard and the others would come to help me lay out Pappa's body. I knew I would be weary by the end of the day, but first I had to go into Town Bank to the lawyer's office to see about the arrangements Pappa had made in his will. It was a task I did not relish, but I had heard from the lawyer that he was ready to receive me. It was uncommon for villagers to pay the lawyer for something like drawing up a will, but Pappa had been accustomed to the ways of England and hired the lawyer to draw up his will soon after we arrived on the cape. He had no doubt changed the will after Mamma disappeared.

The lawyer, who also spent most of his time farming the land behind his home, was at home. He ushered me into the side room, which served as his office. There was a desk and a shelf for books, along with two chairs and several panes of glass in the window, overlooking the street.

As I had suspected, Pappa had left his land, the farm, the house, and all his household possessions, including the animals, to me. The only exceptions were a few items in the apothecary. To my great surprise, he had left those things to Richard.

"Richard Allerton?" I repeated when the lawyer read his name aloud.

"Yes, Sarah. Your father wished Richard Allerton to have the things listed in this letter," he said, handing a letter to me.

It was written in Pappa's sure, capable hand.

*In great appreciation of the help Richard has given me over the recent months, I bequeath to him, for his personal use, one-half pound each of dried basil, hyssop, willow bark, feverfew, yarrow, alcohol, honey, mint, chamomile, and foxglove. I also bequeath to him forceps, a set of weights and a scale, a stone mortar and pestle, an amputation knife, an amputation saw, and two syringes.*

I read the letter twice, then looked up at the lawyer. "Why did Pappa leave these things to Richard?" I asked, handing the letter back to him.

The lawyer, who had been smoking a pipe, set it down on his desk and looked at me intently. "I confess to not knowing the reason. I don't even know who this Richard Allerton is. There are rumors, of course, but ..." he trailed off then, looking sheepish for a moment, as if he had shared something he should have kept confidential.

"Go on," I urged him.

"No, no. I was about to repeat nothing but rumor, and I will not engage in such sinful conversation," he said, shaking his head firmly.

I sighed, knowing he would be no use as a source of information about Richard.

"Miss Hanover, if I may impose upon you, do you know this Richard Allerton?"

"I do," I said with a slight nod.

"Would you be willing to contact him to let him know of your father's bequest? If you send him here to my office, I will give him the letter."

"Yes, certainly," I said. "I shall speak with him today, as he was present when Pappa died and he will be helping to lay out the body."

"That will be fine," the lawyer said. I pushed back my chair and stood, allowing him to assist me with my cloak. I left with a new sense of confusion.

There had been things I didn't know about Pappa—and one of them was the extent of his friendship with Richard. To leave Richard things from the apothecary, things which Pappa had treasured and worked hard to acquire, Pappa must have indeed thought highly of him.

I hurried home as the snow fell in tiny pellets, crunching underfoot and stinging my cheeks. Slipping into the house, I was relieved to feel the warmth from the fireplace. I hung up my cloak and prepared tea for myself, thinking with a pang of hurt how much Pappa had enjoyed his tea when he came in from the cold.

I shook those thoughts from my head so I could concentrate on the task at hand. Richard, Goodman Ames, and Mistress Reeves would arrive soon, and I needed to be prepared to assist in laying out Pappa's body. I readied the water, heating it and adding lavender to it for a familiar and comforting scent. Pappa had loved the scent of lavender. I prepared soft cloths to wash the body, too. Normally combing the hair and beard would be necessary, but since Richard had shaved Pappa to try to rid his body of the fever, there would be no hair to comb.

By midday Mistress Reeves had arrived. She wore her usual black frock, severe and simple in its lines.

She asked me where Pappa's body was, and I told her he was out in the shed attached to the back of the house. She opened the door, her gaze roving about the shed. I saw a shudder pass through her shoulders.

"Help me bring this board into the house," she instructed. I went into the shed, carefully avoiding any glance in Pappa's direction. I helped her lift a large board, carry it into the house, and lean it against the wall. Pappa's body would be placed on the board, the cooling board, for the laying out and visitation. Next we brought two braces indoors—they would be used to support the cooling board. The only other suitable surface in the house was the table, and we needed that to place food for mourners.

She closed the door again. "We will need the men's help to move the body into this room, as it is no doubt frozen from being out-of-doors. But that is good, because it has preserved him. Do you have the washing things ready?"

I nodded, overcome with apprehension at the thought of seeing my father's body for the first time since his death two days ago.

"Let's get the board ready," Mistress Reeves said briskly. I was thankful for her approach, which was detached, without emotion. If she had shown that she was upset, I might not have been able to go through with the task of laying out Pappa's body. Not long after the table had been cleared of its simple implements, both Daniel Ames and Richard came to the door. They made their way directly to the shed to determine how best to bring the body into the house.

Finally the two men lifted Pappa's body and carried it head-first into the main room, where they laid him carefully upon the board.

Standing in the main room, looking at Pappa's body on the

table, I was struck with a breathlessness that threatened to overcome me. Richard seemed to sense how I was feeling, for he placed his hand on my elbow and led me to the rocking chair.

"Your face is the color of chalk, Miss Sarah," he said, placing the back of his hand against my clammy forehead. I winced, wondering if Mistress had seen him touch me. "Let me get you a cup of cider." Two of his long strides placed him on the other side of the room, where he poured a large measure of cider into a cup. He brought it to me and held it to my lips. I drank thirstily, as if gulping the cider might force away the feelings of helplessness and loneliness that grew steadily inside me like a fever.

After I finished the cider, Richard suggested that I get some fresh air. I left the house, doing as he wished, then was able to return to the room where Mistress Reeves was waiting for me to begin.

I looked at her with watery eyes that were ready to overflow, and spoke in a quavery voice. "Mistress, would you mind doing the laying out? I fear I shall not be able to do it and remain conscious."

Mistress Reeves nodded briskly and quickly took charge of the process of cleaning Pappa's body while I stood by, largely unhelpful and trying to keep my emotions from getting out of my strict control. I did not want Mistress Reeves and the others to see me crying. Mistress seemed to sense this, because she asked me to find Pappa's Sunday clothes so she could dress him. I obliged quickly, relieved to have something to do in the other room.

I went into the bedchamber and knelt before the trunk where Pappa kept all his clothes. He had only a small number of pieces, and the ones I thought best were right on top of the pile. I hadn't been able to bring myself to go through his clothes, so I was happy to see his best things within easy reach. I returned to Mistress Reeves carrying a white linen shirt, sleeveless waistcoat, wool stockings, and Pappa's best lawn breeches. It pained me to think I would never see Pappa in those clothes again.

I placed them all in a neat pile near Mistress Reeves, who was standing in the main room, surveying her work. Richard and Goodman Ames stood nearby, watching her and waiting for instructions to help dress Pappa's body for visitation.

Mistress Reeves took the pile of clothes and directed the men to help her in dressing Pappa. I watched with a thick feeling of dullness in my head, and was glad when the ordeal was over. Looking at Pappa's face, I could almost imagine him saying he was ready to go to Sunday service. I blinked back yet more tears and thanked Mistress Reeves and the men for their help.

"Sarah, you gave me one extra stocking." Mistress Reeves handed me a wool stocking she had set on the table.

"Thank you."

While Mistress and I took care of the washing-up things, the men quietly discussed the weather and other innocuous subjects. When the table had been cleaned and cleared of any evidence of Pappa's laying out, I covered it with a thick cloth Mamma had made and served my guests food and drink. They were silent as they ate, then Mistress Reeves stood up.

"I must be getting back to my house, but I will notify my husband that you are ready for visitation. I would expect mourners before nightfall." With a nod that included Richard, Goodman Ames, and me, she left, closing the door quietly behind her.

Goodman Ames was the next to leave. He smiled when I asked about little William, saying the boy was hearty and healthy and growing already. Goody Ames, on the other hand, was still abed, struggling with exhaustion and melancholy. Her headaches had improved, though, so that was welcome news.

"I will bring her something that might help with melancholy," I promised, trying to remember what we had in the apothecary that might be useful to her.

"Thank you," Goodman Ames said. He glanced at Richard, then at me, and opened his mouth as if to speak. But he must have decided not to give voice to his thoughts, and he left.

I was alone with Richard in the small room. I didn't feel as if we were alone, though, with Pappa's body mere inches from us. Richard stood to leave.

"Wait, please."

"Yes, Miss Sarah? I should be going, now that the others have left."

"I have some information for you," I said. "I went to see the lawyer this morning and he tells me Pappa bequeathed to you some items that he kept in the apothecary." I waited for his response, interested to see whether this came as a surprise to him.

It seemed to.

"Your father left me something?" His eyes were wide. I nodded. "How kind of him," Richard murmured, as if to himself. Then he looked at me. "Is it something you wish to keep? Otherwise I shall refuse the bequest."

"You cannot refuse the bequest," I told him. "It is what Pappa wanted. The items are all things from the apothecary—herbs and instruments and the like."

"That is very generous of him." He offered a smile. "I will accept them gratefully."

I told him where the lawyer's house was located and suggested that he visit the lawyer the following day to receive the letter Pappa had left for him. He agreed and said he would return once he had read the letter, then he left. He held my eyes for a moment before he walked into the cold, clear outdoors. "Will you be all right by yourself? I can stop somewhere and ask that someone come to keep you company. I would do it myself, only … only it would not be proper."

"Thank you, Richard. I shall be all right." I lowered my eyes so he would not realize I was lying. I wanted him to stay so loneliness and fear would not crawl into my thoughts, but I could not ask him to do such a thing.

Once I closed the door behind him, I faced the room. My heart thudded in my chest as I gazed at Pappa's body, laid out on the board in front of me. I could feel my hands getting moist from cold sweat; I swallowed hard. Wealthy families, of course, had parlors in which to lay out their dead, but we had no such thing. We had only one room that was appropriate for visitors, and I was standing in it with my father.

I walked slowly over to him and looked down at his face, peacefully set in forever slumber. I missed him dreadfully. I missed the way his eyes crinkled in the corners when he smiled, and I missed the smell of his pipe. I missed the sound of his voice when we read by the fire in the evenings. Several tears fell onto the cold hand I found myself holding. I let go of it for just a moment, long enough to drag a stool over to the table so I could sit next to him.

I held his hand again, telling him how much I would miss him and letting the tears fall. I would have sworn I could feel his hand squeezing mine, but I had heard of such things happening and I knew it wasn't real. Oh, what I would have given to make such a thing happen!

There was a knock at the door and I rose, sniffling and wiping my face with my sleeve as I went to open it. Three women stood in the doorway. I recognized them from Town; they had come to pay their respects. Part of me was glad for the interruption so I could have other people to talk to for at least a short time, but part of me wished I could still talk to Pappa by himself.

The women were silent as they stood by the body, their eyes closed and their lips moving soundlessly. I dared not speak to them while they were in prayer. I stole softly into the apothecary, where I prepared a mixture of herbs that Patience's mother might find helpful for her melancholy. Unfortunately, there was nothing I could give her for exhaustion—she would need to rest until she felt strong enough to move around.

When I returned from the apothecary, the women were talking quietly among themselves just inches from Pappa's body. I wondered if they felt uncomfortable doing so, but it didn't matter since there was no other place for them to go.

I knew that these women marked the first of many visitors I would receive over the next couple of days, so I wouldn't be able to leave the house to take the herbs to Goody Ames myself. Therefore, I made a request of one of the women.

"Goodwife Willoughby, I wonder if you might stop at the Ames house on your way back into Town and deliver this packet of herbs to Goody Ames."

"Certainly, my dear Sarah," Goodwife replied. "We'll miss your father, we will. He was a fine apothecary and a good man." She shook her head and made a *tsk, tsk* sound with her tongue. "It was a sad shame when your mother disappeared. I know your father never stopped hoping he would find her body, but now perhaps they have been reunited in the hereafter."

I wondered with a suppressed grimace if she thought it was making me feel better by talking about *both* my deceased parents.

"Thank you, Goodwife. I shall miss him, too. And of course, I also miss my mother," I managed to say. The other women looked on, nodding sadly. At least they had the good sense not to remind me I was an orphan.

When the three women left, I thanked Goodwife Willoughby for stopping to provide Goody Ames with the remedy I had prepared. I could see other people walking toward my house. I had taken leave of my manners while Goodwife Willoughby and the other ladies were in the house—I had not thought to offer them tea or cider or cheese or any other refreshment. I hurriedly put the kettle on to boil while I waited for the next visitors to arrive.

They were at the door in a matter of minutes, and so it went throughout that day and the following day. Some brought food; some brought nothing but memories. My heart ached more and more with each story that I heard, so that by the time I had closed the door on the last visitor after the second day of the visitation, I was physically and mentally exhausted.

It was not long before Goodman Ames and another man from the village came to take Pappa's body to a barn in Town where bodies were kept until they could be buried in the spring, after the ground thawed. I had already said my goodbye to Pappa in the privacy of the empty house, so I watched in silence as the two men placed the rough-hewn coffin containing Pappa's body in the back of a wagon and rolled away into the gathering darkness. When I returned to the warmth of the house, I was struck by an overwhelming feeling of loneliness that promised to sweep me into despair if I didn't set about doing something quickly. With the food people had brought, I had been able to feed everyone who came after the first three ladies, and I had plenty left over for myself. I would have welcomed the act of preparing a meal, but it wasn't necessary. Instead, I swept the floor with vigor, then went outdoors to milk the cows. When I went back inside I realized how exhausted I was. I sat down to eat of the bounty people had brought and took a long draught of cider before remembering the extra stocking Mistress had handed me after dressing Pappa. I found it on the floor under the table.

I carried the stocking to the bed chamber and knelt once again in front of the trunk in which Pappa had kept all his clothes. We had brought the trunk with us from England. It was our prized possession—carved mahogany with details of birds and flowers. Pappa had refused to let it leave his side on the voyage to Philadelphia and he and Mamma had cared for it lovingly ever since.

I winced, remembering the Sunday clothes I had already taken from the trunk, then lifted the lid and placed my hand on the top piece of remaining clothing, a pair of breeches, feeling the coarse fabric and trying to remember the last time Pappa had worn them. Besides the clean breeches, there was a cloak and a work shirt made of scratchy cloth. Pappa had never minded the feel of the cloth, saying as long as he was busy he didn't notice it. I didn't believe him. There was a warm cotton nightshirt, too, threadbare at the elbows, as well as a pair of suspenders he rarely wore. There was also a scarf he had used only when it was bitterly cold outside, and some woolen under-things. Mamma had made all the clothes for him. Touching them all brought memories of her flooding back, too.

I took each item out and set it on the floor beside me, checking inside the folds of the clothes for the missing stocking. With each piece of cloth, the lump in my throat grew and I almost missed the small, folded piece of paper at the bottom of the trunk because of the tears swimming before my eyes.

I reached for it and unfolded the paper, which was crinkling and yellowed. Spidery handwriting covered the page. I recognized it immediately.

*My dearest William,*
*I am writing to express my concern about Ruth. It seems from her most recent letter that she is afraid of someone in the village of Town Bank, someone who has been subjecting her to threats of bodily harm. She has not shared with me the name of the person who wishes her ill, but I can discern from her correspondence to me how frightened she is. Her letters have become less frequent and more apprehensive, and it pains me to think she may be in danger.*
*Though I am in violation of a promise I made to her not to discuss this matter with you, I feel you are in the best position to help her, to find*

*out who is making her life such a hardship, and to deal with the situation as you see fit.*

*I trust you will investigate the situation immediately upon receiving this letter. I know you would have done so already, had you been aware of the depth of her suffering and fear. As soon as possible, please write to me to apprise me of the outcome of this most severe and distressing turn of events.*

*Oh, how I wish you had never left England!*

*Yours very truly,*

*Mary*

Grandmamma. She had known something about her daughter that Pappa had not known and the information was upsetting to her. I looked again at the top of the letter and saw that it was dated three months before Mamma's disappearance. I read the letter again and again, trying to discern any hint to the identity of the person who had been threatening Mamma, but I could learn nothing more.

What had Pappa done on receiving the letter? Had he asked Mamma about it? It seemed that would have been the quickest way to learn the answers he sought. But he also might have gone looking for answers by himself, not wanting Mamma to know that her mother had betrayed her confidence.

And if he had gone looking for answers himself, what had he discovered? Clearly not the identity of the person wishing harm to Mamma, or he would have notified the village authorities.

He would not have asked me on his deathbed to find out what happened to her. However was I going to fulfill his dying wish?

My exhaustion, combined with the terrifying new thoughts the letter gave me to ponder, was threatening to overwhelm me. Though I was sure I would not be able to sleep, I fell into bed and slumber came quickly. I woke when the sun was high in the sky the next day.

I awoke to someone pounding on the door. The sun was already high in the sky. I called for the person to wait, then I quickly drew a dress over my head and shoved my long hair into my cap. I ran to the door, expecting to see a mourner.

But it was Arthur. I was surprised to suddenly realize I hadn't seen him with the other mourners over the past two days.

"Arthur, please come in," I invited, standing aside so he could enter.

"Oh, no, I couldn't. It would be improper. I merely came because I wanted to offer my sincere condolences on the passing of your father."

"Thank you," I murmured, wondering why it had taken him so long to visit. He seemed to read my thoughts.

"I would have come sooner, but I have been in Philadelphia these past several days," he explained.

"Oh? That must have been quite a trip," I said. I couldn't think of anything else to say.

"Yes," he agreed. "I was talking to a man about my passage to England." He looked at his feet, which he shuffled for a moment, then he looked up at me.

"Sarah, I was wondering if you have had an opportunity to think about my proposal."

I was amazed at his audacity and tried to think of a way to respond that would not be rude or unkind.

"Arthur, I fear that I have not had such an opportunity." I chose my words carefully. "You see, since Pappa fell ill I have been at my wit's end, first trying to find someone who could cure him and then, after he died, I had to prepare his body and the house to receive mourners. There was also the birth of the child William Ames, and all of that, coupled with my grief and exhaustion, have made it impossible for me to give your proposal any thought. Please forgive me for taking so long," I finished.

He regarded me thoughtfully, then nodded. "Of course I understand, and I hope *you* will forgive *me* for asking the question at such an inappropriate time."

"I will consider it now that the guests have left and Pappa's body has been taken to the barn in Town," I promised.

"Do let me know when you reach a decision," he said, and with a slight bow, he turned around and headed in the direction of the Reeves household.

I watched him walk away for a moment, chiding myself for not telling him the truth, that I could not marry him, then turned back to the cold room. I put more wood on the embers of the fire and stoked it until flames were leaping up and I felt warmer.

I didn't want to spend the day in the house because the feelings of despair were just under the surface of my thoughts, waiting for a moment of weakness to burst into the open. As soon as I had tidied the hearth and made up the bed, I went outside to milk the cows, gather eggs, and clean the cow pen. Shoveling the muck from the ground in the pen warmed me up and gave me some much-needed energy, so when I finished I decided to pay a visit to Patience and her family. It was late in the morning and they received me with joy. I spent a wonderful hour with them, holding the baby and watching his face as he gurgled, helping Patience tidy the house, and visiting with Goody Ames. I also took several minutes to tell the younger children a story before taking my leave of all of them with a promise to return the following day.

The visit had, indeed, put me in better spirits. I was lucky to count Patience and her family among my friends.

I was walking home briskly to stay warm when I heard my name being called from somewhere behind me. Whirling around in surprise, I saw Richard striding toward me with his long legs, his arms swinging in time with his steps. It seemed the pain from his wolf bite was gone.

I waited for him to catch up to me, then he slowed down and fell into step with me.

"I am relieved to see you out of the house," he said.

"And I am relieved to be out of the house," I agreed. "It was very close indoors, so I knew I needed company and fresh air."

"Well, I hope my company is agreeable to you." His smile reached all the way to his eyes.

"It is," I answered. I'm quite certain I blushed, so I looked away so he wouldn't see.

"I visited with your father's lawyer yesterday and he advised me to talk to you about the bequest your father left me," Richard said.

"And what would you like to talk about?" I asked.

"I wanted to know your intentions with regard to your father's apothecary. And further, I wanted to ascertain whether the items he left for me are duplicates of ones he already has in the shop."

I confess his queries left me apprehensive and confused. I hadn't given the matter any thought over the past several days, wanting simply to get through the laying out, the visitation, and the overwhelming feelings of sadness and melancholy. I supposed it was time to decide what to do with Pappa's apothecary.

# CHAPTER 11

"I don't know," I said. "I have not thought about it yet."

Richard was silent, perhaps knowing I would continue talking after a time.

"Pappa's apothecary was his life's work," I said. "I would very much dislike seeing it fall into disuse and neglect."

"I am sure your father would agree with that," Richard said.

"What do you think I should do?" My question surprised even me. I had not intended to ask Richard's opinion, but now the question had escaped my lips and was hanging in the air between us.

He raised his eyebrows, evidently as much surprised as I was by the question. After several long moments he spoke.

"I should not offer you advice, but I will share with you my observations. It seems to me that you know the apothecary quite well. Your father must have taught you about his business from a young age."

"He did," I agreed.

"And it seems to me that you are quite adept at knowing what remedies to administer under certain circumstances, so you apparently listened well to your father's instructions and teachings all those years."

"That is also true." I sensed where the conversation was going.

"As I said, I cannot provide you with any advice. But I can suggest that you search your heart and try to discern what is there. You may find the answer you seek."

I looked up at him while I pondered his words. I knew he was telling me that I might consider following my father into the apothecary. But could I, a woman alone, manage such a thing? That would require business acumen I wasn't sure I possessed.

"There's something else I would like to ask you, if you don't have any objection," Richard said, cutting into my thoughts.

"What is it?" I asked.

He took a deep breath. "The night your father died, I heard what he said to you in his final moments. He beseeched you to find out what happened to your mother." He stopped talking, as if to ascertain whether I was amenable to discussing such a topic.

I remained silent as I walked beside him, though my body stiffened somewhat. He noticed.

"Is this topic upsetting to you?" he asked anxiously.

"I do not know yet. I do not know where your words are leading," I replied.

"They are leading to this: would you tell me what happened? Will you tell me what your father was talking about?"

I considered his questions for a long time. Richard may have thought I was ignoring him, but I merely needed time to think about what I would tell him.

I finally decided to tell him the entire story, from the time we knew she was missing to the awful realization that she wasn't coming home. I told the version of the story which left out the anguish, the sadness, the fear and confusion, but I felt quite sure he sensed those things.

"I'm sorry," he murmured when I had finished. By the time I had told the story we were at the door of my house. I invited him inside, not caring whether it was appropriate or not.

He followed me into the room and hung up his cloak, then stood by the fire, warming his hands. I looked at his boots—they were falling apart and were clearly too small—and shuddered to think how cold and sore his feet must be.

I sat down on the stool and offered him the rocking chair. He sat down and regarded me with a thoughtful look. I had to look away from his steady gaze. I found it unnerving, and yet it gave me an unusual fluttery feeling in my stomach.

"So what have you done to find her?" he asked.

"We looked everywhere. In the woods, along the road into Town, throughout the cape, everywhere. Pappa even went to Philadelphia to inquire about her and other people from the village inquired about her wherever they went, too. Of course, no one went very far, but maybe Mamma didn't go far, either."

"What about the ships coming into and leaving the harbor here in Town?"

"Pappa spoke with every captain he could find, every mate. No one saw her leaving. We've always been quite sure she met with a pack of wolves, or maybe even a lone wolf, out in the woods nearby. But we've never been able to find a trace of her, not even her clothes or shoes. It...it's also possible that she was a victim of violence at the hand of a person." I shuddered and told him about the letter I had found from Grandmamma. He listened with an increasingly grave expression on his face.

"This is a concerning development," he said. "Your father never spoke of it to me, but he was my friend and I felt I knew him well. He would have done all he could to figure out who was threatening your mother. He must not have discerned the identity of the person.

"Might your search for information about your mother's disappearance have something to do with your visit to the harbor several days ago?" Richard continued. The question took me by surprise—had it only been a few days since my visit to the bay to glean information about what Captain Eli might know? It seemed like much longer.

I nodded. "Mister Browne, who lives in the village, came by one night to tell Pappa that he had heard Captain Eli mentioning Mamma's name. He seemed to think the captain might know something about Mamma's disappearance. I went down to the harbor to eavesdrop, hoping to get some information about what the captain may know."

"And I gather you didn't learn anything?"

"No," I admitted, looking down at my hands.

"Promise me you won't do that again," Richard said. His voice was stern, but his deep gray eyes were kind.

"I appreciate your concern, but I cannot make a promise like that," I said, sitting up straighter. "I will do anything I can to find out what happened to Mamma, especially now that Pappa has requested it of me."

"Very well," Richard said. "Then at least promise that if you do something so foolish as going down to the harbor again, you will find me so I can assist you."

"I will do that," I said, smiling. "Thank you."

"It would be my pleasure," he said.

"Where shall I find you?" I asked.

"Oh, go to the barrel and sit down. I'll know you're there."

We were silent for a moment while I contemplated his reluctance to tell me where he lived. I supposed it didn't matter as long as he could find me.

"If you're warm enough, shall we go into the apothecary to look for the things my father left to you?"

"If it would be no trouble for you."

While Richard waited behind me in the house, I stood in the

doorway of the apothecary, breathing in the scents of herbs and remedies mixed with traces of Pappa's pipe tobacco. I had been in such a hurry when baby William was born that I hadn't stopped to notice the effect the shop had on me. This time I took my time, savoring the memories of working beside my father and allowing them to permeate my senses with a feeling of calm loneliness. I didn't fight the feelings, but rather embraced them, as if doing so might lessen my pain.

I beckoned Richard to follow me. He carried my father's letter from the lawyer in his hand.

"I don't recall exactly what was in the letter," I said. "Would you mind letting me read it again?"

Richard opened the letter and placed it on a slab of wood Pappa had used for a counter. Richard smoothed the letter and stepped back so I could read it.

I ran my finger down the list, then turned to one of the shelves where Pappa had kept his tools. I rummaged around until I found what I sought.

"Here are Pappa's forceps," I said, handing the tool to Richard. He took it in his hands and placed it gently on the counter.

Then I stooped down to root through one of the boxes which had recently come from Philadelphia. I had forgotten that I had seen another set of forceps and several jars in the box, as well as a number of other items I had seen on Richard's list.

"Most of the items on the list are already in this box. Pappa got the box from Philadelphia just shortly before he died." It was clear that Pappa had planned to give the box to Richard. I was struck with a pang of sadness when I realized Pappa must have suspected that he might get the fever, so he ordered the necessary items and changed his will shortly before he died to include the bequests to Richard.

"How very kind of him."

"Would you mind telling me a little more about why you

were working so closely with my father?" I asked suddenly, straightening up.

Richard looked away, focusing on something outside the window of the apothecary. He was silent for several moments before speaking. Finally he said, "I would rather not discuss that just now, if you don't mind."

I cocked my head, confused, but I decided not to press him on the issue. After all, he hadn't refused to talk to me about it *at all*, just for the present time.

"Will you tell me sometime?" I asked.

"I may," he said. "Let us wait to see what happens."

"What does that mean?" I asked.

"I cannot discuss it with you right now. I apologize for being so confounding," he said.

I turned back to the box and withdrew all the items inside, placing them on the counter. I separated the items on the list from those things not on the list and then filled several jars with herbs in the amounts bequeathed. Finally I pushed the box toward Richard.

"You can use this to carry your things back to Town," I said. "Would you mind terribly if you took the new things from Philadelphia and left the old ones here? Like the forceps? I'd like to keep Pappa's things."

"Of course I don't mind. It's very kind of you to give me the new things." He handed the old forceps back to me.

I handed each new item to him as he repacked the box carefully, putting short lengths of cloth between each of the glass jars so they would not break on the walk back to Town. When the box had been filled with everything listed in the letter, Richard lifted it easily.

"Thank you very much for these things and for helping me to pack them," he said. "I should be going now."

I followed him to the main house and locked the apothecary

door behind us. He hefted the box onto the table to put on his cloak and I had a sudden thought.

"Richard, wait here, please." I hurried into the bed chamber and returned just a moment later.

"I think Pappa would want you to have these," I said, holding out Pappa's boots to him. They had been expensive boots when Pappa had had them made, but they provided warmth to him for several winters before he died.

Richard stared at me, his mouth agape. "Are you sure?" he asked. "Are you sure you want to part with them?"

"Yes," I replied. "He thought of you as a good friend, and just look at your boots. I know you could use these, and what else would I do with them?"

"You could cut them up and use the hide for something," he suggested. I had a feeling the suggestion was only half-hearted, as I had seen the look of eager anticipation in his eyes when he saw me holding the boots.

I laughed. "No, I think you can use them more than I can. Please take them and stay warm."

"Sarah, I don't know how I can thank you for these," Richard said. "This is a priceless gift."

"Don't say any more about it. Just remember my father sometimes when you wear them."

"Every time, I promise you," he said. He sat down in the rocking chair and took off the ragged boots he had been wearing. I hadn't meant to watch, but I saw the holes in his woolen stockings.

"Please let me give you Pappa's stockings, too," I said, already heading toward the bed chamber.

"No, Sarah, you don't have to do that!" he called after me. But I pretended not to hear him.

As much as he protested, I noticed he had removed his stockings when I returned to the main room. I held out Pappa's stockings, including the missing one which I had found, and he gave me a broad smile.

"Thank you," he said, his voice quiet. "Money to buy such things, or to have them made for me, is scarce. I haven't been paid in quite some time."

"Why ever not?" I asked.

He shrugged. "I think my employer has not had enough money. But I will be paid sometime soon, I'm sure."

I didn't ask any more questions, as he did not seem inclined to answer them.

Richard stood up and glanced down at his feet. "They fit perfectly," he said, looking up at me and smiling. "Thank you again. I will take very good care of these."

"You are welcome. I know you will."

He retrieved the box on the table and I opened the door for him. As he brushed past me to go outside, I felt a small flutter again. He gave me a long look and the fluttering intensified.

"What is it?" I asked, my face burning from the attention.

"Please remember what I said about going down to the harbor. I will escort you if you feel the need to go there, but I think we can find other ways to get the information we need to discover what happened to your mother."

"We?" I seized on the word. "Are you going to help me?" I was nearly breathless at the thought of having an ally in my search for answers.

"Of course I am going to help you. If both of us are trying to find out what happened, we're certain to find out more quickly. Do you agree?"

"Yes! Oh, thank you, Richard!"

He chuckled. "I will be out to see you again soon. Maybe I will have some answers for you."

I smiled, almost daring to feel the surge of hope in my chest. The thought of finally learning what happened to my mother was enough to elevate my mood for the remainder of the day and into the evening.

After I finished the outside chores later that day I returned to the main room of the house, where I set about tidying the hearth and the floor of the bedchamber. I should have done the mending that day, but I wasn't ready to mend any of Pappa's things yet. I hoped that, in time, I would be able to mend Pappa's clothes, perhaps for use by someone else in the village or on another farm, without feeling despair and sadness.

Settling into the routine of doing things alone in the house was hard. I kept waiting for Pappa to open the door at supper-time, hungry for his meal. I accidentally set out two trenchers that evening and I didn't realize it until I sat down. Suddenly there was a lump in my throat that made it impossible to eat the dry biscuit and cheese I had in front of me. I took a drink of cider to make the lump disappear, but it only made my throat hurt. Tears rolled down my face and I knew then it would be a long time before I could go about my day normally without feeling the pangs of loss. Things like mending and baking seemed easier because those were chores I was accustomed to doing without Mamma. But Pappa and I had almost always eaten our meals together. I remembered feeling the same way when Mamma disappeared—it seemed like our meals would never be complete without her sitting with us, but in time we grew to accept it. Now I would have to adjust to new ways again.

After my meal I had a sudden urge to read by the fire, but I dared not. Judging from how upset I had become eating my meal, I knew reading the book Pappa had last read would be too much for me. Instead I cleaned up from my meal and went to bed early.

The next day was Sunday. I dreaded going to service by myself, but I knew I must. I put on my Sunday clothes and tried not to remember Pappa laid out in his Sunday clothes, bound for the barn where his body would await the spring thaw for burial.

I moved that morning as if in a fog, barely remembering to eat something before I left for the service. I walked slowly, my heart becoming heavier with each step. How many times had Pappa and I walked the same path on Sundays? How many quiet conversations had we enjoyed on our way to service?

When I reached the home in Town where the service was being held, there were already a fair number of people there. Many of them murmured their condolences again, for most of them had attended the visitation at my house. I accepted their sympathies with a nod of my head, not trusting myself to say anything. I kept my lips tightly closed and clenched my teeth to keep from crying.

Patience and her father and sisters were there, too, seated together not far from me. Patience gave a little wave and I was sorry to see that her mother and the baby had not come. I returned her wave and settled myself in my seat, aware of all the sets of eyes watching me and, no doubt, feeling sorry for me. Indeed, I felt very sorry for myself.

I had never been so relieved for service to begin. That kept people from saying anything else to me, at least until it ended.

After the service I hurried over to where Patience was standing so other people would not come in search of me to share their condolences. I couldn't listen to any more of it today. I touched Patience on the shoulder and asked if she could come over to my house later in the afternoon. She nodded and I left hastily.

I prepared a small midday meal for myself, as I was not hungry. I knew I should eat, though, in order to keep up my stamina. I sat down in the rocking chair and fell asleep while I waited for Patience.

She arrived by mid-afternoon. The sun was shining, though it was still very cold outside. Patience sat down before the fire to warm herself while I poured us mugs of cider, then I sat down across from her.

"Would you like to read this afternoon?" I asked. It had been some time since Patience and I sat reading in my house.

Her eyes lit up. "I would love to!" she exclaimed.

I took one of the books down from the shelf above the door, not the book Pappa had read most recently, and we sat down by the hearth, the fire crackling brightly behind us. I drew the lamp closer so we could see to read, then I handed the book to Patience. She took it from my hands very gently, as if she were holding a holy thing. She gazed at the cover reverently, tracing her fingers over the gilt script on the cover. Her eyes shone as she turned the pages to the place where we had left off the last time we read together.

She began reading slowly, haltingly, looking to me every few words for reassurance. I would nod at her and she would continue reading, then we would repeat our actions again and again. It wouldn't be long, I was sure, before Patience felt confident enough to read aloud without my encouragement. She was making steady progress; it still seemed strange that I had taken Mamma's place as Patience's mentor.

She continued reading for a short while, but eventually she closed the book and looked up. "I should be getting home to check on Mother. She will need my help this afternoon."

"Patience, wait. There's something I've been meaning to tell you."

"What is it?"

I took a deep breath. There was no point in prolonging the conversation. "Arthur asked for my hand."

Patience's eyes grew wide as the news sunk in. "I knew it!" she cried. "I knew he would ask you! When did he ask you? Why didn't you tell me?"

"He asked many days ago. So much has happened since then that I haven't even thought about it. I hope you'll forgive me."

"Of course! When will you be getting married?"

"That's part of the reason I didn't tell you as soon as it happened." I splayed my hands before me. "I told him I didn't know, that I needed time to decide."

Her eyes grew even wider. "You didn't accept?" The incredulity in her voice obvious.

I shook my head. "I couldn't. I don't love him."

"But you would grow to love him, I'm sure."

"I don't know. I don't feel about him the way Mamma and Pappa felt about each other when they were married, that much I know."

"How do you know?"

"Because Mamma always told me they were in love from the time they met. I certainly can't say I'm in love with Arthur."

"So you're going to reject him?"

I hated to think of it that way. "I just can't accept. I don't love him."

"Give it some time. You'll grow to love him," Patience assured me. But I knew I would not.

Someone knocked on the door, and I opened it to find Mistress Reeves, who was holding a basket covered with a linen cloth.

"Good afternoon, Mistress Reeves. Please come in," I invited.

She saw Patience sitting on the floor next to the hearth and her eyes flicked to the book she was holding. "Am I interrupting?" she asked.

"No, not at all," Patience said. She stood up and bowed her head toward Mistress Reeves, then handed me the book. She gave me an arched brow which Mistress couldn't see. "I was just leaving."

"I brought you a bit more cheese and some bread I baked a few days ago," Mistress Reeves said, turning her attention to me.

"That is very kind of you. Thank you."

Patience was putting on her cloak and she turned to

Mistress Reeves and me. "Thank you for letting me read with you today, Sarah. I'll see you soon. Good day, Mistress," she said.

"Goodbye, Patience," Mistress and I said in unison.

Once Patience had left Mistress offered me the basket and as I placed it on the table she moved about the room, looking out the window and coming to stand at the hearth. "What were you two reading?" she asked.

"It's a lovely book my parents brought from England. Mamma taught Patience to read, as you may know, and I'm simply helping Patience continue with her studies."

Mistress Reeves nodded. "I see," she said. "In our home we read nothing but the Holy Book on the Lord's Day."

"I also read the Bible," I said.

"Did your father allow you to read other books on the Lord's Day?"

"Yes. He encouraged me to read other books all the time. He always said there was much knowledge in books, but that books also held great potential for expanding our imaginations."

"First my father, and then my husband, have always been able to teach me everything I need to know," Mistress said. I thought that rather sad, but did not say anything.

"You should be reflecting on the things you learned in the service today from my husband's sermon, Sarah."

Embarrassingly, all I could recall of the sermon was how bored I had been.

"Thank you again for the cheese and bread," I said, not knowing what else to talk about. "Would you care to sit for a while?"

"I would, thank you," Mistress Reeves replied. She sat in the seat Patience had vacated and I also sat down. We looked at each other for an uncomfortable minute before she cleared her throat.

"Sarah, I would like to discuss something with you," she said.

# CHAPTER 12

"Certainly, Mistress Reeves. What is it you wish to discuss?" I had an idea, but I didn't mention it.

"I wish to discuss Arthur's proposal."

I suppressed a groan. My hunch had been correct, though Arthur was most definitely *not* a topic I wished to discuss with Mistress Reeves.

I swallowed. "Yes, Mistress?" I waited for her to begin speaking. She sat up straighter and looked out the window, then turned back to me.

"I know, of course, that he proposed to you and that you have asked him for some time before giving him your answer. You and I both know what that means—you do not wish to hurt him, but you do not wish to marry him, either. You can't be blamed for leading him by the nose the way you have, since your mother is no longer here to guide you and … well, your father, God rest his soul, probably did his best with you."

I held my breath, in part because her words had incensed me to the point where I needed to hold my tongue and in part because I was waiting to see where this conversation was leading.

"I think it would be to the good of everyone if Arthur is made to understand that you would not be a suitable wife for him."

I stared at her, my mouth hanging open. When I realized how simple I must look, I closed my mouth.

"I know this must come as a surprise to you, but I think Arthur would be better off with someone a bit younger than you, Sarah."

I was taken aback. I was too old for Arthur? He was older than I by several years, and I was eighteen.

"My husband and I believe it would be wise for Arthur to find a younger wife who is willing to travel to England with him. May I ask why you did not accept his proposal of marriage when he asked?"

I squirmed on my stool, trying to think of a polite way to tell Arthur's mother why I didn't want to marry her son. I didn't say anything for what seemed like ages.

"Please do not misunderstand my motives in not accepting Arthur's proposal immediately," I said after a long moment. "You see, I simply felt that Arthur and I do not know one another well enough to be married."

Mistress Reeves nodded, and I was unsure what she was thinking. She pursed her lips, looking pensive, then spoke.

"I find it interesting that young women nowadays seem to find it necessary to be on inappropriately familiar terms with their betrotheds," she mused. "When Pastor Reeves and I were betrothed, we had only met a small number of times, and each time we were fully within sight and hearing of our elders. That method has worked well for us, as we have grown fond of each other over the years."

"Begging your pardon, Mistress, but my parents knew each other well before getting married, and theirs was a union filled with joy and happiness, not merely fondness."

Mistress Reeves nodded once, slowly. "There is more than

one way to go about entering into marriage. Your parents took one route; my husband and I took another route. As for Arthur, I think he requires a wife who has seen less tragedy, less heartache. You understand, of course."

"Certainly, Mistress," I said. I didn't know whether to feel relieved or indignant. After all, here was Arthur's mother solving my problem of having to tell Arthur I could not marry him. But her reasons for objecting to a marriage between me and Arthur left me hurt and sad.

Mistress Reeves seemed to sense that my feelings were at war with themselves.

"My dear, you cannot be blamed for feeling sad and lonely following the deaths of your parents," Mistress said. "But you understand, don't you, that Arthur has a gentle constitution and might not know how to cope with a wife who brings such despair to a marriage."

I was striving to keep my mouth shut. It seemed that Arthur should be permitted to make such decisions for himself. I had to remind myself that this was a good outcome, one that I knew was best for both me and Arthur. I suppose I merely wanted to reject Arthur's proposal in my own time, on my own terms.

"What do you suggest I do about the proposal?" I asked.

"I am going to speak to Arthur about it," she replied. "I will tell him that his father and I do not approve of the marriage for the reasons I have given you. There is no need for you to tell him anything further."

"Thank you for coming today, Mistress Reeves," I said, standing up and waiting for her to do the same. Implying that she should leave gave me a feeling of strength. I was only a little surprised when she stood up and walked toward the door.

"Thank you for cooperating, Sarah," she said. I nodded and held the door for her. I wanted to slam it behind her with the power of an ocean wave in a thunderstorm, but I forced myself to remember that, however humiliating her visit, it was saving me from the pain of having to reject Arthur's proposal.

I needed something to do to stay busy after she left, so I put on my cloak and went into the apothecary. I left the door open so the warmth from the fire would penetrate the frigid air in the shop.

Being so cold turned out to be good for me. I moved about the shop quickly to keep warm, and I was able to tidy up a number of boxes and packets that Pappa had left undone when he died. I worked in the apothecary until the afternoon shadows began to darken the windows, then I went back into the house, surprised at how warm I had become in the shop. I knew I should not be working on the Lord's Day, but I couldn't bear the alternative—sitting in the house, thinking about my parents and sinking in grief.

Before leaving the shop, I took Pappa's ledger from the shelf where he kept it under the counter. As I ate my evening meal, I looked at the ledger next to me on the table. If my parents could have seen me trying to read while I was eating, they would have despaired, but there was no one to scold me, no one to tell me I should pay attention and be thankful for the food in front of me.

No one to eat with, no one to talk to while I ate ... I blinked tears away furiously, then turned back to the book, with its columns of numbers and notations.

After I finished eating I took the ledger over to the fire, bringing a lamp with me so I could see better. I spread the ledger on my lap so I could read it better. There, as before, were the columns of numbers that didn't seem to make sense for an ordinary apothecary. Pappa's strong script listed amounts that had come in and amounts he had spent for supplies and medicines. The profit was quite large. I knew Pappa kept his money in a locked box in the bedchamber, but I had not even thought to count it since his death. I would have to remember to do that in the morning. It was too dark now to count it correctly.

When I counted the money the next day, I found more coins than I had even realized. My father had been frugal with his spending, and that left me with enough money to live for a moderate time without worrying about coin.

But I needed to make a decision. Richard had started me thinking about the shop, the medicines, and all the time Pappa had spent teaching me about herbs and remedies and medicines. Could I really run the apothecary? A woman, alone?

I wasn't sure. What would people think? Would they scorn me for not being as smart as a man? For not having the business acumen one needed to run such a shop? For having the audacity to think I could turn a profit as my father had?

My thoughts turned to Richard. He seemed to think I should take over the apothecary and keep it running. And I *did* need a source of income, for as much as Pappa had left behind, it wasn't enough to sustain the apothecary for a long time. I didn't need much money, but there were certain things I would need and eventually the coins he left would run out.

What else was I capable of doing? I could do all the things most women could do—I could bake, mend, sew, clean, and do farm chores. I could plant and harvest vegetables. But could I make a living doing any of those things? Probably not.

Maybe I *should* continue Pappa's practice of helping others and easing the pain of the unwell on the cape. There was no other apothecary for many miles, so I would be providing a valuable service to the people who lived in the village. Mamma always told me I was quick to learn, so maybe I could run Pappa's shop.

I made a decision that day—I would try it.

And once the decision was made, I was excited. This gave me a new reason for hope and purpose, and I could hardly wait to begin telling people.

I planned to tell Patience first, but something happened to alter my plan. The next day I was cleaning in the apothecary when there was a tap at the window. Glancing up, I saw Richard smiling at me through the clean glass. I hurried to let him inside.

"Richard, I must thank you for giving me encouragement the last time I saw you," I began, my words tumbling out in my excitement.

"Encouragement? Of what sort?" He took his hat off as he entered the room.

"I have come to an important decision. I am going to continue my father's work as the apothecary."

Richard's smile warmed me to my very bones. "I am very happy to hear it, Sarah. I hoped you would reach that decision. I think you will make a fine apothecary."

"Thank you." I am quite sure I blushed. "What brings you here today?"

"I thought you might like to get out of the house and go for a walk with me."

"I would certainly enjoy that," I said.

"Shall we be off, then? I'll wait while you get your cloak."

I hurried to retrieve my cloak from its peg near the front door of the house, then I called to Richard, "Would you please make sure the door is bolted in the apothecary?"

I heard the bolt slide across the door and a moment later Richard joined me in the house. He offered me his arm as we went out the front door and I slid my arm under his. His strong arm kept me from slipping on the ice outside the door.

It felt so different from the time Arthur did the same thing.

We walked along the road leading to Town, not speaking except to comment on the weather. It was a pleasant walk. When we neared Town, I put my arm down at my side, lest anyone think I was the kind of young woman who would gad about with any man who arrived at my door. Richard was different—he was my friend, but the people in Town didn't know that.

Richard stopped walking for a moment. "I have an idea. Let's to go the tavern and toast your decision to take over your father's role as apothecary."

"That isn't necessary, Richard. I do not wish to make a fuss over myself."

"You won't be making a fuss. I will. Would you allow me to do that?"

I smiled. He seemed so keen to do this simple thing, so I agreed. He opened the door of the tavern for me and I preceded him into the cozy darkness of the large room.

There were only a few people inside, owing to the early hour of the day, but all eyes were upon us as we sat down on two stools at a rough-hewn table. Richard nodded to a table where three men were sitting, not saying anything to each other. Each of them nodded to him in return. They were frightening. They were covered with dirt, and I could smell the odors from their clothes from across the room.

Richard gestured for me to take the stool with my back to them so I wouldn't have to look at them. He ordered two flips from Mister Ellis, the tavern keeper, and I watched as Mister Ellis plunged the hot fire poker, or flip-dog, into the mixture of ale, rum, molasses, and cream to make it frothy and warm. He served the drink in large mugs, and I wrapped my hands around my mug, breathing in the delightful scent of the steam. It was pleasantly warm in the room. Richard toasted my success as the new apothecary and I joined him in sipping the flip. It slid down my throat, warming me from the inside out. I sipped the drink slowly so I could savor every drop.

After a quarter of an hour, another person came into the tavern. We all turned to look at the newcomer; it was Ada, she of the braying laugh. She spoke coquettishly to the tavern keeper for a moment or two, then slid a piece of mail across the counter to him, and was gone. As the tavern keeper was charged with holding the mail for occasional delivery to and from Town, he knew everyone. Very shortly after she left, the town's cooper came inside. Richard noticed him with a look of recognition and turned to me. "Would you excuse me for just a moment? I do need to have a word with that gentleman."

"Of course."

Richard approached the cooper with a smile and, taking the man's elbow gently, led him outside. I looked down at my flip, wondering what his business with the cooper could be, then looked up again and took in my surroundings. The keeper was behind a long counter, cleaning something. A fire burned cheerfully in the fireplace, which was much bigger than ours at home. The tavern felt safe and warm.

The three men behind me were talking in low voices, and I didn't mean to eavesdrop on their conversation—until I heard one of them utter the name "Eli." I was immediately alert.

I leaned back on my stool just a tiny bit, straining my ears to hear anything they might say. They didn't seem to notice that I was listening.

"Aye, he's a hang in chains, that you can believe. And he's been so for years. There's talk that the auld buzzard was overfond of a woman right here in Town a couple years back," one of them said. I held my breath so my breathing wouldn't impair my ability to hear.

"The poor woman," one said with a laugh.

"Aye, he says she would have sailed off wif him, too, if she hadn't disappeared."

"I'd disappear if the likes of him came lookin' for me," the third said with a cackle.

They were talking about my mother. The implications of their words set my mind spinning.

I was too stunned to move. I must have looked ghastly,

because when Richard came back into the tavern with the cooper, he took one look at me and rushed to my side.

"What's happened, Sarah?"

I could only shake my head. Sound rushed about between my ears and I had the feeling I was going to faint. I took great gulps of air as Richard demanded a cold drink from the tavern keeper. The man rushed over with a tankard of ale, and Richard held it to my lips. There was so much commotion that I couldn't hear anything else from the table of men behind me. I tried turning my head to look at them, to see their faces, but Richard was holding the tankard to my mouth again. I took a sip and coughed until Richard set it down on the table, an anxious look in his eyes.

"Sarah, can you tell me what happened?"

"We have to leave here now," I sputtered.

He took several coins from the pocket around his waist and left them on the table. He turned to help me rise from my stool, but I was already standing on my own, ready to leave. I cast a backward glance at the three men at the table behind me, and all of them were looking at me with bold stares. Richard gave them a dark look and they looked down at their own drinks. Then Richard took my arm and we left the tavern.

Outside in the cold air I began to feel better. I didn't feel faint anymore and I was eager to go home. I only wish I hadn't become so agitated, because I might have been able to hear more.

"Sarah, can you tell me what happened?"

"Richard, those men behind me. Those men at the table. They were talking about Captain Eli and *my mother*."

His eyes widened. "How do you know that?"

I repeated what the men had said. "There is only one woman who went missing from Town two years ago, and that was my mother."

"They could be mistaken," Richard said. The tone of his voice suggested that even he did not believe what he was saying.

I shook my head vehemently. "No, it was my mother. Richard, how could she have allowed any attentions from a man other than my father? How could she have allowed it and not said anything?"

"We don't know that she didn't say anything to your father. It's possible that your father knew about it."

I was reminded of the letter from Grandmamma. The thought that Pappa may have known about the captain calmed me a bit, though I was still distressed to think a man like the repellant Captain Eli had been bothering my mother.

"Where do you suppose he wanted to sail with her?" I asked.

Richard shrugged. "From what little I know of Captain Eli, he frequently sailed to and from the West Indies."

"Where are the West Indies?" I asked.

"Far south of here. The weather is beautiful there."

I wondered for a terrible moment if my mother would have liked to live in a place with beautiful weather. "Do they have winter there?" I asked.

"No. It's warm all the year through."

Mamma would have liked that. She had often said the winters were her least favorite part of living in New Jersey. She had always said the winters in England were preferable because they were milder. Warm weather in the winter might have appealed to her. I shuddered again.

"Sarah, you must remember that your mother loved your father and you and would never have left either of you."

"How do you know?" I winced at the challenge in my voice.

"I know because of what your father has said about her. He talked about her often, you know. He loved her and she loved him. Even if the weather had been perfect all year somewhere else, she never would have given a thought to leaving her family behind."

I looked down at my hands, embarrassed that I had had the gall to question my mother and that Richard, who had never known her, was sure in his conviction that she would never have left her family behind willingly.

Willingly.

We had been walking briskly, but I stopped suddenly when a sinking fear overcame me. "Richard! I've had a terrible thought. Do you suppose Captain Eli took her away? Do you suppose he took her somewhere against her will?"

"I suppose we would have to find out where Captain Eli was before he settled on this cape. If he sailed somewhere directly following your mother's disappearance, it is certainly possible that your mother was aboard that ship."

I gasped.

"Let's not make rash assumptions," Richard cautioned. "It could be that Captain Eli was in port for months after your mother went missing. In that case, I am sure she was not kept a prisoner on his ship. Too many men would have been aware of it and word would have spread."

"Are you sure?"

"I am sure."

"How do you know?"

"I have ways of knowing which needn't trouble you."

I frowned. I didn't like Richard's implications. It sounded to me like he was involved in something nefarious, something I would be better off not knowing.

I shook the thought off, though, grateful instead that there was someone helping me to solve the mystery of what happened to my mother. His secrets were none of my business.

But still … I kept wondering about him long after he left my house that day.

Neither my inquisitiveness regarding Richard nor my frustration over not knowing anything more about Captain Eli abated over the next several days. I thought constantly about ways to find out more about the captain, but I discarded each idea as foolhardy or dangerous or both.

While I tried to come up with a way to get the information I needed, I had plenty to keep me busy in the apothecary. I dusted and cleaned jars and bottles, and peeked inside boxes and packets to see what I might find. I discovered that my father had a physick book he kept in the apothecary, probably for research on ailments and remedies. I found it fascinating, and I settled down in the afternoons to read it by the fire. It wasn't a story, like the other books we had brought with us from England, but instead it contained facts and information that would be useful to someone treating illnesses.

As word of my new position as apothecary had spread throughout the village and to the scattered farms surrounding it, people who had stopped coming to the apothecary upon Pappa's death started to return. Some were clearly unsure of a young woman taking over her father's business, so I knew it would take time for them to trust me and to understand that Pappa had taught me well. If I could persuade them, I knew I could do a good job taking care of them and their families when someone was ill or hurt.

Less than a week after my fateful eavesdropping in the tavern, I had occasion to return to the tavern to leave a letter for the post to Philadelphia. It contained an order of supplies that I required in the apothecary and I hoped someone would retrieve the mail soon. The tavern was quiet on the day I visited. I had held out hope that the men whom I had heard talking on my last visit would be there again, but no one was inside except for the tavern keeper who was standing behind the gleaming wooden counter. He and I exchanged pleasantries for a few moments, then I gave him the letter and bid him goodbye. The street was nearly deserted when I went back outside. The wind was blowing fiercely, so I turned away from the wind to turn up the collar of my cloak. I was surprised to see Richard striding toward the water, coughing into the scarf he wore tightly wrapped around his neck. His form was unmistakable, and I fancied I could see Pappa's boots on his feet from where I stood.

Something in my mind urged me to hurry after him—this might be an opportunity for me to find out more about this man who revealed so little about himself.

# CHAPTER 13

*R*ichard was clearly in a hurry, or possibly it was the cold that was urging him to walk with such haste. I didn't want him to see me because I didn't want him to think I was following him, so I kept my head down and remained a discreet distance behind him. I practically had to run to keep pace with him.

At the end of the street he hastened down the scree- and scrub-covered embankment to the sand below. I hurried to watch from the street above as he strode toward a dinghy that was held fast on the sand. He pushed the dinghy into the water, jumped in, and rowed quickly away from the beach, teetering on the tops of waves that crested white as they rolled onto the shore. I had to hide my face from the icy wind that was whipping off the water, and because Richard faced the land as he rowed. I watched as he continued to row toward a large boat that was moored just a short distance away.

Slipping on the icy ground atop the beach in my kid shoes, I struggled to see as he drew closer to the boat. One of the men already on board waved to him and he waved back. They exchanged some words I couldn't hear and both of them appeared to laugh. To my astonishment, Richard tied the dinghy to the side of the large boat and, without a moment's hesitation, climbed the rope ladder that the man on board had tossed over the side.

Once Richard was aboard the boat, he disappeared from view. I had no idea what he was doing. I watched for another minute or two, and when he didn't reappear, I turned around to walk home. As I turned to leave, though, a voice called my name.

"Sarah? Sarah?" I whirled around to see who was calling me and I saw Mister Browne coming up the hill toward me from the sand.

"Good day, Mister Browne," I said.

"Good day, my dear. What in the name of heaven are you doing down here in this unsavory place by yourself?" To my surprise, he grasped my elbow and pulled me away from the edge of the small cliff.

"I ... I was trying to locate a friend of my father's," I stammered, unwilling to tell him I was following Richard. I prayed God would not strike me down for lying. Well, it wasn't really lying so much as it was being deceitful, for Richard *had* been a friend of my father.

"You should never come down to the bay alone, Sarah," Mister Browne cautioned. He lowered his voice. "That ship you were watching? Rumor has it that it's a ship full of pirates." He said the word *pirates* as if it hurt his mouth to say it. "And one never knows who might be watching them on behalf of the governor."

Pirates? How could that be? Richard wasn't a pirate.

Was he?

I stumbled on a piece of dirty ice in the street. Mister Browne grasped my arm just in time for me to avoid falling.

The word *pirates* was one reserved for whispered conversations, overheard and resulting in nightmares of seagoing brig-

ands inflicting their own peculiar brands of villainy on
unsuspecting ships sailing under legal flags. It couldn't be
possible that Richard was one of the blackguards of whom I had
heard so much since coming to New Jersey

As soon as we were safely out of sight of the cliff, I thanked
Mister Browne for his advice to stay away from the bay when I
was alone. I hurried home, lost in thought.

What, precisely, did I know about Richard?

I knew he was from England, like me and my parents. I
knew he and my father had been friends and engaged in some
kind of business together. I knew he wore Pappa's old boots and
had been given apothecary items when Pappa died. I knew he
had spent some time in the medical college in London. I also
knew his eyes were enchanting and I felt warm and safe with
him. But what else did I know about him?

I couldn't think of anything else. Was he a violent person?
He certainly didn't seem to be. I had never seen him raise his
voice or his hand. Was he a brigand and a marauder? I had
never seen an indication that he was anything other than a
gentleman. He was polite, he did not eat with his hands as I had
heard pirates commonly did, he did not use foul or embarrassing language. He treated me with respect and dignity, which
was the opposite of how I had always heard pirates treated the
fairer sex. Was he devilish? I didn't know, but he had been polite
to Mistress Reeves the few times he had had occasion to speak
with her.

I couldn't bring myself to believe that Richard was one of the
black-hearted men I had heard so much about in civilized
conversations among citizens of Town and Cape Island.

But yet ... why was he on that ship? Mister Browne would
certainly know which ships were full of pirates and which
ones were full of law-abiding sailors and captains. He was
down at the bay all the time, inspecting ships and cargo and
talking to all the men who milled around. He was the one who

had alerted us to Captain Eli's unholy obsession with Mamma.

I needed to talk to Richard. I didn't care anymore if he scoffed at me for wondering about him, or thought me brazen because I followed him to the bay. I simply needed to know what he was doing on that ship.

But Richard did not come to the house again for over a week. I grew more impatient with each passing day, and I had no excuse to go anywhere to see if I could find answers to my questions about Mamma and Captain Eli. I saw Arthur once, from a distance. I waved to him, but he turned around and I didn't know if he had seen me. My cheeks grew hot with embarrassment at the mere memory of the event. Patience was only able to talk for a few minutes all week long because she was so busy taking care of the new baby with her mother still not feeling well. I worked in the apothecary and found that it took my mind off Richard, Pappa's recent death, and even Mamma's disappearance, as long as I was busy. I mixed several tisanes for Goody Ames in the hope that one or more of them might help her with her melancholy. I spent my spare time reading the physick book, learning all I could about diseases and ailments that might afflict the people of the cape.

Late one afternoon I chanced to visit the tavern to see if there had been a mail delivery. I left the tavern empty-handed after just a few moments and headed in the direction of my house, walking swiftly and with purpose, hoping that no stranger would speak to me and that I could get home before it was completely dark outside.

I had only gone a short distance when someone grabbed my elbow from behind. Letting out a gasp and whirling around, I found myself facing Captain Eli. There was a strange glint in his eyes, as if he had taken to drink.

"I've been looking for you, girl." His breath reeked of rotting teeth.

"What for?" I asked, trying to yank my arm out of his grasp.

"I hear that Josiah Browne, that n'er-do-well, was telling tales about me and your lovely mother."

I avoided gagging by turning my face from him. "Mister Browne is not a n'er-do-well," I said primly, letting my arm go limp. I thought he might let me go if he thought I would not try to get away.

"Ha!" he laughed, spittle flying from the corners of his mouth. He kept his grip on my elbow. "You look like your mother, did you know that?"

"So I've been told." I refused to look at his face. Those eyes of his were positively frightening.

"She was real pretty, that one."

"Captain, please let me go. I do not care to discuss my mother."

"She was real nice, too, if you know what I mean," he said, winking at me. I could feel my face getting hot and my breath was coming faster. I did not, in fact, know what he meant, but I could guess. The thought of my mother giving this monster the briefest notice was enough to make my skin crawl. I didn't believe a word of it. He was just trying to goad me into saying something about her.

"I do not know what you mean, sir, and I will thank you to leave me alone." I finally gave my arm a forceful twist and he let go in surprise.

"You're a feisty one, aren't you?" he asked, his mouth curling into a sickening grin.

I turned on my heel and stalked away toward my house, hoping with all my heart that he was not following me. After about a hundred feet I gathered the courage to look behind me to see if he was still standing in the street.

He was, and he was watching me warily. I shuddered. I never wanted to see that man again.

But as I drew closer to home, I chided myself for not asking him the questions I had about my mother. Just how did he know her? Did he know what happened to her? Where had he sailed before retiring from his life on the sea? I wondered if my father had told my mother not to go down to the bay by herself, worried that she might run into Captain Eli. It probably did not matter that I didn't ask the old man any questions about my mother—surely he would have lied to me.

My poor mother. Had she known of the particular dangers that Captain Eli posed? Had he been threatening her, as Grand-mamma had suggested?

The thought sent shivers up and down my spine. I practically ran the rest of the way home, looking behind me every few moments to be sure the captain hadn't followed me. When I was inside, I slammed the door and slid the bolt into place so I wouldn't worry about anyone getting in while I slept.

I couldn't eat supper. My mind and my stomach were churning—my mind with anxiety over my brief encounter with Captain Eli, and my stomach with worry over what and how much he knew about my mother's disappearance.

I slept fitfully that night, unable to find a comfortable position and freezing despite the warm covers on the bed. I rose more than once to check that the bolt was safely across the door. As long as Pappa had been alive, I had never been afraid to sleep in my house. But now that he was gone, all my dark and grim thoughts took flight during the darkness.

I dragged myself out of bed the next morning, did my chores as if in a trance, and finally sat down to eat something. I was hungry for the first time since the midday meal the previous day, and there was warming porridge in the kettle that hung to the side of the fireplace. I needed to stay busy, so I went into the apothecary to retrieve the physick book.

That afternoon I sat in front of the fire, studying the book by the light thrown from the flames.

My eyes were beginning to close from sheer exhaustion

when I put the book away and decided to organize the bottles in the apothecary. At least the cold in the room would keep me awake. I hadn't been working long when there was a knock at the door. Turning around, I was surprised to see Richard standing outside, blowing on his hands to keep them warm. I had been waiting for so many days to see Richard and to talk to him, and now I was suddenly nervous at the prospect of possibly finding out he was a pirate. I gave him a weak smile as I unlocked the door to let him into the shop.

"Hullo, Sarah," he said, his voice jolly.

"Good day, Richard," I replied. "Would you like to come in by the fire? You must be cold."

"I would, indeed, if you don't mind," he said.

I locked the apothecary door again and led the way into the house. Richard dragged the stool in front of the hearth and I sat down nearby.

"I apologize for not coming 'round sooner, but I've been sick," he said. "I had an awful hacking cough and sore throat, and many of my friends suffered the same affliction, I am afraid. I didn't want to come over here and take the risk of making you sick, too."

"Thank you for that," I said. I remembered him coughing forcefully into the scarf wrapped around his neck when I saw him on the wharf. "You are feeling better now, I trust?"

"Much better. Your father provided me with a cough remedy months ago, and I still had some left. It was very effective."

"I am glad of it," I said. I was growing more nervous. What was I going to say to him?

"Have you any news of Captain Eli?" he asked.

I took a deep breath and told him of my encounter with Captain Eli in the village. He listened in astonishment, his eyes growing wider and his jaw dropping.

"Sarah! I'm so sorry I wasn't there to escort you from the tavern. Perhaps you should not go there by yourself anymore."

"I don't think that will be necessary," I said. "I think it so happened that Captain Eli and I were on the street at the same time. I do not believe he was following me. He watched me as I walked toward home, but he already knows where we live."

"Did he hurt you?"

"Not physically." Richard opened his mouth to speak, but there was another matter pressing upon my mind, and I needed to speak of it at once or I might never say anything.

"Richard, I saw something that surprised me last week."

"What was that?"

"I happened to be walking down by the bay and I saw you row out to a ship that was moored there."

Richard gave me the merest hint of a wary look, then encouraged me to continue.

"Yes?" he asked.

"I thought nothing of it, but Mister Browne told me it was … it was … rumored to be a pirate ship." I stopped talking, suddenly unsure of how, precisely, I should word my question.

He raised his eyebrows. "Before I discuss what I was doing on that ship, I have a question for you. Was Mister Browne your escort down by the bay?"

I hesitated before answering. "Not exactly, but he escorted me away from there."

"What were you doing down there by yourself? I am grateful to Mister Browne for taking you away from that disreputable place."

I suddenly realized he was prevaricating. He didn't want to answer my implied question, so he was carrying on with a question of his own. I gathered my determination and replied to him.

"Yes, it was fortunate that Mister Browne was nearby. Now, though, shall we get back to what I was saying? I was saying that Mister Browne told me the boat you boarded is a pirate ship. Is that true?"

I was almost afraid to hear the answer, then he was silent for so long I thought he might not answer me at all. But finally he spoke.

"Sarah, I have not known you for a long time, but I would like to take you into my confidence. Will you allow me to do that?"

"Yes," I answered, hesitation forcing me to draw out the syllable.

Richard took a deep breath and set his hands on his knees. "The truth is that I do work on a ship. And yes, it is an outlaw ship. I—"

"But, why?" I interrupted.

"Let me finish, Sarah. I am the ship's doctor. Though I have not completed my medical studies, the owner of the ship hired me to live with the other men, to treat their injuries and illnesses, to make sure that his investment is secured with men that are able-bodied and hale."

"You're a *pirate doctor*?" I asked, barely daring to trust my own hearing.

He nodded. "I am. But you must understand that this life was not my choice. When I was a boy in England, I was orphaned. I was taken in by a generous benefactor and he paid for me to attend two years of medical college.

"Sadly, he died of fever when I was nearing the end of my second year. It happened very suddenly, much like your father's death. And unfortunately for me, my benefactor had never put into writing the nature of his provision for me, so there was no money for me to continue my studies upon his death. His family, who had never approved of his actions in taking in a poor boy, received all his money, his estate, everything.

"And, since I was practically grown, I had to find money quickly. I needed it to live, to eat, to obtain shelter. When I was approached by the owner of the ship you saw me board out in the bay, his offer seemed too good to be true." Richard paused and took another deep breath.

"What was his offer?" I asked.

Richard looked past me, gazing into the fire as if remembering the occasion of the man's offer, before turning his attention back to me. I waited, my hands folded on my lap.

"He said that he had a ship that was engaged in certain trade across the Atlantic Ocean. He said that if I would sign on as the ship's doctor, I would receive a place to live, quality medical supplies, and a portion of the proceeds of the ship's profits.

"I was not wise enough to discern his meaning. I know I should have realized he owned a ship that plied an outlawed trade. But, not realizing what I was getting into, I signed on."

"And you can't get out of it?"

He gave a raw laugh. "You haven't met many pirates, have you?" Then he shook his head. "No, I'm in this until I've served the term of the contract."

"And how long is that?"

"Four years. I'm three years in."

"How often do you sail?"

"We sail whenever the sea complies. When we leave I never know how long we'll be gone. Or if we'll be back." An involuntary shudder ran up my spine and my breath caught at the thought of him not returning from a voyage. I hoped he hadn't noticed.

"Where do you go?"

"Usually south and east."

"Do you always return to New Jersey?"

"Not always. That's why you've not seen me until recently."

I couldn't explain it, but I felt a sadness just then that lay over me like my counterpane. Except, unlike my counterpane, the feeling left me cold and fearful.

Richard reached out to touch my hands, where they still lay clasped in my lap.

"Are you disappointed in me, Sarah?"

"Well, I wish you weren't practically a prisoner to the man who owns the ship, but I certainly understand why you had to sign on."

"Thank you."

"How did you come to know my father, then?" I asked.

A hint of a smile played around Richard's lips. "I met your father in the tannery, soon after my arrival in Town Bank. I had made an enquiry of the tanner whether I might find an apothecary in town, and it was providential that William was there. Your father was understanding of my predicament, more so than most. He had heard the rumors, of course, that my ship is one of outlaws and rakes. And he knew that the governor has made many attempts to roust pirates from the coastline here along the cape and in other places. But he also knew that as the doctor on board, I needed certain supplies and remedies that only he could supply."

"So you struck a bargain with him?"

"I did. He agreed to provide me with the things I need for my medicine chest and I agreed to pay him handsomely."

I thought back to Pappa's apothecary ledger and the trouble I had had believing the numbers I was seeing. Now it made sense: Pappa was being paid by pirates. I didn't know how I felt about that.

Richard seemed to sense my thoughts. "Your father did a brave and noble thing, Sarah. He knew the ship would sail with or without medical supplies, and he knew men would sign up to join the crew with or without an equipped medicine chest, so he did what was right to make sure that those men could be treated for a number of various ailments and wounds."

"I see."

"You surely understand, then, why your father and I conducted much of our business after dark," Richard said. "Between the rumors and the governor's stated antagonism toward pirate ships and crews, neither your father nor I wanted to be discovered doing business together."

"It makes much more sense now," I said with a nod.

"Do you also understand why your father left me the items in his will?" Richard asked.

"I do. He wanted to make sure your crew had crucial supplies, just in case you couldn't find someone else to provide you with the necessary items."

"Precisely. Now comes the awkward question: now that you know of his activities, are you willing to continue in the bargain he made with me?"

My alarm at the prospect of supplying a pirate ship with medical necessities must have been evident in my face, for Richard hastened to add, "You don't have to do anything you don't want to do, of course. I would never ask you to do that."

"I need to think about that, Richard," I said.

"That is fine. I can return in a few days, if that is long enough for you, and you can let me know what you've decided. I hate to put such a condition on your decision, but I'll need time to find a way to get the supplies I need if you decide this is something you would rather not undertake."

I nodded. "Thank you for giving me some time, Richard."

He rose to leave. "And I thank you, as well. Thank you for your willingness to think it over."

I rose, too, and opened the door for him.

"Is it dangerous, Richard? Being on a ship like that?"

He touched the scar on his face. "It can be." I nodded and he left without another word. When I turned around to go back inside, I found I didn't want to go back into the apothecary. I needed to sit down and sift through the things Richard had just told me.

I sat down and let my gaze drift to the low flames in the fireplace. It calmed my mind and I could think more clearly about what I had learned.

I had been right—Richard wasn't the type of person one typically associated with pirate crews. He didn't say so, but I presumed he did not participate in any of the evil deeds attributed to crews of brigands.

But what if he had? He certainly wouldn't tell me, not unless I insisted upon knowing. I had a feeling that he would tell me the truth if I asked for it. Did I really want to know it?

And what of the governor's hatred of pirates? Though they brought goods and riches from their plunders and townspeople liked the business they brought to the village, they were outlaws and criminals. Common thieves, and dangerous ones, at that. It was well known that the governor was attempting to stifle any pirate activity along his shores.

But the question I now found myself asking in uncertain situations was *What would Pappa do under the same circumstances?* And for that question I had an easy answer: Pappa had cast personal prejudices aside and helped the pirate doctor, knowing that the doctor's job was to try to save the lives of the men who created such havoc on the high seas. Pappa hadn't been able to turn his back on men in need, even if they were men he would never want in his home. Even if they were men he didn't want his daughter to see or hear.

I thought about Richard's request for much of the time over the next several days, while I was doing chores, while I was idle, while I walked to Patience's house to talk with her and see Baby William.

And eventually, Pappa's own actions dictated what mine would be under similar circumstances. Of course I was a woman whereas he was a man, and I was new to the business of being an apothecary whereas he had made it his life's work. But if he could decide to help the pirate doctor when he had a daughter to protect, I could do the same thing with no one but myself to protect.

Richard was pleased when I told him of my decision.

"Sarah, this takes a great weight from my shoulders. I had high hopes that you would carry on in your father's footsteps, but I could not influence your decision. It had to be yours alone. But now that you have decided to continue helping me, I will offer you the same payment terms that I had with your father. Would that be sufficient?"

"I do not know the payment terms you and my father arranged," I answered. True, I knew Richard was paying Pappa handsomely to provide medical supplies for the ship, but I hadn't been able to discern the prices for medical items from the notes Pappa had made in his ledger.

"Your father made a percentage of the profits brought in on a voyage," Richard said. He watched my reaction closely, as if unsure how I would feel about such an arrangement.

In my heart, I was surprised that Pappa had agreed to that type of payment, but I was careful not to let my face betray my surprise. I thought for a moment: it was merely a business decision by Pappa. If he was going to help pirates, he had to accept payment in the form in which they were able to pay. I made my decision quickly and firmly.

"I'll take the same percentage you offered my father," I said, lifting my chin ever so slightly. Richard smiled.

"You'll make a tidy profit, I can assure you of that, Sarah."

"I know. I've seen the ledgers Pappa kept."

Richard smiled again. He reached out to shake my hand to seal our business deal, and though it felt awkward, I shook his hand. I was surprised at the softness of his skin. I had expected it to be rough and calloused, the hands of a pirate. Then I began to wonder why I had any expectation of what his hands might feel like. I blushed. When he unclasped his hand, my fingers were warm and my stomach quivered with something I didn't understand.

"I need to get back to the ship," he said. "I'll continue making a list of the things I still need for the medicine chest, and I'll bring it to you. You should be able to get everything on the list before we set sail." Again, that strange and uncomfortable feeling of unease and sadness swept through me like a wave.

"Very well," I replied, not wanting him to know the effect his words had had on me. "As soon as I have your list I will set aside or send away for the necessary supplies."

"I must be going," Richard said. "Thank you for helping me like this. We can continue to do business the way I did with your father, under the cover of darkness, and no danger should come to either of us." He left then, turning to wave at me, and I watched him until he disappeared around the bend in the road.

Why did I feel sad whenever he mentioned setting sail? I supposed it was because he and I had become friends and I didn't like the thought that something could happen to him while he was away at sea. It wasn't anything more than that.

Was it?

## CHAPTER 14

*P*atience knocked on my door the next morning.

"Care to go for a walk?" she asked. Patience didn't like winter and usually wanted to sit in front of the fireplace when she visited. I thought it odd that she wanted to be outside in the wind and cold.

"Certainly," I replied. She waited in the doorway while I threw a long cloak over my shoulders.

She hooked her arm in mine while we walked. I finally asked her why she didn't want to stay in my house where the fire was burning.

"I suppose I'm feeling restless today," she replied, casting a long sideways glance at me.

"Patience, tell me the truth. Something is wrong and you don't want to share it with me. But really, you do want to discuss it, or else you wouldn't have asked me to go walking with you in this frigid weather."

Patience sighed. "You're right, Sarah. I don't want to tell you what I've learned, but I have to." She lowered her voice. "It's about Captain Eli."

Immediately all my senses were alert. My breathing quickened. "What about the captain?" I asked, pressing her arm a bit more tightly against my side.

"Father overheard Captain Eli talking to men down by the water. He said the captain was filled with drink, his lips flapping. He was in quite a state, according to Father, and he was talking about your mother and father."

It took all my power, but I remained still. My voice quiet, I asked, "What did he say about them?"

"He said that your mother didn't know enough to come with him when he asked her to go. He said he was a better man than your father." My fists curled when I heard what the old man had said about my father.

But those men at the tavern had been right. Captain Eli had asked my mother to go with him somewhere.

"Where did he ask her to go?" My voice betrayed my frantic thoughts.

"I'm not sure, exactly," Patience replied. She looked at me sadly. "I wish I knew."

"What else did he say?" I asked, exasperated.

"Like I said, he was drunk," Patience said, as if warning me not to give credence to what she was about to say. "But there was one interesting thing he said before my father had to leave to go to the tanner's. The captain said that the moment your mother refused him, he was seized with such a rage that he could easily have killed her."

"What? So did he hurt her? Did he kill her? Refused him what? I can't bear this, Patience!" My voice had risen several notes and my breath came quickly. It seemed less and less likely that a chance encounter with wolves had been responsible for my mother's disappearance. I buried my face in my cold hands, dropping Patience's arm from my side.

"We'll figure it out, Sarah. We'll talk to Captain Eli when he's not been drinking and we'll demand to know what he was talking about."

"And how are we going to do that? What could he possibly have meant?" I asked, now wringing my hands.

"My father asked him what he meant, but he just shook his head and kept talking to the other men. Sarah, it's possible that he doesn't know what he's saying. Father says the captain has been declining from drink. But he'll ask him again, of that you can be sure."

*I can't be sure of that, but I can be sure of one thing. I am going to find out what happened to Mamma, even if it means seeking out Captain Eli and confronting him by myself.*

Patience took my hand in hers. "I probably should have waited to tell you what Captain Eli said until I had more information, but I thought you would want to know."

"I appreciate that, Patience. Thank you."

"What will you do now?" she asked.

"I'm going to talk to a friend to see if he can find any more information."

"What friend is this?"

"His name is Richard. He was present when my father passed. You must have seen him at my house when you arrived that night. He's helping me to find out what happened to Mamma. He is ... he knows certain people who might be able to give us more information."

"Be careful around him, Sarah. He looked disreputable to me."

I chuckled for the first time in what seemed like days. "I'm being careful, I promise. He's not disreputable. Really. I trust him."

"Very well, as long as you're sure," Patience said with a sigh. "Now that I've told you what I know and I'm far less anxious, shall we turn around? I'm frozen."

"Yes. Let's go back to my house. It's almost noonday and you can eat dinner with me. I still haven't gotten used to cooking for just one person, so I have too much food."

We turned around and went back home, where the room was warm and comfortable. Patience sighed as she walked through the door. "Ah. This is much better than being outside."

We ate dinner together while she told me that her mother was starting to show signs of improved health. She was holding the baby now, which she had refused to do for several days. She was also getting out of bed and helping Patience prepare meals for the family. Patience was thrilled with her mother's progress, not just because she wanted her mother to be well, but because she was ready for some help taking care of the house, the meals, and the rest of the family. When she was ready to go back home, I went to the apothecary and gave her some herbs I had read about in the physick book that were supposed to help in healing.

She left with a promise to see me again at the church service on Sunday. I spent the rest of the afternoon working in the apothecary and reading the physick book. I was finding more and more useful information that I hoped to put to use as patients came in.

The next day I went into the village early in the morning in the hope of seeing Richard. I wanted to talk to him about the things Patience had discussed with me. I didn't want to go as far as the bay and set tongues wagging about why I might be there again after having been told so many times not to go there by myself, so I lingered on the street closest to the water until I decided Richard was not going to show himself that day. When I returned to the house, I found two people waiting for me at the apothecary door.

When I had provided them with a remedy for sores inside the mouth and a cough, I was surprised to find two more people coming into the shop. And so it continued throughout the day, with a trickle of customers that left me pleasantly busy and thankful that people weren't staying away because a woman was the apothecary now.

I tried going into the village even earlier the following day. I had a strong sense that Richard might know what to do with the information Patience had given me, so I needed to find him. And this time I saw him leaving the tanner's shop, long before anyone else was about on the street.

"Richard!" I called, hastening to catch up with him. He turned around and looked at me, his eyebrows raised. His eyes darted this way and that, and I realized he probably didn't want anyone to know he had been at the tanner's shop.

"I'm sorry for calling your name aloud," I said when I caught up to him.

"That's all right," he replied. "You see, the arrangement I have with the tanner is similar to the one I had with your father and now with you, so I do much of my business with him when people aren't around."

I lowered my voice. "My friend Patience told me something interesting about Captain Eli and I wanted to relay it to you." I waited for him to respond, because I was sure he didn't want to discuss Captain Eli out on the streets of Cape Island.

"Come with me," he said, taking my elbow and leading me away from the tanner. He didn't say anything else until we were standing on a plot of land at the end of the street, a goodly distance away from any other buildings and where we could see any people who might be coming toward us from any direction.

"This is fine," he said. "No one to overhear us. So tell me. What did your friend have to say?"

I repeated my conversation with Patience while Richard listened, nodding his head once in a while and not interrupting.

"And you have no idea what the captain might have been talking about?" Richard asked when I had finished. I shook my head in reply.

"Let me think about this, Sarah. Maybe I can gather more information."

"I would be very grateful," I said.

"I will be in touch with you. Now, it won't do to have a young lady such as yourself seen with a rogue like me, so let us go away separately. I will go to the bay, and you go that way," he pointed to the west, "to get back to your house. Are you all right by yourself?"

"Certainly. And thank you, Richard."

To my great surprise, he reached down and took my hand lightly in his. He raised my hand to his lips and kissed it gently, then bowed toward me. I turned around and practically fled toward my house, not daring to look back to see if he was watching me go. My hand tingled where he had kissed it. I was not accustomed to such a feeling—I had certainly never felt anything of the sort when I was with Arthur.

I finally slowed my pace when I was no longer in sight of the village. I directed my steps toward home, but I was barely conscious of where my feet were taking me, so lost was I in my own confused thoughts.

By the time I was home I had talked some sense into myself. Of course Richard had kissed my hand. That was something gentlemen did in parting. It was ridiculous to have such fanciful thoughts about it. The tingling had probably been nothing more than my freezing skin. But then, it hadn't tingled before he kissed me …

It was with great impatience that I waited to hear from Richard with news of Captain Eli. I couldn't be still. In the apothecary I rearranged bottles and packages I had already organized. In the main room of the house I swept the already-clean floor. In the bedchamber I washed the bed linens that were already clean. I tried reading the physick book, but I couldn't concentrate long enough to retain anything I was supposed to be learning.

Finally I could stay at home no longer. I prepared a basket with bread, cheese, and a few packets of herbs and set off toward Widow Beall's house. It had been a while since I had heard news of her, and I wanted to make sure she and her children were well. I shuddered to think she might be too embarrassed to ask for help if she could not afford remedies for sickness or injury.

When I arrived at Widow Beall's house, she and all her children came to the door to greet me. She seemed pleased to have a visitor, and after I had handed the basket to the children to look through, she shooed them away and invited me to sit down. She poured tea for both of us and we sat talking.

She told me of different times my father had been kind enough to help her, and she even spoke to me about her memories of my mother. Though I would rather not have talked about either of my parents, it seemed to bring her joy to remember them to me.

"Why, I even remember the day your mother—" she began, but there was a loud knock on the front door. "Excuse me, Sarah. I don't get a visitor for weeks, and suddenly I have two!" I sat in front of the fire, gazing into my tea, when I heard raised voices. I jumped up and ran to the door.

To my great surprise, Captain Eli stood in the doorway. He was listing to one side, his eyes unfocused, and Widow Beall was giving him a talking-to.

"You know better than to come to my front door with your dirty clothes and your dirty mind and your filthy habits. Now go on back to Town!" She slammed the door as he turned around, but not before he saw me inside and opened his mouth as if to say something.

She turned to me. "I'm sorry about that, Sarah. He's drunk as a sot."

"Is he bothering you, Widow? We should report him to the authorities."

"No, my dear. Let him be. He's a harmless old fool, but I don't want him in my house."

I had the sense that I need not worry about Widow Beall. She was a strong woman.

"He scares me," I said. I hadn't meant to say anything, but the words escaped my mouth.

"And rightly so," she said, ushering me back to the table where our tea was getting cold. I glanced at her, wondering if she was going to elaborate.

"I miss your mother, Sarah. Do you know how much you look like her?" The widow looked out the window at something far away that I couldn't see. She sat that way for several long moments, then turned her attention back to me. "And because you look like your dear mother, I'm afraid the old captain might get some unseemly ideas."

My hand went to my throat and I was keenly aware of every sound in the house. I stared at the widow, waiting for her to continue. She looked at me sadly.

"Captain Eli is always influenced by drink. And he spews hatred and lies, which is why I'm going to tell you something."

I held my breath, still waiting.

"The captain had a dark obsession with your mother, Sarah. I know it because I've heard him talk about her many times."

"What kind of obsession? Did he hate her? Did he love her?"

"I rather think it ran to lust, if you want the truth."

I blushed. I couldn't bear to think my mother might have been the subject of Captain Eli's lusty thoughts. The very idea of it was enough to bring waves of nausea washing over me. I gripped the armrests of my chair.

"I know this isn't womanly talk, but I think you deserve to know how miserable the captain can be. I would hate to see his ugly obsession turn its attention to you."

"I thank you for telling me, Widow. I should be ... I think I should be going."

"Now, don't you worry about what I said. I don't think the old man has the gall to bother you, with you being so young and all. You just make sure your doors are locked up tight at night."

"I will, Widow, I promise."

"And you let me know if you need any help." She laughed. "I do believe the old man is afraid of me."

"Thank you, Widow. I'll let you know if I need help."

I walked home briskly, checking behind me every so often to make sure Captain Eli wasn't in the vicinity.

I was mending later that afternoon when there was a knock on the door. I jumped, upsetting the mending basket and dropping my needle on the floor. I walked slowly to the door while the person outside knocked again. My throat was dry and my hands sweating.

"Who is it?"

"Richard."

A flood of relief washed over me. I slid the bolt aside and opened the door to let him in.

He looked at me and immediately I could see the concern in his eyes. "Are you all right, Sarah?"

"Yes. I feared someone else might be at the door."

"Who?"

"The captain."

"Eli?"

I nodded. "The widow told me today that she fears he might turn his dark attentions to me because I look so much like my mother."

"What do you mean by that?"

I started gathering up the things that had spilled from my mending basket while I talked. I didn't want him to see my face. "He said, that is, he felt, uh … inappropriate things about my mother."

Richard nodded, seeming to understand what I was talking about.

"Has he come near you again?"

"No. But I visited the widow today at her house and he called on her while I was there."

Richard frowned. "What did he say?"

"I didn't hear him, but I heard her yelling at him to go away." I smiled at the memory. "He did as she told him."

Richard chuckled. "He needs to hear that more often."

"Especially after talking to her, I am convinced he had something to do with Mamma's disappearance. 'Obsession' was the word the widow used to describe the captain's feelings toward my mother."

"And you look like her? In that case, you need to be especially careful about bolting the doors when you're not in the house or the apothecary."

"I will, Richard."

He stared at me for a moment, smiling.

I found myself squirming under his intense gaze, so I asked him, "What brings you here today?"

He frowned again. "I've heard something that I believe I need to share with you." His voice sounded ominous.

"What is it?"

"I had occasion to speak with one of the captain's old mates. He mentioned a place where Captain Eli used to meet certain women," Richard said. He shifted on the stool, not meeting my eyes.

"What women?" I asked. Then realization dawned on me and I gasped. "Captain Eli? With women like that?"

"I'm afraid so," Richard said. "The man I spoke to did not know where Captain Eli took the women, but I gathered it wasn't far from here."

"I can't believe there are women like that in Town or anywhere on the cape!" I exclaimed.

"There are women like that everywhere," Richard said. "Some of them have no other way to support themselves."

I hadn't thought of those women that way. I nodded,

ashamed at having passed judgment on them. "How awful," I murmured.

A terrifying thought seized me and I gave a start. "Richard, you don't think anyone believes my mother was a woman like that, do you?" I could hear my heart's anguish in my words.

"No, not at all," he said in a soothing voice. "Your mother was a well-respected woman. We need to learn more about the captain and I would like to be able to find this place the men talked about."

"I have no idea where it could be," I said, raising my hands and letting them fall back into my lap.

"I'll see if I can gather any more information. In the meantime, stay alert to any mention of a place that might be useful to the captain for such purposes."

"I will. Thank you, Richard."

"I wish I could be of more help to you, Sarah. I hope we are able to solve the mystery of your mother's disappearance before I set sail."

*Before he sets sail?* "Do you know when that will be?" I asked, my heart giving a little jump.

"I do not have the exact date, but it will not be long now."

I saw him to the door and opened it for him. He stepped out into the cold, then turned back. I gave him a questioning look and he responded by reaching for my chin and bending his head toward mine. He tilted my chin upward and kissed my lips ever so lightly. I was astonished, but not so much that I pulled away. My toes tingled and my heart thumped in a wild rhythm. When he straightened up he smiled.

"I hope I haven't offended you."

"Not at all." I was more breathless than I would like to have admitted.

"I have grown very fond of you, Sarah. I've wanted to do that for a long time, but I didn't want to do it before you made your decision about helping me with the medicine chest. I didn't want it to influence you in any way."

I nodded, still trying to catch my breath. I had never felt like that before, even when Arthur asked for my hand in marriage. It was a strange, delightful feeling.

He walked down our path toward the road, his hands swinging jauntily at his side. He turned to wink at me and I waved to him, then shut the door. I felt like I was flying as I bustled around the room, trying to find something to keep me busy. My hands were shaking, but not from fear or nerves. They were shaking with happiness, a happiness such as I had never known.

## CHAPTER 15

*I* should have finished the mending that day, but there wasn't much left to do and my hands would never have been able to hold my needle, which I had found on the floor after Richard departed. I was bursting with energy, so I went outside to muck out the cow pen and the chicken coop. They were in sore need of attention, and I spent the rest of the day working outdoors.

By the time I went in for my evening meal, it was practically dark outside and I was exhausted from so much hard work. But it was the blessed kind of exhaustion, the kind that promised good, heavy, dreamless sleep.

My arms and back were sore in the morning, but I didn't mind. When I went outside to gather the eggs and milk the cows, I smiled at how clean the pens were. Pappa would have been very happy.

When my thoughts turned to Pappa, as they often did, I usually tried to push them out of my mind, to think of something else that wasn't so painful. I knew, in time, that I wouldn't be so sad every time I thought of Pappa, just as I remembered

Mamma without grief and anguish, but with deep love and sweet memories.

But today I wanted to think about him. I wanted to know what he would think about Richard kissing me. I wondered if Pappa would approve, or whether he would warn me away from Richard.

Before Pappa died, he had invited Richard into the house while I was there. Richard had even eaten a meal with us. He had done business with Richard, too. When I thought of all these things in combination, I knew Pappa had respected Richard as a man of medicine, a man of business, and as someone who wanted to help his fellow man.

But I knew there had been times, too, when Pappa did not want me to know about Richard. Was that because he was afraid for my sake, or was it because he didn't want me to know he was doing business with a pirate? I didn't know the answer.

But I couldn't deny what I had felt when Richard kissed me.

Patience visited that afternoon, with news that her mother was continuing to improve and that she wanted to pay me for the medicines I had taken to her while she was bedridden. Patience held out some coins, but I refused to take them.

"Patience, tell your mother those herb mixtures were a gift. I wanted her to have them because I wanted her to feel better, for her own sake and for the sake of the rest of your family."

"But I can't take the coins back to her. She'll be mad at me for not giving them to you."

"Then I'll write her a note telling her myself. If your mother wants to pay me, tell her the best thing she can do is to tell other people about my remedies. I've been getting some people from Town into the apothecary, but not as many as I would like. Perhaps if your mother helps to spread the word, more people will be able to accept that a woman is the new apothecary. Better yet, don't tell her. I'll write it myself in the note."

I retrieved a small piece of paper from the shop, along with a quill and inkwell. It seemed silly to write to Goody Ames when she lived nearby, but I didn't want to leave the house to talk to her just then in case anyone from the village came to the shop needing assistance.

I carefully penned the note and folded it, then handed it to Patience. For just a moment I longed to tell her about Richard, but something stopped me. Patience gave me a look that told me she knew there was something on my mind, but she didn't ask about it. She had a lot on her mind, too, with her parents' growing family and her increased roster of chores.

After she left I turned my feelings over and over. Why hadn't I told Patience about Richard kissing me? I knew she would be thrilled if she knew, but I didn't know what it was that had held me back from saying anything.

Was it that Richard was an outlaw and I didn't want her to know his secret? Was it that I was ashamed that he was forced to conduct his business in the dark? Was it that he had not been to a Sunday church service since I had met him?

I finally decided that I had avoided telling her simply because I wanted to keep it to myself, to savor it, for just a while.

I was compiling a mental inventory in the apothecary when there was a knock at the shop door. I turned around with a smile on my face, ready to greet whomever was there.

But my smile vanished when I saw Captain Eli standing outside the door.

It was too late to run over and lock the door. I cursed myself for leaving the bolt open. I could see the captain reaching for the door handle, then he rattled it and, finding it unlocked, pushed it open and came into the shop. He had a pronounced limp.

I watched him warily from where I stood near the door leading into the house. I debated whether I should flee into the house and lock the door behind me, but the last thing I wanted was for him to be loose in the apothecary and trying to get into my home. Instead, I stood my ground, my chin slightly lifted. The captain thankfully could not see that my knees were quaking and my heart was beating wildly, as if it might hop out of my chest and onto the floor at any moment.

"What do you want?" I asked.

"I need summat for ma knee," he rasped. His eyes were bleary as he took in the surroundings of the shop.

I didn't move. "I'm afraid you'll have to find what you need elsewhere."

"And how am I supposed to do that? I can't barely walk."

"I'm sorry. I cannot help you."

He took a wavering step toward me and I backed up into a counter along the wall. "Why won't you help me?" His voice held a sneer that scared me.

"Because I do not treat your ilk. Now, please leave or I shall be forced to tell the authorities that you refused to go." How dare he think that I might treat him, knowing what I did about the way he treated my mother? Knowing that he might even have had something to do with her disappearance?

He let out a laugh that sounded like a dark barking. "You're the apothecary. Where else am I supposed to go?"

"I do not know, and I do not care." I nodded toward the door. "You can find your own way out." I watched him, waiting for him to turn around and go.

But he stood still. "Can you at least give me summat for the pain?"

I heard a pathetic plea in the tone of his voice, and it brought forth a thought I would rather not have had. Pappa, one of the most knowledgeable and honorable apothecaries on these shores, agreed to do business with a pirate because he wanted to ensure that the men who signed up to go to sea, the men who supported families with the money they earned in such a despicable manner, were not left without medical equipment and medicines for their diseases and injuries. Would Pappa treat Captain Eli's wound, whatever it was?

I had to begrudgingly admit to myself that he probably would. Could I, then, do any less?

"What happened to your knee?" I finally asked.

"Hurt it."

"Yes, I gathered that. How did you hurt it?"

He looked at the ceiling of the shop, then out the window. "It doesn't matter, now, does it?"

"May I at least look at it? I can't give you anything for it until I have an idea of how you've injured it."

He limped toward me and stopped several feet away. Bending down, he pulled up the leg of his breeches and it was all I could do not to gasp in dismay at the oozing mass of yellow-green liquid seeping from an obviously deep, purple wound.

"Oh, my!" I exclaimed, quickly forgetting my loathing. I hurried over to the cabinet where Pappa had always kept his instruments used for cleaning out and cauterizing wounds. I bade the captain sit on a stool I placed near the cabinet and gave him a roll of cloth to bite. He would certainly need to use it, judging from the look of his wound. Cleaning it out would be an extremely painful endeavor. He sat down heavily, holding the roll of cloth, and pulled up the leg of his breeches again so I could see the wound more closely. It gave off a rank odor, even worse than the odor wafting from the captain's skin and clothing.

"This is going to hurt, so please put that roll of cloth in your mouth and use it to bite down hard when I tell you to. It will help to stifle any noise you make and to prevent your teeth from breaking." I suppressed a shudder at the thought of his rotting teeth.

I selected two instruments that would be useful and set them on a cloth on the floor next to me. I experienced just a moment of hesitation, when I worried that the pain of the procedure might make the captain kick me with his other leg, but I quickly pushed that fear aside and reached for the first instrument, a wooden handle with a small, curved piece of metal at the end. I held it firmly, then told the captain, "Now."

He bit down on the cloth while I peeled apart the ragged skin that flapped around the wound. He gasped in pain, but did not scream—yet. The skin had become gray around the edges and looked dead to me. I knew I would have to cut the dead parts off before he could leave the shop. Crusted blood, the color of a robin's breast, was smeared up and down his leg.

When I held the instrument near the wound, I sensed rather than felt him wince in apprehension. And with the first pass of the metal through the pus coming out of the wound, he screamed in pain. I shot him a look of exasperation and said, "Please, use the rolled cloth. If you startle me while I'm working I might make a mistake." He was a bit quieter after that. I might have chosen to use much more soothing language if my patient had been anyone else, but I suppose there was a certain amount of superiority I felt under the circumstances. I knew what Mistress Reeves would say: *pride goeth before a fall.* And I was feeling a swelling sense of pride in agreeing to and being able to treat this man's injury.

I decided it would be best to finish the job as quickly as possible so as not to prolong the captain's suffering or my danger in being so close to him when he was wild with pain, so I got to work scraping the pus, dried blood, and ooze from the mouth of the wound. The captain kept up a steady moaning, alternating every few seconds with gasps and screams. I found myself almost feeling sorry for him, but every time I thought about how much pain he must be in, I thought also of the pain he may have put my mother through, and I dug a little deeper.

After many long minutes of cleaning out the wound and clipping the dead skin around its opening, I reached for a jar of honey I had placed on the floor near me. I slathered a goodly amount of honey all over the wound and then bound it securely with a clean roll of cloth. The captain looked ashen when I had finished, but nodded and managed to thank me for my services. When I named my price for the procedure, he winced again, as if in more pain.

"I do not have any money," he said, his face grim and white.

"Then how do you expect to pay me for my services?" I countered.

"Would you take payment of sugar or tea?" he offered. "I can get those things for you."

"Very well, I'll take both." I surprised myself with my own forthright response, but it was a good feeling—telling this man, who had caused me so much recent anxiety, how much would be required to pay me adequately.

He seemed subdued when he nodded his agreement. "Come back tomorrow and I'll change the dressing for you. That will be included in the price of the procedure," I added.

"Thank you." The words seemed to come from a cold place deep within him that was not accustomed to giving thanks.

I walked toward the door and opened it for him, then stood holding it open while he limped slowly across the floor, his face twisting in pain with every step.

When he was gone I locked the door behind him, not wishing to talk with him again if he decided to return. He would be in a great deal of pain until the wound healed, *if* it healed, and I did not want to be the recipient of his ranting if the pain was more than he expected or could bear.

I wondered how he had sustained such an ugly injury to his leg.

One thing gave me satisfaction. If his leg healed, he would hopefully tell people I was the one who helped him, saving his leg. And if he didn't tell people, I would. That surely would help my apothecary business.

The next day I had to go to Town early in the morning to see if the general store had any honey. I was running low in the apothecary and wanted to replenish my supply before the next delivery from Philadelphia. I was pleased to see that the store did, indeed, have several jars of honey for sale.

While I was in there, I was also looking at bolts of fabric that were piled on a counter in the back. I was examining the weave of one of the fabrics when two men came into the store. They were both disreputable-looking, with dirt on their faces and an odor which preceded them into the large room.

"I'm telling you, he was barely able to walk last night," one was saying.

"Serves the old bugger right. What happened?" his companion asked.

"Word has it that he was attacked by someone."

"Woe be to the man who attacks Captain Eli. He's not one to let that go unanswered."

My hands froze on the fabric when I heard who they were discussing. Captain Eli had been attacked. By whom? And where? And why? It made sense, having seen the extent of his injury, and I was bursting to ask questions, but the men stopped talking and purchased a packet of tobacco between them. I managed to stay calm and leave the store without making a fool of myself by chatting up the two strangers.

I was walking home, lost in thought, when I heard someone hailing me. I turned around to see Richard walking toward me. He was wearing Pappa's boots; I felt a flutter of happiness at having been able to help him in a way that offered him such physical comfort.

"Hullo, Sarah!" he called as he approached.

"Good morning," I replied, smiling.

"What brings you outside this morning?" he asked.

I held up the basket containing my honey and explained that my supply was running low in the shop.

"And what brings you here?" I asked.

"I was coming to see you at your house. I suppose I've given up on trying to look proper and not go inside your house, but since you're now a woman of business, I suppose no one would think twice if they saw me come out of the house."

"I suspect you are correct." In truth, I suspected people would still talk and gossip, but I found that I didn't care. It was a good feeling.

"I have news," I said.

"What is it?" he asked.

"Captain Eli paid a visit to the apothecary yesterday." I leaned toward him as if I were sharing a secret.

His eyes widened and his mouth hung open for a moment. "Surely you jest."

I shook my head. "He came in with a positively grisly leg wound. He was obviously in a great deal of pain. I will admit that, upon first seeing him, I insisted that he leave and try to find someone else to help him, but eventually I agreed to treat it for him."

"I wish I had known. I would have been there to make sure he did not try to harm you."

"Truly, I wasn't worried once I saw his leg. He was barely able to walk, and if he had tried to attack me I would have simply run from him. He never could have caught me."

"How did he hurt his leg?"

"He wouldn't say. It was awful. It required me to clean out the wound, snip away the decaying skin around it, and bandage it after covering it with honey. I gave him a roll of cloth to clamp between his teeth while I worked. I'm surprised he was able to do that, since his teeth are in such a dismal condition.

"But here's something of interest that I have just now learnt, Richard. While I was in the store for the honey, two men came in and they were talking about Captain Eli. One said someone attacked him. I can certainly believe it, based on the seriousness of his injury. But that is all I was able to overhear and the men left."

"You must take special precautions not to be alone near him, Sarah. I worry for your safety."

"If Widow Beall can take care of herself, I can, too. Don't worry about me, Richard."

"But I do worry. Sarah, I have news, too." Something in the tone of his voice chilled me.

"What is it?"

"We set sail in two weeks."

I could feel my heart sinking, sinking, as if it might pull me along with it. I was unable to speak for a few moments. That was one bit of news I had not been prepared to hear.

"Sarah? Did you hear me?"

I nodded, then blinked. "Where are you going?"

"Jamaica first. After that, I do not know."

"How long will you be gone?"

"I don't know. It could be weeks, it could be months. We go with the weather, and we go where the other ships go."

I did not say anything for a long time, but finally I had to say something or I would start crying. "I wish I could pay for you to leave the boat." I looked straight ahead because I could not look into his eyes.

"I wish I did not have to go, but I have a responsibility to earn the money I owe. And I have a responsibility to the men aboard the ship. They depend on me to heal them, even save their lives, when they take sick or are injured."

We had reached my house and I entered through the apothecary door, with Richard following close behind me. I slid the bolt closed when we were inside, then headed straight for the apothecary ledger.

"What are you doing?" he asked.

"Getting my ledger. I must make a list as soon as possible of everything you'll require for the voyage. I may need to send away for certain things in Philadelphia, so I will have to send that letter immediately."

"I haven't made a complete list yet," he said. "I shall return to the ship, compile a list, and be back with it later this day."

"Very well," I said, turning away from him to replace the ledger where I kept it. I had suspected he had not prepared a list yet, but I felt the need to do something with my hands, to do something that would keep my mind from dwelling on his departure from New Jersey.

When I turned back to him I was startled to find him standing right behind me. He reached for my hands and held them to his lips.

"I don't want to leave you, Sarah, but I have to go. You understand that, don't you?"

I nodded mutely.

He leaned down and kissed my lips and again I had a strange sensation of falling, but this time it felt wonderful knowing there would be strong arms to catch me. The fluttering in my stomach didn't stop when he did, and I blushed, breathless. He had an unsettling effect on me.

"I want to marry you, Sarah. Will you wait for me to return?"

I gasped. I covered my mouth with both hands—I don't know why. Perhaps to keep from screaming. Richard laughed.

"Do you want to marry me?" he asked,

"Yes, of course! I'm just so surprised!" My words rushed out, tumbling over one another.

"I knew from the night your father introduced us that you were going to become very special to me," he said. "I just had no idea how special. And I've tried to stay away, to give you time and space to grieve for your father, but I haven't done a very good job, have I?"

"I'm glad you haven't stayed away."

Everything was happening so quickly. Did I love him? Did I feel about Richard the way I was sure my parents had felt about each other before being married? I knew the answer to both questions was a resounding *yes.*

He took my hands in his and kissed them again, then kissed me again. I felt like I was flying. And I knew in that instant that Pappa wanted me to experience that feeling, and that not only would he approve of me marrying Richard, but that it would have been his wish.

"Do you know something?" I asked. "I think Pappa would be very happy right now."

"I think he would, too," Richard replied, and I saw the smile coming from his eyes, his mouth, his heart.

# CHAPTER 16

*N*ow I *had* to tell Patience. It wouldn't wait. As soon as Richard left that morning, I hurried to the Ames house.

When Patience opened the door to my insistent knock, she knew something was different. She grasped my hands and drew me into her house.

"What's happened?" she asked.

"You'll never believe it, Patience. I'm going to be married!"

She dropped my hands and stared at me, her mouth agape. She sat down on a stool directly behind her, as if her legs would no longer hold her up.

"To Arthur?" she asked, giving me a confused look.

"No. Do you remember Richard, the man you met at my house?"

"Yes. That disreputable-looking young man with the shabby boots."

I laughed. I didn't care how she described him. "That's him. He asked me to marry him and I've accepted! Oh, Patience, I'm so very happy!"

"But I don't understand. Who is he? Where is he from? How come you haven't mentioned him more often?"

"He's from London, where he attended medical college. He became friendly with my father when they did business together, and when I decided to take over the apothecary he asked if I would continue my father's business association with him. I have spent only a short amount of time with him alone, but that is all I needed. He brings me joy, even as I grieve for my parents."

"I'm so very happy for you, Sarah." But she didn't sound happy.

I was taken aback at the disappointment in her voice. "What's wrong, Patience?" I asked.

"You and I are close friends, or at least I thought we were. I suppose I'm just shocked that you didn't care to tell me more about Richard before announcing your engagement."

"Please don't be offended, Patience. It's all happened so quickly, and I didn't recognize the feelings I was having toward him. He makes me feel more special than Arthur ever did."

"Those are the types of things I hoped you would tell me when the time came for you to meet the man you would marry. Not merely introduce me to him and then shortly afterward announce that you're marrying him."

"I'm sorry, Patience. I thought you'd be happy."

"I *am* happy. Really, I am. I just wish I had been included in your happiness before now."

"What can I do to make you feel better?" I asked.

"You can tell me about every time you met with him. I want to know everything."

I laughed. "Most of the times we spoke together it was about business or my mother or my father. It has only been recently that my feelings have become ... different."

"So tell me about those times!" she exclaimed. I could tell from her voice that I had been forgiven for not including her from the time I met Richard, and I proceeded to tell her all about our more recent meetings, but I left out the parts about his job and his indentured servitude.

I knew she would ask, though.

"And how does he earn his living?" she asked.

I had been thinking about how I would respond to such a question.

"He treats people with injuries and illnesses."

"So he is an apothecary, too?" she asked, her eyes wide with surprise.

"Not exactly," I said.

"Oh, of course he is a physician. You said he attended medical college in London."

"He is a type of physician, yes."

"But what type?" she pressed.

"He was not able to finish his studies. Not yet. He works on a ship, treating the men aboard."

"Oh, I see. What a thrilling job!" she exclaimed. It was clear from her reaction that she did not understand the full implication of what I had told her. She did not realize he worked on a pirate ship.

*Should I tell her the full truth?* I decided to give it some thought before making a commitment to tell her.

"When will you see him again?" she asked.

"Later today. He's coming to the shop to give me a list of the provisions he requires for his next voyage."

Patience was silent for several long moments while one of her younger sisters came to sit on my lap. I played a game with her before setting her back on the floor.

"Are you afraid he won't come back from his voyage?" Patience finally asked. Her sister was out of earshot.

I felt a stab of something—was it fear? Helplessness? I didn't know, but I didn't relish the feeling. Of course it was something

I had thought about, but I hadn't expected to hear the question spoken aloud.

"I can see it in your face. Of course you're afraid," Patience said. "I'm sorry I asked the question."

"Don't be sorry," I assured her, reaching for her hand. "You're right. I am afraid, but I will hope and pray that he returns safely. He will be in God's hands."

"You are so brave," Patience said.

*Not even brave enough to tell you he's a pirate*, I thought, suppressing a grimace.

I rose and walked to the door. "I wanted you to be the first person to know about the engagement," I told my friend. "I have to go back to the house. Captain Eli is coming today to have his wound redressed."

"Captain Eli?" she cried. "Don't be there alone with him, I beg you!"

"If you could see him, you wouldn't worry," I told her. "He's so badly wounded that he couldn't catch me even if he gave chase around the apothecary." I chuckled.

"How did he get hurt?" she asked.

"That is a good question."

I returned home to find Captain Eli waiting for me at the apothecary door. He was leaning against the door frame, his face flushed and sweating despite the cold wind that was buffeting the house. He held a large sack in his hand.

"Come in," I said briskly. I unlocked the door for him and waited as he limped inside. His coloring was better than it had been the day before, so I knew his condition hadn't worsened.

He mopped the sweat off his forehead with a grimy sleeve.

"Girl, this hurts summat fierce."

"My name is not *girl*. It is Miss Hanover. And I know your

leg hurts. You have a serious injury. But you did the right thing in coming here for help, and I'll examine the leg when I unwrap the bandage. I'll wrap the leg with a fresh one and then you'll need to come by again tomorrow to have it dressed again. After that, maybe not every day. We'll see how it looks tomorrow. Now, let me see that leg." My mind screamed in protest again over treating the man, but in my heart I knew I was doing the right thing.

The old captain seated himself heavily on the stool he had occupied the previous day. He set his sack on the floor and lifted the leg of his breeches.

I reached for the dressing and he pulled his leg away just a little bit, eyeing me warily.

"I have to put fresh bandages on your leg." I looked down at the filthy cloth on his leg, then met his eyes. He scowled. He reminded me of an animal in pain—aware that I was trying to help, but fiercely protective of himself.

"And you won't tell me how this happened?" I asked.

"It's none 'o yer business."

Slowly and carefully so as not to jar the injury, I unwrapped the cloth from around his leg. I reached for a magnifying glass I kept nearby and examined the wound closely.

"This is better than it was yesterday," I said, almost to myself.

"Then why isn't the pain going away?" he asked harshly.

"You need to give it time. Injuries like this can take a long time to heal. You're lucky you don't have to go to sea anymore."

"Nothing lucky about it, Gir—Miss."

I raised my eyebrows ever so slightly and suppressed a smile.

After I had satisfied myself that the wound was no worse, I slathered another measure of honey on it. I had been crouching next to the stool where Captain Eli was seated and I had to straighten up to reach the roll of clean bandages that sat on the counter just a few feet away.

Captain Eli used my awkward stance to reach for my arm. He grabbed it with a strength I would not have expected and squeezed—hard.

"What are you doing?" I cried. "Let go of me!" I tried flailing my arm to loosen his grip, but he only squeezed harder.

"Tell me why yer asking people about me."

"I haven't asked anyone about you," I said, squirming.

"I know you have. I've gotten wind of it."

"Well, it is not true." I grunted as I continued struggling to free my arm. I could feel my breath coming faster. I had assured Patience that this man was no match for me in his injured state, but that had obviously been untrue. He seemed to have lost none of the strength in his arm and hand.

I gave one mighty heave of my arm and, by the grace of God, he lost his balance and toppled off the stool. He was trying to push himself up when the apothecary door opened and Richard swept into the room, his eyes taking in the scene in an instant.

He rushed over to where Captain Eli was grunting in pain, still trying to right himself, and yanked him up by the arm.

"What the devil do you think you're doing?" he said in a low, deadly voice. If he hadn't been protecting me, I would have been afraid of that voice.

"Nothin'," the captain sputtered. "I just lost my balance, that's all." He shot me a look that warned me not to say anything, but Richard knew the truth.

"Did you try to touch this young lady?" Richard demanded.

"Of course not," the captain said, a trace of false indignation in his voice.

"You're lying. Let me tell you something, Eli. If I ever catch you near Miss Hanover again, I'll tear your limbs out one by one myself. Do you understand that?"

"Yes," growled the captain. "Now let go of me."

Richard didn't let go of the captain's arm yet, but turned to me instead. "Are you done with this good-for-nothing wretch, or do you need my help to restrain him while you work?"

"I'm done," I said in a clear voice. My confidence had returned with Richard's arrival.

Richard released the captain's arm with a rough shove. "Now out you go. And don't come back here."

"I have to come back tomorrow to have me dressing changed," the captain whined.

Richard turned to me again. "Do you have some clean bandages you can send with him?" I nodded and reached for two rolls of cloth. Richard took them and thrust them at Captain Eli.

"Take these. You'll be changing your own dressing from now on. Now be gone." He glowered at the captain, who looked suddenly meek and harmless. We both watched the captain as he made his slow way to the door and closed it behind him.

I heaved a sigh of relief, not realizing I had barely been breathing since the captain grabbed my arm.

"I'm so grateful you came when you did," I said to Richard. "I didn't think he would be a danger to me, but I was wrong."

"I hope you won't have any more trouble from him, but you must remember to keep the apothecary door locked from now on. That way you don't have to let him in if you see him standing out there. And don't open the door in the house unless you know who's standing outside, either." He gathered me to his chest. "I can't bear the thought of something happening to you."

I smiled into his shirt. "I'll keep the door locked," I said in a muffled voice.

"Good."

"Do you have the list of things you'll need for the trip?" I asked, pushing myself away from him with reluctance.

He pulled a small piece of paper from his coat pocket. "Here it is. Paper is hard to come by, so I had to write everything on this little scrap. I'll read it to you."

As he read the list of items he would need, I was surprised and relieved to learn that I already had all the necessary supplies and I would not require a delivery from Philadelphia. I gathered everything into a pile on the counter against the back wall. There were dental pelicans, dressings, syringes, and cupping glasses. I shuddered when he asked for an instrument that he would use for bullet extractions.

When I had gathered everything on his list, he helped me pack it securely into a wooden box. He lifted the box and set in on the floor, then he moved around a number of other boxes and hid his box behind the rest.

"When will you be back for it?" I asked.

"Tonight, long after dark. If you'd like me to hide it some-where outside so I don't wake you up, that would be fine. I don't think the captain will be back anytime soon, so you don't have to worry about him finding it."

"I won't be able to sleep, knowing you're coming for the box. I'll be awake. That way I can at least help you get it outside," I answered in a murmur. There was no reason to lower my voice, since we were the only ones in sight, but somehow the secretive nature of our movements made me wish to keep my voice low.

"Then I look forward to seeing you in the middle of the night, my love," Richard said, leaning down to kiss me. I felt that same thrill I had the last time—would I feel that thrill for the rest of my life? I thought it very likely. We agreed on a secret knock for him to use.

I watched him walk away, his footsteps crunching in the snow. I gazed for a moment at my father's boots on Richard's feet and made a decision. I would sort through the rest of Pappa's clothes— there weren't many—and decide what might fit Richard and what could be given to someone else. Perhaps Richard would know of someone on his ship who needed clothes in my father's size.

But first I peeked into the sack Captain Eli had brought with him. Indeed, there was a large packet of sugar in the sack and two tins of tea leaves. I wondered where the captain had obtained such fine items, but then I remembered that he had spent many years at sea. He probably had a large supply of sugar and tea at his home.

I stored the sugar and tea on the shelf near the fireplace and then turned my attention to Pappa's clothes.

Going through the trunk again reminded me painfully of the letter I had found written to my father by my grandmamma. At the time I had found the letter, I had been too overwrought to do much of anything about it, but now a plan began to formulate in my mind.

Mister Browne was the person who had pointed the finger of suspicion at the captain. Did he know more than he was saying? Was Captain Eli the person Grandmamma had been referring to in the letter?

I needed to find Mister Browne and ask him to divulge any information he had about the captain, even if he thought it was too rough and disturbing for my ears to hear.

I was careful to fold the letter along its original creases, then I put it in my pocket before leaving the house to go into town. I knew where Mister Browne lived with his wife and children and I intended to go straight to his home to ask for his help. I hoped I would find him there.

The Browne family lived on a narrow street that ran parallel to the water. The house was two stories tall and painted an exquisite shade of blue the color of a robin's egg. It was one of the only painted houses in town.

I marched up the front steps and knocked on the door quickly, before I could lose my determination. While I waited for someone to answer my knock, I turned around to survey the rest of the street. There were three other houses, also two stories each. One was on the same side of the street as the

Brownes' house and the other two stood facing them across a muddy path that served as a road.

The door opened behind me and I whirled around to face a woman wearing servants' dress and staring at me expectantly.

"Yes, hello. My name is Sarah Hanover and I'm here to see Mister Browne, if I might. Is he home?" I took a deep breath, wondering how I had managed to state my business without stammering.

"Just a moment. I'll announce you," the young woman said. She left me on the porch as she closed the door and retreated inside the house. She was back in just a few moments. She beckoned for me to follow her and I stepped into the warm, inviting hallway beyond the front door.

She led me to a parlor to the left of the door and invited me to sit while I waited for Mister Browne. Presently he came into the room, a perplexed look on his face. I stood up quickly.

"To what do I owe this honor?" he asked, bowing slightly in my direction.

"I've come to ask some questions about Captain Eli, sir," I responded. "I know you have heard … things … about him and I was hoping you could share them with me."

"What sorts of 'things' do you mean?"

"I mean, you told my father that Captain Eli had made some unsavory remarks about my mother. I would like you to elaborate, if you would be so kind."

Mister Browne rubbed his beard as he sat down on a settee, gesturing for me to be seated again in the chair opposite him. I complied.

"I am not sure you really want to hear the things Captain Eli said about your mother," Mister Browne said. "To be frank, they were vulgar remarks that have no place in polite society. But then, Captain Eli has yet to show a desire to be a part of polite society."

"I realize that, sir, but I believe my mother was the victim of a violent act at the time of her death. I want to know if you are aware of her ever being threatened bodily by the captain."

Mister Browne rubbed his hand along his beard again, as if trying to decide if he should tell me anything. I waited, my hands folded in my lap, my face a mask of patience. On the inside, though, I was agitated and anxious.

Finally he spoke. "Captain Eli has always believed your mother loved him. Ever since she arrived in New Jersey."

I let a tiny gasp escape before I remembered to maintain my pretense of calm. Mister Browne gave me a sharp look, paused for a moment, then continued.

"Of course everyone knows it's rubbish, but the man has persisted with such rants since he met her. I'm afraid, Sarah, that it's nothing more than a case of lust, combined with his obvious madness."

I took a deep breath to steady my nerves. I knew Mister Browne would not like my next question.

"Mister Browne, do you think Captain Eli could have been behind my mother's disappearance two years ago?"

Mister Browne was silent for a long time. I was afraid he wouldn't answer me. When he spoke, his shoulders fell and his eyes took on a troubled look.

"I wish I knew, Sarah. But I have no idea. He's never admitted to anything, of course, and I don't know of any other instances when he has been violent toward a woman. Men, yes. But women, none of which I am aware."

That didn't help me very much. But it made sense that a man who made terribly lewd comments about a woman, especially a married woman, might go to great lengths to take her for himself if he thought he could get away with it. I thanked Mister Browne for his information and returned home. He promised to let me know if he heard anything else about the captain.

I was rounding the bend in the road by Widow Beall's house when I was shocked to see Captain Eli making his way into the woods from her farm. I could tell from his distinctive limp. I hastened to Widow Beall's front door, hoping and praying that the captain had not been causing trouble for her.

I am afraid I startled her when she opened the door. "Widow Beall!" I cried. She took a step backward in surprise, so I tried to speak more calmly. "I just saw Captain Eli traipsing into the woods beyond your farm. Has that unctuous ruffian been tormenting you?"

Widow Beall smiled. "That old toad? He knows better than to meddle with me. Don't you worry about us, Sarah. We're fine here."

"I'm so glad to hear it, Widow. Please, if he bothers you, let me or Goody Ames know. One of us will make sure the captain doesn't come round again."

"Thank you, dear." I waved at the woman and continued on my way.

Mistress Reeves was waiting at the apothecary door when I got home. She was wringing her hands and when she spoke to me her voice shook ever so slightly.

"It's Arthur, Sarah. He's sick. He can't move, can't eat, can't speak. What do you have that will help him? And what do you have that might prevent the rest of us from getting it?"

Mistress followed me as I hurried to the back of the apothecary where I kept the jars and bottles of liquids and powders that might be useful in such a situation. I tried not to think about Pappa, about his fever and the things I tried that didn't work to save him. *No,* I repeated to myself. *I cannot let another person die.*

# CHAPTER 17

*I* ran into the house for my physick book and turned to the small section on lockjaw. It sounded to me like Arthur was suffering from it. I ran my finger down the text to see if there was anything the book suggested that I hadn't already known, but there wasn't. Mistress Reeves didn't know of any injuries or wounds Arthur had sustained, but there had to be something. There were only a few options to treat lockjaw: one was with cold water and the other was with bloodletting. I took up a lancet from the counter and bound it in a piece of clean cloth, then grabbed some other things that might help with the pain after the procedures.

Mistress Reeves and I hurried to her house, where we found Arthur lying on a sleeping mat in the bedroom. His body, rigid as a board, looked like something not of this world. I had read about lockjaw, of course, and knew my father had treated it once or twice, but I had never witnessed it myself. It was terrifying in its taut severity.

Pastor Reeves paced the floor, his lips moving in silent supplication to the Lord. I knelt down next to Arthur and explained to him what I was going to do. The first thing I had to do was the bloodletting. I put a fillet around his upper arm to force the blood to the surface in the crook of his elbow, then I lanced the skin where the blood made a bulge. I had brought the bleeding bowl from the apothecary and the blood began spurting into it from Arthur's arm. I heard a rustle behind me and knew Mistress Reeves had fainted from the sight of the blood coming from her son's arm, but Pastor Reeves assured me he had caught her and did not require my attention. In a beseeching voice he bade me to continue working on Arthur. Arthur had made no sound since I entered the room, but his eyes followed my movements closely. I explained each step of the bloodletting method to him. He couldn't have asked any questions if he had wanted to, so terrible was the condition of his rigidity.

Once I had taken an appropriate amount of blood from Arthur's arm I sewed the skin together and bandaged it carefully with the clean cloth I had brought. Next I asked the preacher to fetch me water and to add a good deal of snow to it. I breathed a silent prayer of thanks to God that this had happened in the wintertime, when snow was plentiful and cold water would be easy to come by.

The preacher had been tapping his wife's cheeks with his fingers, and slowly her eyes fluttered open. She took one look at Arthur and they briefly rolled back in her head again, but the preacher rather harshly told her to get ahold of herself while he went to fetch the water and snow. After that she was able to sit in a chair quietly.

Pastor Reeves was only gone for a few moments before returning with a bucket of water and snow. He handed it to me and I quickly poured it over Arthur's body, beginning with his head and continuing down to his feet. When the water was gone the preacher ran for more and I poured a second bucket of water on Arthur.

We sat, waiting, while the water did its work. Presently Arthur began shaking: his entire body convulsed over and over again with increasing strength. His mother screamed, his father dropped to his knees and began crying loudly to God, begging Him to save his son. Mistress Reeves joined in his supplications and before long their other two children had joined them.

It was a sight more horrifying than Arthur's lockjaw. The four other family members, rocking on their knees and heels, crying and lamenting Arthur's condition. They set up a keening noise that set the hairs to prickling on the back of my neck. I was trying to focus my attention on Arthur as this went on, and I thought I noticed the tiniest movement of his hand, once his shaking at last subsided.

"Look!" I cried. "He's moving!"

Arthur's hand was shifting, ever so slowly, across the sleeping mat on which he lay. Mistress Reeves stood up from where she had still been kneeling near the hearth and rushed over to her son.

"Arthur, can you hear me?" she asked, her voice tremulous and scared.

An almost imperceptible nod from Arthur.

A brilliant smile spread across Mistress Reeves' face and she turned to her husband. "God has given our son back to us!" Her eyes shone wet with tears.

Pastor Reeves wept with relief. He placed his hands on Arthur's cheeks and bent down to kiss his son's forehead.

I let out a short cough to remind them I was still there. "We need to keep Arthur warm now," I cautioned. I sounded brisk and efficient, but on the inside I was weak with relief. I had no idea why the bloodletting and the cold water worked, but somehow they had. My task now was to make sure Arthur kept moving, even if only a tiny amount.

"Pastor Reeves, would you mind holding Arthur's hands while I try to move his legs?" I asked. He nodded, reaching gently for his son's hands. I could see that he was holding them with a soft grip, but that was all I needed.

"If his hands move, let me know," I told him. I moved to the end of the sleeping mat, where I grasped both of Arthur's ankles and pushed them toward his upper body, trying to make his knees bend. They inched up his body. Mistress Reeves let out a tiny squeal of excitement behind me and the pastor's face glowed with happiness.

"His hands are moving just a bit," the pastor said. I grunted my approval as I continued to push on Arthur's legs. The pastor and I continued these motions for quite some time, until I had satisfied myself that Arthur's muscles were moving, albeit clumsily.

It was time for me to leave the family to themselves. I gathered my instruments while I gave them instructions to move Arthur's limbs regularly throughout the day and night. "We have to get the blood moving," I said. "Once that happens, the rest of him should start to move more, too."

The family thanked me for coming and I left. I went home with a lifted heart, grateful that Arthur would no doubt be up and walking around soon. I hoped he wouldn't work too hard, since he needed as much rest as he could get over the coming days.

Back at home I cleaned the instruments I had used at the Reeves household and put them away in the apothecary shop. I turned when I heard a knock on the door. It was Mister Browne.

"Come in, Mister Browne," I said, unlocking the door and opening it for him. "I hope you're not ill."

"No, Sarah, I'm fine. I just thought of something I heard Captain Eli say a long while back and I thought you might like to know."

"What is it?"

"He said he'd watched a woman being torn apart by wolves once and it was the most horrible thing he'd ever seen." Mister Browne lowered his eyes, as if sorry he had told me. I hesitated, my throat constricting, then took a deep breath. If Mister Browne felt I could not be trusted to remain composed in the face of such information, he might decide not to help me in the future.

"Thank you, Mister Browne. I appreciate you telling me. It could be that Captain Eli was not responsible for my mother's death, but knows something about it nonetheless." And there *had* been threats against her, according to Grandmamma. I wondered with a shudder if Captain Eli had watched Mamma torn to shreds by wolves without trying to help her; he might well have done so if he had been filled with a murderous rage at her refusal of him.

"I wouldn't have told you, but there's been speculation since your mother's disappearance that she was attacked by wolves. I don't exactly reckon when Eli told me this, but it might have been right around the time your mother went missing."

He was being very careful not to say *death* or *died*, but I knew in my heart that Mamma was gone. Not just missing, but deceased. She would never have let so much time pass without contacting me or Pappa unless she had died that day she disappeared those two long years before.

I thanked him again for the information and locked the door behind him after he left. I was exhausted. Between doing the work of the apothecary, taking care of the house and tending to the farm chores, I was tired all the time. But it was a good tired. It kept the dreams away at night and I slept deeply, as though I couldn't get enough slumber.

After Mister Browne left I went into the house and sat down in the rocking chair in front of the fire.

I wondered if Pappa had written back to Grandmamma. The

only way to find out was to write Grandmamma and ask. I didn't know that she'd tell me even if he did. With Mamma and Pappa both gone, she might feel the confidence she betrayed should go no further.

With Captain Winslow at sea, I knew any letter could take many months to reach Grandmamma. I decided against writing to her, hoping the questions about Mamma's disappearance would be answered much sooner.

Despite all the activity of the day, I could not rest knowing Richard was coming to pick up his box of supplies later that night. I lit the oil lamp and studied the physick book until he arrived. When I heard the secret knock I wasn't startled.

He followed me into the apothecary and lifted the box from its hiding place, then he returned to the main room. I closed the shop door behind him. We didn't speak the entire time. I don't know why—I suppose it was the gravity of the situation, the necessity of having to conduct business in the dark. But Richard finally spoke.

"Thank you, Sarah. I am very grateful to you for doing this. I know it makes you anxious, but do not worry. One day it won't be like this anymore. I will be back to see you before we sail."

I slept fitfully that night.

The next morning I called on Arthur at his house to see how he was feeling. His mother answered my knock.

"Good morning, Mistress Reeves. I've come to see how Arthur is doing."

She looked over her shoulder. "He's doing much better, praise be to God." She stood aside to let me enter the house.

Arthur was still lying on the sleeping mat in front of the hearth, but his color had returned and he turned his head rather easily, I thought, to look in my direction.

"Thank you for coming, Sarah," he said. "Thank you for everything you did yesterday. I'm still very weak, but I'm feeling much better and I can move every part of my body."

"That's wonderful, Arthur. Do you mind if I look at your arm where I drew the blood?"

In response he used one hand to roll up the sleeve on his other arm. It was a pleasure to see his limbs working as they should. I knelt down next to him and examined the place where the blood had been extracted.

"It seems to be healing nicely." I turned to Arthur's mother. "Make sure you keep it bandaged with clean cloth for the next couple days. He should be just fine after that." I turned back to Arthur. "And don't do anything physically strenuous. You need to regain your strength before you do any work outdoors, so make sure you're eating plenty."

Mistress Reeves spoke up. "Don't worry about that. I am making all his meals and he loves being indoors with me, don't you, Arthur?" I glanced at her and she was beaming at her son. How lucky she was that her favorite child had survived his bout with lockjaw. The love I saw pass from her eyes to his warmed my heart. I had feared that coming to check on him might make him uncomfortable, given that I had not accepted his proposal of marriage, but it didn't seem to be affecting him in the least.

I knew my decision had been a wise one.

On the way home I stopped to see Widow Beall. I felt it my duty to check on her to see if she needed anything, since Pappa had helped her often when he was alive.

As usual, she opened the door with children crowded around her skirts. She invited me into the house, where it was cluttered but tidy. A pot of something that smelled good hung from the rod in the fireplace, and one of her daughters was stirring it.

"That smells good," I said with a smile. "What are you cooking?"

"Stew with rabbit meat and a sugar cake," she said. It sounded delicious. I was surprised—it seemed a lavish meal for a poor widow, but she or one of her older children had probably trapped the rabbit and perhaps someone had given her sugar as a gift.

And when she invited me to stay for a meal, I couldn't resist. I enjoyed the hearty stew and the sweet cake with the family and helped clean up afterward.

"Widow Beall, you and your girls are wonderful cooks," I said, scrubbing one of the bowls.

"Thank you, dear. Sometimes I would feed your father when he fixed things around the farm for me, and he was always grateful. Said he enjoyed our cooking."

"Well, I know I'm not as good at fixing things as my father, but I'd be happy to help you on the farm if you need it. Is there anything I can do for you today before I go home?"

"No, no, Sarah. We're fine."

"When I passed your old barn on my way here, it looked like it could use some mucking out around the door. There's a lot of dead grass there. Couldn't I at least do that for you?"

Widow Beall looked at me for a moment, as if weighing my offer, and finally shook her head. "No. That'll be fine. I can do that myself."

She was certainly an independent woman. I smiled, thinking how I would love to be more like her.

She and her daughters accompanied me to the door when it was time to go. As I neared the road that passed her house, I turned around. Her daughters had gone back inside, but she was still watching me. She waved. I wondered if she was too proud to ask me for apothecary supplies that she might need. I chided myself for not asking her directly. She had probably used up the herbs I had given her on one of my other visits.

When I next saw Richard, several days later, he looked harried and worn. He came to visit late one evening, again using our secret code when he knocked on the door. I drew him into the house, worried over the dark circles around his eyes and the skin that drooped on his cheeks.

"What on earth is wrong?" I asked, bading him sit near the fire. He rubbed his hands together.

"I've been running around every night getting supplies for the trip, and I have been busy during each day, setting up the medical room on board and checking each man for disease." He closed his eyes and leaned back into the rocking chair. "I'll be glad when I don't have to do this anymore."

"Can you rest here awhile?" I asked.

He shook his head and opened his eyes. "I'm afraid not. I have come to pick up a few more supplies that I didn't put on the list I gave you, and then I must be off again. We sail in just two days."

I unlocked the door to the apothecary and led him inside with the aid of a lantern. When we had gathered the items he had come for and tied them in a sack for him to carry easily, I extinguished the lantern and led the way through the house and to the front door.

"Someday it won't be like this," he said. "Sneaking about the village in the dead of night, hoping not to be seen by any people who might want to curry favor with the governor."

I nodded, my face grim. I didn't even want to think about Richard being caught. The governor would surely send the ship away to other waters farther up or down the coast; that is, if he didn't order the arrests—or worse—of all the men on board. I shuddered to think that I might never see Richard again.

He set the sack on the ground and held me an arm's length away from him. "I will do everything I can to come see you again before we set sail, but I cannot promise I'll be able to come. Just in case I can't come, promise me you'll be careful while I'm gone. I'm coming back for you when this voyage is over and I have served my time as the ship's doctor. Then we'll be married. We can stay here in New Jersey or go wherever you want to go. I will see you again."

He kissed me and was gone into the darkness.

Sadness was like a weight on my chest at the thought of not seeing him again for a very long time, but at the same time there was a hopefulness that I allowed to bubble at the back of my mind. I didn't know what was going to happen, but I had faith that God would return Richard to the shore of this cape and to me.

The next morning brought a surprise, one that left me shaken and afraid.

Captain Eli pounded on the locked door to the apothecary, bringing me running with alarm. Without thinking, I opened the door with what was surely a flushed face and looked at him angrily.

"What's the matter?" I asked. "You couldn't knock like everyone else?"

"Not everyone else has a secret like mine, girlie," he said with that ghastly grin. His breath almost caused me to gag. I beckoned for him to follow me to the counter where I kept the dried herbs and I handed him a fistful of mint.

"Chew this."

He put it all in his mouth and grimaced, but his eyes held a bright hint of menace that I could not ignore.

"What do you want? And do not refer to me as *girlie.* I have told you that once before."

"I hear there's a boat moored in the bay. A special kind of boat. One that the guv'ner don't want plying the waters around this cape."

I felt a tiny prickle of anxiety on my arms, but I stood up straighter and lifted my chin ever so slightly.

"And? Why should that interest me in the least?"

"Because I understand you know one of the crew, if you get

my meaning." He gave a vicious wink with his rheumy-looking left eye.

"I'm sure I have no idea what you mean."

"I think you do, gir ... I think you do."

I stared at him, wondering how much he knew about Richard. He stared at me, too, and we stood in the same spot in the apothecary until he finally spoke.

"I happened to see that selfsame crew member leaving here last night, carrying some little bundle. What do you suppose was in it?"

My heart began thumping in a rhythm I was sure he could sense. It was pounding so that I could hear nothing but a buzzing sound in my ears.

I couldn't let Captain Eli see me react to his revelation. I turned around so he couldn't see my face and made believe I was searching for something in the jars and bottles and packets behind me on the counter.

"What do you suppose was in the bundle he was carrying?" the captain persisted.

I took a deep breath to steady myself and turned to face him. "I'm afraid you're mistaken, Captain. I was sound asleep last night and I would have heard if someone had been in the house."

"Who said he was in the house?"

I almost bit my lip. I hoped my misstatement hadn't given Richard away. But it didn't matter—clearly the captain knew about Richard. My only hope was that he didn't figure out that there were medical supplies in the sack. I didn't want to be reported to the authorities for aiding pirates; it would be bad enough if Richard were to be caught. If I were caught, too, there would be no way for me to help him out of such a predicament.

"May I ask what you were doing around my house last

night?" I asked, hoping my haughty voice and the change of subject would be enough to halt his questioning.

"I needed a new bandage for me leg," he said, "but once I saw who was here I didn't come any closer. I know enough to stay away from them pirates."

"Certainly you don't believe there are pirates taking shelter in the bay below Town Bank." My ploy to change the subject hadn't worked.

"I know there are, girlie, and so do you."

"Don't call me …" I sighed. "I will give you a new bandage now, but you will have to pay me for it. Then I must ask that you leave and not come back."

"What should I tell people who are asking about you and the pirate?" he asked, his voice low, threatening.

"Tell them whatever you like. I have no knowledge of any pirate," I said. I couldn't keep my hands from trembling as I handed him the rolled bandage.

"Yer hands are shaky, girl." He spoke in a soft voice of which I would not have considered him capable.

"I haven't been eating well," I said in a rush of words.

"Here's some tea for you," the captain said, pulling a grimy tin out of his pocket. "Maybe it'll help you, but I don't think so. Yer problem's bigger than that." He gave me another foul wink.

"Be off, Captain." I opened the door for him and held it until he had left. I noticed that his limp, which had previously been so pronounced, was improving.

I closed and locked the door, then leaned with my back against it, taking big gulps of air. I needed to speak to Richard. He needed to know that there were people in Town who suspected his ship of carrying outlaws. I hurried to put on my cloak and left the house a few minutes later.

I was glad Captain Eli had disappeared from sight, so I wouldn't overtake him on my way into the village. He must have slunk into the woods to return to Town.

I hastened directly to the harbor, not caring who saw me. But when I arrived at the top of the embankment, something was wrong.

Richard's ship was gone.

Though I had known he would be leaving, I believed he would have time to visit me once more before his trip. Seeing the space where the large boat had been moored sent my mind reeling and I grasped the nearest tree for support.

I must have looked ill, because a man came running from the end of the street. "Are you all right, girl?" he called.

"Yes, yes ... thank you," I stammered.

"This is no place for a young lady like yourself," he scolded. "Your parents should know better than to let you come down here alone." He shook his head in disgust. He was a stranger, so he couldn't have known that I was an orphan. *My parents*, I thought with a cruel stab of sadness, *have no idea where I am.*

"When did that boat leave?" I asked, indicating the space where Richard's ship had been.

"Middle o' the night. Must have heard a good weather report," the man said. "You get along home now." He returned to where he had been working.

I was truly alone now. Patience had become so busy with duties in her home that she no longer had time to spend with me. Richard was gone, my parents were gone. Sadness swept over me like an ocean wave.

My walk home was slow. I couldn't bear to think of the long weeks, perhaps even months, stretching ahead of me without Richard and without Patience. Of course I could visit her, but it wasn't the same as before Baby William's arrival. We couldn't go for a walk or stand outside talking as we had just a few short months ago. It only gave me a small bit of comfort to know that William wouldn't be a baby forever and eventually Patience could spend time with me again.

I passed Widow Beall's house on my way home and was

reminded to give her some things from the apothecary for herself and her children. I did that when I got home. I prepared a bottle of mint syrup for stomach aches, a bundle of basil for simple headaches, and a few bandages for small scratches and scrapes that occurred on any farm. I put everything in a basket and filled the rest of the space with some bread and butter, then covered it all with a square of wool and set off for her house.

# CHAPTER 18

*I* knocked on the front door of the widow's house and stood waiting for someone to open it. I heard feet shuffling inside, so I knew someone was there.

"Hello?" I called. "It's Sarah, Widow. I've brought you some things from the apothecary shop." I waited another minute, all the while hearing footsteps just on the other side of the door.

Finally it opened just a fraction of an inch. Eyes peered at me from a spot closer to the ground. One of the widow's daughters.

"Hello, Millicent. Do you remember me?" I asked.

She nodded and opened the door a bit wider. She gave me a shy look.

"Is your mother inside?" I asked. The little girl shook her head.

"Where is she?" I asked.

A shrug.

I could hear the back door slam and one of the widow's older daughters came to the front door. "Millicent," she scolded. "Why are you standing there with the door open?" Then she noticed me standing on the other side of the doorway.

"Oh, Miss Sarah! I'm so sorry! I was in the privy and I didn't know you were here. Come, Millicent, step aside and let Miss Sarah in."

Millicent moved out of the way and I stepped inside. The warmth felt good on my hands and cheeks.

"Your mother isn't here?" I asked the older girl. "I brought some things for her from the apothecary, but I can leave them with you."

"That's very kind of you. I don't know where Mother is," the girl replied. She looked around and I could see her other sisters and her brothers had come from wherever they had been and were standing nearby. The other youngsters shook their heads.

"Then I'll leave the basket with you. There's bread in there, and butter, and some simple remedies for aches and pains."

"Thank you very much, Miss Sarah," the eldest daughter said, taking the basket from my hands. "I'll make sure Mother gets this when she gets home."

I thanked her and bade all the children good-bye.

I had rounded the bend just beyond the Beall house and was surprised to see Widow Beall coming around from the back of the barn in the field behind her house. I waited by the side of the road and waved to her when she lifted her head.

She was obviously startled to see me. She looked toward me, looked away, then jerked her head back and looked toward me again. Finally she returned my wave. I watched as she bent her head into her cloak and hurried toward her house.

The next several days passed quickly with a number of patients who visited the apothecary needing remedies and advice for different illnesses. When Pappa had been alive, I had noticed that apothecary visits for injuries increased in the summer, when everyone was working hard outside, and visits for illnesses increased in the winter, when everyone was indoors and in close quarters. The same pattern seemed to be repeating itself this winter. I hoped, not for the first time, that

Richard had stockpiled enough medicines for himself and his crew to remain healthy throughout their journey.

After a few days had passed I called at the Reeves household again to check on Arthur's progress. I hoped he was continuing to heal; I assumed he was, since no one had been round to the apothecary for help.

And when I saw him standing behind his mother as she opened the door to invite me inside, I knew immediately he was healing nicely. His color had returned and he was moving and walking without assistance.

He gestured for me to be seated opposite him at the table in front of the fire, and I noticed that he seated himself with little trouble. His face held the hint of a wince as he lowered himself onto his chair, but otherwise his smile never faded.

"I'm pleased to see that you're doing so well, Arthur," I said.

He nodded. "I must thank you again for the help you provided. I am most grateful."

Mistress Reeves and her husband stood nearby, listening to us. "I don't need to remind you, Arthur, that it was God's will that you survived and have healed so quickly," Mistress said, giving him a pointed look. The pastor nodded.

"Your mother is right, my son. Without God's help you never could have lived through such an ordeal, whether the apothecary was here or not." I nodded in agreement, though the words of Arthur's parents had diminished my happiness. If I hadn't been present to perform the bloodletting and provide guidance on the cold water treatment, would Arthur have survived? I doubted it. But I maintained my placid expression.

"Sarah, I would like to share some good news with you," Arthur said with a glance toward his parents. They were both smiling.

"What is it?" I asked, looking around at the three of them.

"I am going to be married."

His words hit me like a clap of thunder. I must have looked surprised, because Arthur asked, "Are you all right, Sarah?"

"Yes, yes. I'm fine, Arthur. That's wonderful news! I'm very happy for you. Who is the lucky young woman?"

"Ada Hutchinson. You are acquainted with her, I assume?"

*Braying Ada?* I hoped my shock didn't show in my face. I couldn't imagine a more ill-suited couple. And how had it happened so quickly? I chided myself inwardly, remembering how quickly I had come to realize that I loved Richard. Perhaps I had been wrong about Ada, about Arthur, or both. I was again glad I had declined his proposal.

"Yes," I said. "A lovely girl." My face was no doubt flushed at having to lie, and I hoped no one noticed it. I was tempted to share the news of my engagement to Richard, but I thought better of it, knowing Arthur deserved time to bask in his happiness.

"I'm so sorry, Arthur, but I must be going. I have chores to do outside before it gets dark," I said. I stood up to leave. Arthur and his father bowed and thanked me for coming to check on him while Mistress Reeves walked me to the door.

"You must be shocked at the news of Arthur's engagement," she said in a low voice.

"I *am* a bit surprised," I admitted.

"She is such a sweet, simple girl. We are thrilled with his choice," she said, and she raised her eyebrows at me ever so slightly, as if inviting a challenge. "She may not be able to read, but she can provide comfort to Arthur in the way he deserves." I gave her a sharp look. I wouldn't have expected such a forthright remark from her, one that left no doubt of their feelings about me or about Arthur's fiancée. I wondered how they would have reacted if I had accepted his proposal. Something told me they would not have been as thrilled.

I went home lost in thought, and I was glad for the diversion of chores in the cow pen and the chicken coop to take my mind off Arthur's upcoming marriage. I had a nagging urge to run to Patience with the news. She would be incredulous. But I didn't finish the chores until it was almost dark and I did not have enough time to run to her house and return to my own house before the road would be in complete darkness.

That night I read by the light from the fireplace, wishing I had company. Truth be told, I was feeling a bit sorry for myself. My parents were gone forever, Richard was gone and would likely not return for many months, and Patience was too busy with her own family to spare me any time. I wished she could join me in front of the fire—she loved reading and would have relished the chance to improve her skills.

When the knock sounded on the door, I jumped right out of the chair, startled. I glanced quickly at the door, thankful that it was locked. Another quick glance confirmed that the door to the apothecary was locked, too.

I crept to the door as quietly as I could manage. I stood next to the crack in the doorway, breathing heavily, trying to decide whether to answer the knock.

I took a deep breath. "Who's there?" I asked in a loud whisper. *Why am I whispering?* I thought. *There's no one else here and it's quite likely the person on the other side of the door knows that.*

"It's me, Miss Sarah—Mister Browne."

*What is he doing here?*

I opened the door slowly, peering around it to make sure it was, indeed, Mister Browne.

It was. He stood outside with his hat in his hand, looking behind him. "May I come in?" he asked.

My gaze followed his as he glanced over his shoulder; I shivered. Was he worried that he had been followed?

I opened the door to let him in, then stood back as he came into the room. I gestured toward the rocking chair, but he remained standing.

"Miss Sarah, I have learned something about Captain Eli that I thought you should know."

"What is it?" I asked, my senses alert.

"He was not on the cape the night your mother went missing."

*But he had to have been nearby!* My mind was reeling. *How else could he have watched my mother being attacked by wolves? How else could he have been responsible for her death?*

"Are you all right, Miss Sarah?"

I sat down hard in the rocking chair I had just offered to Mister Browne. I stared into the fire for a long moment, trying to collect my thoughts.

"How did you learn this?" I asked, looking up at him. His gaze was sympathetic.

"Your mother's name came up at a meeting among some of the men from the church. They were talking about Arthur Reeves and his fiancée, and someone mentioned that you had turned him down." Here Mister Browne had the grace to blush at such a statement, since the entire affair was clearly none of his business, nor the business of any of the men from church, save perhaps Pastor Reeves.

I suppressed a grimace and nodded, encouraging him to continue.

He cleared his throat. "One of the men suggested that you might not have declined Arthur's proposal if you had had a mother to advise and guide you. Talk then turned, naturally, to what had happened to your mother. I suggested that perhaps Captain Eli might know more about her disappearance than anyone had realized, but one of the men said Captain Eli was in Philadelphia at the time. He remembered it specifically because he witnessed the captain hearing about Ruth's disappearance when he returned to Town and the captain was overwrought with emotion."

So the captain was not responsible for Mamma's disappearance, and since her clothes and shoes had never been found and had certainly not been eaten, it was also likely that wolves had not been responsible for her disappearance.

*So who was?*

I stood up on wobbly legs and thanked Mister Browne for coming by at such a late hour to give me this bit of news. He put his hat on and touched the brim as he went out into the cold night.

"I am very sorry about this, Miss Sarah. Though I didn't want to think any of the gentle folk in the area was responsible for your mother's disappearance, it appears the perpetrator may be in our midst. I would like to see the culprit brought to justice. And Captain Eli—well, he's not exactly of a gentlemanly caliber. I would have thought if anyone in the village or hereabouts were responsible, it would be him. I'm sorry you have to start at the beginning again."

"Thank you, sir. It may take the rest of my life, but I will never stop looking for the person responsible for my mother's disappearance."

Mister Browne nodded once and turned toward the road. I watched him leave, my heart heavy. I had hoped the mystery would be solved and Captain Eli would be brought to justice for his lewd and errant ways.

But it was not to be, and I would have to find the answers I sought another way.

I slept poorly that night. My conversation with Mister Browne weighed on my mind and every time I fell asleep my dreams were full of violence, of hungry wolves, of Captain Eli's unpleasant face.

I lay abed until the sun was high in the sky the next morning. I knew the animals needed food, that their pens needed to be cleaned, that there were other chores to do, but I simply couldn't bring myself to get up.

It was the urge to use the privy that got me up finally, and as much as I wanted to return to my bed afterward, I was hungry, too. I dressed slowly, retrieved two eggs from the chicken coop, and fried them over the fire. I paired my eggs with toasted and buttered bread, and I was finishing my meal when there was a knock at the apothecary door.

I hastened into the apothecary and was surprised to see Arthur standing outside the door. I opened it and invited him inside.

"Arthur!" I cried. "What are you doing this far from your house? You'll tire yourself."

"I've come because my mother is in need of help," he said in a rushed voice, his eyes worried.

"What's the matter?" I asked.

"We don't know. She's burning up with fever and can only utter words that make no sense. Please, Sarah, can you help her?"

"I hope so," I answered, already rushing about the shop and gathering herbs and syrups in a small basket. My mind churned with memories of my father's brief illness. I hoped Mistress Reeves wasn't suffering from the same ailment.

I followed Arthur down the road toward his house, noting his slow gait even as he tried to hurry. He urged me to go on before him, but I couldn't do that. If I left him alone on the road and something happened to him, my guilt would be paralyzing.

So I waited for him. Despite my impatience, I hid my frantic desire to get to his house to examine and hopefully treat his mother.

When we finally arrived at the house the pastor was just getting there, too. Peter, the younger son, had run into Town to fetch him while Arthur went to the apothecary.

"What is wrong with her?" the pastor asked his son.

"Fever," was the terse answer.

We all hurried into the house. "How long has she had the fever?" the pastor asked Arthur.

"It came on suddenly about two hours ago," Arthur answered.

The pastor turned to me. "Sarah, can you do anything to help her?"

"We'll start by letting some cold air into the room," I instructed. "Open the front door so air begins moving through here. Cooling down her skin might help cool the fever." I hurried to examine Mistress, feeling her wrists and cheeks. Though hot, their color was normal.

"Pastor, would you please get a mug of cold water? I'd like to get her to drink some, if she can and will," I said. He hastened from the room to fetch the water. When he returned, I added a few drops of hyssop essence to the water and held it to her lips.

"Mistress, it's me, Sarah. Here, please try to drink this. It might help you feel a bit better."

Mistress moved her head slightly so she was facing me. Her eyes were closed, her lips pressed together. She shook her head.

"Mother, please take a drink like Sarah asked," Arthur pleaded. "She's brought something to help you."

Mistress clearly wanted to say something, but didn't seem to have the strength to do so. Her hand waved limply against the coverlet.

"Mother, please," Arthur repeated.

The pastor stepped up to the bed and took one of his wife's hands in his. "Wife, what is it you want to say? We're listening." Once again she waved one flaccid hand toward the door to the bedchamber.

"Perhaps she wants the door closed," Arthur suggested.

"I think it is necessary to leave the door open for another minute, just to cool down the air in the house," I said. Mistress waved her hand again, this time with a bit more strength.

"Do you want us to leave the room, my dear?" the pastor asked.

Mistress, exhausted from the effort of gesturing with her hand, lay back against the pillow and moaned.

"We can't all leave," Arthur said. "Someone has to stay with her."

"I'll stay," I offered. "That way I can continue to examine her and perhaps get her to sip some water and oil from the mug. And while I'm in here with her, would you, Arthur, return to the apothecary and bring me some more hyssop oil?" I fished in my pocket for the key to the door and held it out to him. "And if you wouldn't mind, Pastor, could you perhaps hasten to the general store in the village for a packet of needles? I am out of them in the apothecary and I may need them."

"For my wife?" he asked.

"I do not yet know, but it is possible."

"Very well. We'll be back quickly. Arthur, take Peter with you. He's faster and can run back with the oil if necessary," the pastor said. Arthur nodded his agreement. They left the room hurriedly.

When they had both departed I left the door open and peeled the coverlet from Mistress's body. Her bedclothes were dry to the touch, so she hadn't been able to sweat out any of the fever. I raised the mug of water and hyssop oil to her lips again, beseeching her to take a sip. Her eyes followed my movements and she managed a frown.

"I know it doesn't have a pleasant taste, Mistress, but you must try to drink some," I said. I sat down in a straight-backed chair next to the bed. "Please. Just one sip, and then you can rest. Once you take one sip it becomes easier to drink more."

She shook her head.

"Please. Just try," I urged her.

She opened her eyes and glared at me. I sat back in the chair, surprised. I set the mug down on the floor next to the bed and leaned toward her.

"Very well. I won't ask you to drink the medicine just yet. Can you speak?"

She continued looking at me out of eyes that flashed with ... something. Was it frustration? Was it peevishness? I was a little surprised that she could summon the strength to exhibit any emotion in her fragile state. I pulled the chair closer to the bed so I could better hear her if she tried to say something.

"Is there something else I can do for you, Mistress?" I asked.

In response, she reached for my hand and held it in a shockingly strong grip.

"What is it? What are you trying to say?" I asked, bewildered.

She nodded slightly toward the door to the bedchamber. "Close the door," she rasped. I did as she asked and returned to the chair next to the bed.

There was a bright look in her eyes. "You think you're as good as God," she said. Her voice was stronger than it had been just a moment before.

"No ... no, I don't," I stammered, not knowing what else to say. Mistress was delirious.

"You think that because you have the tools and remedies to help people heal, you are God. You are not. You are nothing but a village apothecary, the daughter of another rural apothecary and a heathen woman who didn't obey God's law."

I stared at her, the realization dawning on me that this woman had gone mad.

"Mistress Reeves," I said in the most soothing voice I could muster, "you are ill. You need to rest. You must stop trying to speak." All that was true, but her words were scaring me, too. I didn't want to hear any more.

She ignored me. "I am not half as sick as you think I am, Sarah Hanover. I've tricked you. God cannot be tricked. Therefore you are not God."

"Mistress, I would never say I was God. I would never pretend to be God. I *could* never come close to being like God."

"You lying wretch," she seethed. "When was the last time you prayed?"

"Last night," I answered honestly. "I always pray at night before I go to sleep. I always pray after I read my Bible, too."

"Girls such as yourself have no business reading the Bible. It is the charge of the upright men of the community to teach women what it says."

"I don't agree, Mistress. I am very grateful to be able to read the word of God for myself, along with any other books I can get my hands on."

"That's just your problem," she said. Her voice was getting higher as she became more agitated.

"What is?" I asked.

"Your heathen practice of reading books not of God's own word."

I didn't know what to say. Was she actually accusing me of being a heathen because I read books other than the Bible?

She lay staring at me, clearly waiting for me to say something.

"I'm sorry you feel that way, Mistress, but God gave me the ability to read and I consider myself lucky to have that privilege."

Her eyes narrowed; her nostrils flared slightly.

"Do you know what will happen to you?"

I shook my head and looked toward the door, wondering if Pastor or Arthur and Peter had come home while I was in the bedchamber with Mistress Reeves.

"You sent them away, so no one will hear you," she said, raising herself onto one elbow and reaching for the coverlet. She wasn't nearly as ill as I had assumed. Her actions now explained why her coloring had been normal and there was no sweat on her body. A chill ran through me like a shudder and my hands grew clammy and cold.

"What are you talking about?" I asked. I stood up and moved

away from her, eyeing her warily as she swung her bare feet onto the floor.

"Just like your devilish parents, you will end up in the place of eternal damnation for your practice of reading drivel that mocks God!" she cried, now standing next to the bed.

I was horrified. Surely my parents were not suffering through all eternity for teaching me to read. "That is utter nonsense," I told her, sticking my chin out and hoping she didn't sense the fear coursing through my body.

"Is it?" she sneered. "Then why did God allow your mother to die in such a horrible way? Why didn't He protect her from attack? I'll tell you why—because she alone was responsible for teaching the girls of this land to read and thus to disregard the teachings of God!"

"That's not ..." I stopped. How did Mistress Reeves know Mamma had died in a horrible way? No one knew why Mamma had disappeared. Certainly we assumed she had been attacked by something—either wolves or a violent scoundrel—but no one had ever found any evidence of it.

As I hesitated, my mind racing to figure out what Mistress Reeves was saying, she took a step toward me. This was not the feverish woman I had found when Arthur bade me visit his sick mother.

"What are you doing?" I asked.

"I am going to make sure the women and girls of this village are not subjected to your wicked teachings any longer. I am going to make sure you join your witch of a mother and your evil father in the fires of hell." This she spoke in a low, deadly tone, her voice filled with hatred and madness.

"My parents are not in hell!" I cried. The very thought of it was paralyzing.

"I know they are," she whispered.

"No, you don't!" I cried. I had to get away from this woman, but her words kept me rooted to the spot.

"I lured your mother here under the pretense of illness and I saw the light of her life go out. I *know* she is in hell. I heard her screaming about the fires when she died." Mistress Reeves's calm voice teetered on the cusp of lunacy.

I wheeled around to grab the door handle. I had to get away from this woman. But I wasn't fast enough and she reached for my hand. Her strength was astonishing, given the limp state in which I had found her.

"Let me go!" I cried.

"Of course I will not! You will die just like your mother did, in this room, in flames that will escort you straight to the devil himself!"

I gasped and the room started spinning. My mother, in flames? Is that how she had died? Is that why no one found evidence of her clothes? Because they had been burned?

I felt myself falling and the room went dark. The last thing I remembered was trying to think of something from the apothecary shop that might help me escape the darkness, but there was nothing. It didn't matter, anyway.

# CHAPTER 19

When I awoke I was on the floor, my hands tied behind my back and my feet bound with thick rope. Mistress Reeves was kneeling next to me, pushing me toward the fireplace. Flames leapt in the corner of my vision and my skin burned from proximity to the fire.

I screamed and Mistress slapped me across the face. I stopped screaming simply out of surprise, my face stinging, but then I began anew, using every bit of strength I could muster to scream and wrestle myself out of her grasp. She tried slapping me again, but I twisted my head just in time and she missed, striking the floor instead. She shook her hand as if to toss away the pain.

A cry of rage escaped her throat and a look of pure wildness lit her eyes. I squeezed my eyes shut and rolled toward her, knocking her off balance. She fell to one side, her knees coming out from underneath her skirts. She was very thin—her strength wasn't coming from her muscles, but from within, from a place of sick depravity.

She used her legs then to push me toward the fireplace once more. With my hands and feet bound, there was little I could do to escape her, save for writhing on the floor to get away from her. The wooden floor planks ripped my skin as I tried to slither away from her, but she rose to her feet and used her body to push me toward the fireplace.

I was exhausted. In a tiny corner of my mind I began to wonder if it would be easier to let Mistress Reeves push me into the flames, to give myself up to the fate that had met my mother. Surely if I allowed death to overcome me I would meet my mother and father again. That tiny thought began to grow and I could feel my muscles losing the battle, my breath coming in shallow rasps. Mistress obviously felt it, too, because she began pushing harder. My body was only protesting from reflex now, from the natural tendency to avoid a painful death. I closed my eyes again, wondering how long it would take, how terrible the pain.

But in another tiny part of my mind, I could suddenly hear Richard's voice struggling to make itself heard. He was promising to return to me after his voyage at sea. I saw his face in that part of my mind, his bright eyes, his gentle smile. And before I knew what was happening, that part of my mind began to overtake my thoughts of death, of joining my mother and father in eternity. I wasn't ready to die, and certainly not at the hands of a madwoman.

The scream that erupted from my mouth was so piercing and so shrill that it surprised even me. Mistress Reeves was clearly taken aback, since she stopped pushing me and stared into my eyes for the briefest of seconds.

And in that moment, she knew something inside my mind had changed. I saw the fear rising in her eyes, the momentary uncertainty and the renewed determination to kill me rather than accept the fate that surely awaited her if I survived.

But her determination wasn't as strong as mine, and it wasn't enough to dislodge the thought of Richard from my mind.

Rolling onto my side, I kicked her legs, sending her tripping and sprawling backward onto the wooden floor. As she scrambled to rise again, I used my feet to drag a chair between us. When she was standing and moving toward me again, I kicked the chair toward her, knocking her down again and hurting her this time. She grabbed her ankle and howled in pain; I could see a huge lump forming over the bone almost immediately. She stood and advanced toward me again, limping and using the chair to help support herself, I wriggled under the table and lay on the floor on the other side of it, panting from exertion and fear. She was moving more slowly now, the pain making her wince with every step, and as she came around the table, I rolled underneath it to the other side, out of her reach.

Her eyes burned with fury when she wasn't able to reach me. She looked around and a monstrous smile spread across her face as her gaze alit on the fireplace poker. Using a wall for support, she limped over to where the poker stood up against the side of the fireplace. She gripped it in both hands and turned around to where I lay on the floor. I looked around wildly for a place to escape where she couldn't reach me with the poker, but it was a small room. I rolled farther under the table again as she took her first swing toward me.

The whizzing sound the poker made as it narrowly missed my head was the only sound I heard for a moment, but it was quickly followed by a loud *thump* as Mistress Reeves lost her balance and fell forward into the edge of the table. She whimpered as she hit the ground, probably due to the pain in her ankle but possibly because she had hit her head, and I took the only chance I had.

I rolled toward her with a speed that I wouldn't have thought possible, gathering slivers of wood from the floor in my skin as I moved. She was searching for the poker with her eyes and making grasping motions toward it with her hands. I was wearing shoes, so it didn't hurt me when I found the poker with my feet and kicked it out of her reach. Then I aimed my feet at her and wriggled forward, pushing her toward the fire in the grate with every ounce of strength I had. She was still crying out in pain from having fallen into the table, and I hardly think she knew what was going on, such was her surprise when I kicked her hard in the back.

She slumped toward the fireplace and I caught a quick glimpse of abject terror on her face. She screamed and I think the shrill, horrifying sound of it spurred me to further action. I kicked her again, and this time her hand flung into the fire as I pushed her body closer to the hearth.

Her shriek was bone chilling.

"Stop, please stop!" she cried. She looked at her hand as if it was something she didn't recognize and screamed again, and this time the front door flung open and Arthur and his father rushed in.

Taking in the macabre scene in a single second, they pulled Mistress Reeves out of the fire; the pastor tended to her while Arthur ran to where I was weeping on the floor, panting and spent.

"What happened?" he cried. He looked over his shoulder at his mother. "Mother, are you all right?"

She could only shake her head and sob into her skirts. The pastor looked stricken with confusion and shock.

"Father, put her hand in water," he ordered. The pastor stared at his son for a moment and then stood up and reached for a bucket that was on the floor. He ran outside and was back in an instant, snow filling the bucket to the brim. He gently picked up his wife's hand and placed it in the snow as she screamed in protest, and as her hand touched the frozen water she fell back in a stone faint.

I lay on the floor watching the scene with relief and gratitude for their arrival. Arthur finally noticed that my hands and feet were bound and he grabbed a knife that hung around his waist. He quickly cut through the rope and threw it aside.

"Why are you bound?" he asked. He looked at me with a complete lack of comprehension.

"I fainted and your mother tied me up!" I yelled. It wasn't Arthur's fault; my shock was fading, being rapidly replaced by furious wrath.

"Why did you faint?" Arthur still didn't seem to grasp the gravity of what had happened while he, his younger brother, and his father were away from the house.

"She killed my mother!" I shrieked. The pastor's head jerked up from where he was trying to revive Mistress Reeves. Both men looked at me and then glanced at each other, clearly appalled at my words.

"That's nonsense," the pastor said. His voice was quieter than I would have expected.

I took a deep breath. I was safe, Mistress Reeves couldn't hurt me anymore. I needed to calm down and speak so I could be heard and understood. I lowered my voice. The pastor tapped his wife's face again, trying to get her to wake up, but he was watching me as I spoke.

"Mistress Reeves admitted to killing my mother," I said in as calm a voice as I could muster. "She said my mother was teaching heathen practices to the girls and women of Town Bank. She killed her." I slumped, finally allowing the realization of Mistress Reeves's actions to permeate my mind. I bent forward and began to cry into my skirts, much as Arthur's mother had done just a few minutes before. I let the tears flow in a torrent of sadness, grief, and shock, not caring what either Arthur or his father thought or said. When I looked up at them they were both staring at me. The looks on their faces told me everything I needed to know: they knew I was telling the truth.

When Mistress Reeves awoke, she immediately started screaming again from the pain in her hand. Arthur and his father looked at each other again, clearly at a loss over what to do to give her some relief.

I staggered from the stool where I was sitting and made my way over to her on the floor. She cowered when she saw me moving toward her. She called for her husband and he stood up with a start, but I motioned for him to be seated, explaining that I was going to help her.

I examined her hand without touching it. The silent screams inside my head begged me to let her suffer and die where she lay on the floor, quite possibly in the same spot where she killed my mother, but something else inside me couldn't let her perish when it was within my ability to help her.

I grasped the fireplace poker and she let out a scream. I held it away from her as I explained that using a hot object to draw more heat out of the burning wound would help her heal. When I had explained that to her, I turned to her husband and asked him to fetch wine. His eyes narrowed in suspicion, but I explained that wine was necessary for healing. When he still looked skeptical, I explained that no one would be drinking the wine—I was going to pour it on his wife's skin.

That seemed to appease him and he left in search of wine while I turned to Mistress Reeves.

"Arthur, I want you to hold her arms so she doesn't inadvertently touch the poker," I instructed. He looked at me with something akin to horror.

"Arthur, you must. If she moves, she might very well touch the poker with her burned skin and she'll be burned all over again."

Mistress whimpered. Arthur let out a long, labored breath and knelt on the floor next to his mother. She cried out loudly when he grasped her upper arms, but she held still while I held the poker over her hand. Before long she was begging me to stop, saying the heat from the poker was making her burn worse. Just then her husband arrived with the wine, so I put the poker aside and grasped the bottle. I poured it in a slow stream over Mistress's hand as she howled in pain. To my utter relief, she fainted again.

That made my job easier, so I continued pouring wine over her hand as Arthur collected the runoff on a cloth he held under her arm, casting anxious glances at her face as he waited for her to wake up again.

When I had used all the wine in the bottle to soak her burns, it was time for me to leave. I had stayed for as long as I could, looking at her loathsome face and treating wounds that I secretly hoped wouldn't heal. Without another word to Arthur or his father, I fled from the Reeves house and back to my own. I was still weak from my ordeal at the hands of Mistress Reeves, but my urgent need to get to safety in my own house was too great to be impeded by physical pain and exhaustion.

Once in my house, the trembling began. How I wished my parents or Richard were with me. The shock of Mistress Reeves's words hadn't abated. I still flinched in horror every time I thought of her telling me she had killed Mamma.

Mamma, who had been the kindest, gentlest, most generous woman I had ever known. Dead at the hands of a pastor's wife.

I knew what had to happen.

When I got to the lawyer's house in Town Bank, he received me immediately. As he listened to the details of my encounter with Mistress Reeves, the expression on his face grew from grave interest to shock to horror.

"My dear Miss Hanover!" he cried. "We must go to the authorities with this information straight away!"

There was a problem, though, since one of the main enforcers of the law was Pastor Reeves himself. The lawyer made the decision to go to the town officers immediately. They, like him, were astounded by the account of my torment at the hands of Mistress Reeves and promised to send an officer of the law to the Reeves household at once.

It was much later that night when there was a knock at my door. I was seized with an icy fear that wouldn't let go of my throat.

"Miss Sarah?" a voice called. "It's me again, Mister Browne."

I trudged to the door in my stocking feet, unsure of what awaited me when Mister Browne came into the house.

I opened the door slowly and faced the man standing outside in the cold, clear air of midnight.

"What can I do for you, sir?" I asked. "Forgive me for not inviting you inside, but you can see I am ready for bed."

"That's all right, Miss Sarah," he said. "Several men from the village took a vote and elected me to come tell you."

"Tell me what?"

He hesitated. "Mistress Reeves is dead."

I should have been surprised, but I wasn't.

"How did it happen?" I asked.

"She threw herself into the fire when the men from town went to arrest her, and she died shortly afterward."

So she had died in the same way my mother did. It was strangely comforting.

"Thanks for letting me know, Mister Browne. If you don't mind, I'm going to bed now."

"Wait, Sarah. There's more."

"There's more?"

He nodded. "A woman from one of the farms hereabout came to my office yesterday. She told me a gruesome tale of being attacked recently by Captain Eli in Widow Beall's barn."

I let out a gasp. "Is she all right?"

Mister Browne nodded. "Her husband found out about it and beat Captain Eli, causing serious injury."

*So that's the story behind the captain's leg injury,* I thought grimly.

"It seems, upon further investigation, that Captain Eli had a spot set up in the barn where he would receive certain female visitors," Mister Browne continued.

"Did Widow Beall know about it?"

Mister Browne sighed. "It appears that she did. He paid her to keep that part of the barn cleared for him. It also appears, however, that she was unaware of his attack upon the woman recently."

I couldn't believe what I was hearing. I now understood how Widow Beall could afford the ingredients for sugar pie, despite having no discernable income. And I also understood why she had declined to let me clean up the area outside her barn. She was protecting her income. Then I was struck with a more horrible thought.

"Mister Browne, do you think my father knew about this ... this arrangement?"

"I doubt it, Sarah. He would sooner have given Widow Beall money than let her earn money in such a disgraceful way." I knew in my heart that he was right—my father would never have let her stoop to such depths for money if he had known her predicament.

"Is Widow going to be brought up on charges?" I asked.

Mister Browne shook his head. "We understand it was her way of surviving to provide for her children. She'll suffer from the things people will say about her once word gets around, but we won't make her suffer any more than that. Captain Eli, on the other hand, will be leaving Town at daybreak. I'll make sure of that. I've spoken to him, and for once he wasn't taken with drink. He told me that he did try to get your sweet, gentle mother to go away with him, but she refused. He didn't bother her again after that, though his obsession never diminished. I'm embarrassed to say he was no more than a lustful and contemptible wretch who lied about his dealings with her."

I could do nothing but nod, overwhelmed with all I had just learned from the magistrate.

"You take care of yourself, Miss Sarah." He gave me a sympathetic look and turned away. I closed the door and sat in front of the fire for a long time, missing my parents, concerned for Widow Beall's future welfare, and wishing Mistress Reeves had never been born. I thought back to the letter I had found in Pappa's trunk. I wondered if Mamma had been afraid of Mistress Reeves, or whether it had been Captain Eli to whom she had referred in her letters to her mother. I supposed it didn't matter anymore, now that both Mamma and Mistress Reeves were gone. I shuddered at the thought of Captain Eli, relieved that he would be leaving the cape, never to return.

The village was abuzz for days with the death of Mistress Reeves, and I received another round of visitors who came to tell me how very sorry they were to hear about the gruesome way my mother had died.

I should have been grateful for their good intentions and their expressions of sorrow, but I wanted it all to end. I wanted Richard to return. I wanted to be left in peace to attend to the people who needed me in the apothecary. I wanted to tend to the animals on my small farm. I wanted my parents back.

And one day the visitors stopped coming. Almost every resident of Town Bank and the surrounding farms had come to the house over the past two weeks and I knew it was time for me to move on.

I gathered up the books my parents and I had brought from England and set off for Patience's house, where her mother awaited her first reading lesson. Following the death of Mistress Reeves, I could think of but one way to continue honoring my mother's memory, and that was by teaching the women and girls of the cape to read. All of them, if possible.

# CHAPTER 20

*M*onths passed. Life had settled into a routine that was almost comfortable, but not quite. Only one thing could have made it better.

Patience's mother had a difficult time learning to read, but was finally beginning to make progress. Patience's sisters were better at it, and they helped their mother with extra lessons in the evenings.

Baby William was growing into a chubby little boy with cheeks the color of English roses. He crawled everywhere and his sisters quite often found themselves giving chase if he was left alone for even a moment.

When I wasn't busy in the apothecary I was teaching the women and girls from the village, often mothers and daughters together, how to read and write. It was slow work, but after every lesson I returned home with a smile on my face and I left smiling pupils in my wake.

But that one thing that would make everything better eluded me still ...

Until one Sunday.

I had been to service in the newly-constructed church and I

was sitting outside the door to my house in the rocking chair. Since coming to New Jersey, I had often dragged it outside in the summertime in order to catch the breeze while I read and rested.

I must have been dozing, for I awoke with a start when I heard a shuffling noise coming from the side of the house. I was immediately alert.

"Who's there?" I asked as I stood up.

I stood still, waiting for a response, but all I heard was the buzzing of summer insects.

I stepped quietly to the corner of the house and peered around, hoping I wouldn't come face-to-face with a wolf.

But it was a man.

I could see only his back. His long dark hair was pulled back at the nape of his neck and he crouched on the ground, tying a scraggly ribbon around a small bouquet of wildflowers.

He turned around when I gasped.

Richard had returned.

～

# AUTHOR'S NOTE

I have taken certain creative liberties with some parts of the story. For example, the language used by European settlers in Cape May County in the early eighteenth century was more formal than that we use today. For the sake of clarity, I have chosen to use language that is less archaic for the modern reader.

In my research I have not found evidence that there was a tavern in the tiny settlement of Town Bank, though there is substantial evidence that alcohol was in profligate use at that place and time. I placed a tavern in the village for purposes of the story.

There was probably no apothecary nearby to serve the needs of the citizens of Town Bank in the late seventeenth and early eighteenth centuries, though there is some evidence that at least one resident of the town had been banished from New England for practicing witchcraft, which she may have continued to practice in Town Bank. At the time witchcraft could have been considered a dark healing art, but I have chosen not to address such practices. An apothecary would have been a valuable member of the small society. In fact, in the year 1714 (when the fictional William Hanover dies of a sudden fever), there was a plague that swept through Cape May County, killing a full ten percent of its citizens. Though medical knowledge at that time was rudimentary at best, an apothecary's skill with herbs and medicines may have been quite helpful.

Similarly, the presence of a full-time lawyer would have been unlikely in Town Bank. However, the lawyer in my story was primarily a farmer, and it is entirely possible that such a person existed to help with the legal needs of the citizens, and in particular for assistance with land deeds and business dealings.

I hope you've enjoyed *Cape Menace: A Cape May Historical Mystery*. Would you consider leaving a review? Reviews are important for authors because they increase a book's visibility. It's easy—just a couple sentences will do. Consider the following if you need some inspiration:

Did you like the characters? Did you care about what happened to them?
Did you like the setting? What did you like best about it?
Did you learn anything about eighteenth century Cape May?
What was your favorite part of the story?

Remember, the best way to help an author is to leave a review and tell someone else about a book!

On the next pages you will find the Prologue and Chapter One of *Trudy's Diary*, Book One in my Libraries of the World Mystery series. I hope you enjoy it!

# TRUDY'S DIARY

## A LIBRARIES OF THE WORLD MYSTERY

### PROLOGUE

*D*aisy Carruthers left New York City because of a murder investigation.

When her boyfriend, Dean Snyder, fell from their ninth-floor balcony to the deserted Brooklyn sidewalk below late one evening the previous year, it was Daisy who had been named the prime suspect in his death. It was Daisy who spent the better part of a year trying to clear her name, trying to get people to stop thinking of her as a ruthless criminal, trying to get everyone to understand that Dean's tragic fall had been accidental.

Trying, most of all, to grieve the loss of someone she had loved so completely.

As long as she was a suspect, she couldn't move away from the city, couldn't start fresh. She couldn't bear the thought that she might be remembered as a black widow of sorts, killing her mate so she could continue life unencumbered by a weighty relationship.

But the day came when a witness stepped forward to

confirm what Daisy had been saying all along: that Dean had been alone on the balcony that night and that he had fallen over the railing trying to catch a cocktail napkin which had blown out of his hand. The witness had not realized for many months that there was an investigation surrounding Dean's death because it had so obviously been an accident.

The witness's story confirmed what Daisy had been saying all along.

Dean's death was finally ruled an accident, and Daisy was no longer a suspect.

By then, she was ready to leave the city that had been so cruel to her. She wanted to start fresh in a city she had never visited with Dean.

So she packed her bags and moved to Washington, DC.

# TRUDY'S DIARY

## CHAPTER 1

### ONE YEAR LATER

*D*aisy stood pouring herself a much-needed cup of coffee in the galley kitchen of the Global Human Rights Journal offices. Rain from her jacket dripped onto the linoleum floor.

Jude Laughton, the senior editor, looked up from the table where she was reading the headlines on a discarded newspaper and frowned. "You're getting water all over the floor. Are you going to wipe it up?"

Though Daisy had worked for the journal in Washington, DC, for almost a year, Jude was still as cold as she had been the day Daisy interviewed with her.

"Of course I am. Just give me a minute."

"Why don't you carry an umbrella?" Jude asked.

"Because I keep forgetting to put one in my tote bag," Daisy answered, a hint of annoyance creeping into her tone.

"It's not that hard to remember. I keep one in my briefcase all the time." Daisy rolled her eyes and walked to the paper towel dispenser on the wall. She pressed the lever several times, tearing off a long sheet of the barely-absorbent paper toweling, then wadded it up and placed it on the water that had fallen from her coat. Jude's lips curled in a tight grimace, but she didn't say anything.

Daisy threw away the paper and left the kitchen without another glance at Jude. She walked into the small conference room between her office and Jude's office and took several manila folders out of her tote bag, spreading them on the table in a circular pattern. Jude walked by, steam curling from the mug of coffee she carried. "What are you doing?" she asked. Nothing escaped Jude's curiosity about Daisy and her assignments.

"Just organizing my work. My desk isn't big enough," Daisy answered with a sly peek at Jude. She started moving folders around, standing back with her arms crossed. She knew it irritated Jude that the Editor-in-Chief, Mark John Friole, had given her so many assignments, and laying everything out for Jude to see gave her a jolt of devilish glee. Jude, though higher in the pecking order at Global Human Rights Journal, wasn't as good a researcher as Daisy and she didn't hide her jealousy well. But it was only natural that Daisy, as a Master's-level anthropologist, should be the better researcher--if she weren't, it would just be embarrassing.

Daisy pulled out her laptop and sat down to wait for it to boot up.

"I have a meeting in this room today, so you won't be able to keep your stuff in here," Jude said.

"I'm not planning to. As soon as I get these folders organized, I'll work in my office." Daisy was pretty sure Jude didn't have a meeting later.

Jude was just turning away to go back to her office when Mark John came into the conference room.

"Update me, please. What are you working on?"

Jude stood up a little straighter and gave him a big smile.

"I've made significant progress on the clean water story," she said brightly, batting her eyelashes.

"Good," Mark John said, nodding. "Daisy?"

"I'll be ready to submit my current story today, then I'll dig more into the story about childbirth centers."

"I have an idea I'd like to run by you, Daisy, if you would please hand off the childbirth center story to Jude."

"Sure," Daisy answered, suppressing a slight grin at Jude's scowl. "Do you want to talk about it now?"

"Yes. In my office, please." Mark John left.

"Don't be long in Mark John's office," Jude said. "I need to talk to him about something."

Daisy gathered up her notebook and sharpened pencils and left the room without another glance at Jude.

Mark John wasn't in his office when Daisy knocked on his door, which was partially ajar. "Mark John?" she asked, poking her head into the room. There was no answer. She went inside and sat down in one of the chairs in front of his desk. She idly flipped through her notebook, then cracked her neck and checked her watch. When five minutes had passed and Mark John still hadn't appeared, Daisy stood up and wandered around his office, picking up and setting down various mementos from his travels. She went to the window behind his desk and looked down onto the ground far below, at the people scurrying about with their umbrellas up, hiding their faces. She felt another surge of annoyance that she had forgotten her own umbrella that morning. As she turned away from the window, a photo of Mark John and his wife, Fiona, caught her eye. She picked up the photo and gazed at it for several moments, focusing on Fiona's wide smile. In her time at Global Human Rights, Daisy had only heard Mark John mention his wife's name a few times. Daisy wondered what she was like. She set the photo back in its spot and sat down to wait.

Mark John came into the office a minute later.

"Damn secretary can't do anything without asking me twenty questions about it," he said, settling into his chair.

Daisy didn't reply.

"This won't take long," he said. "I've been thinking--we should do a feature about women's roles in this country. You know, how they've changed since the time when the United States was an agrarian society."

"Sounds interesting, but that's going to take up more space than just one article."

"I know. I'm thinking we'll do it in three parts."

"All right."

Mark John sighed. "You're probably going to have to tell Jude about this, but take your time telling her. The last thing I need right now is listening to her complain about why I gave you the assignment instead of her."

Daisy grinned. "I'll keep it quiet as long as I can." She looked at her watch and chuckled. "I give it about two minutes. Maybe three."

Mark John ran his hand over his forehead and squeezed his eyes closed for a long moment. "Well, I don't feel like dealing with it today. I have a headache."

"If you prefer, we can talk about particulars of the assignment later," Daisy said. "In the meantime I'll get started on some preliminary research."

"Sounds good." Mark John looked around his office, puffed out his cheeks, and let out a sigh.

"You okay?" Daisy asked.

"Yeah," he said, rubbing his face with both hands. "There was a burglary in my neighborhood last night. A house just across the street and a couple doors down from us. A bit unnerving, you know?"

"I'm sure it is," Daisy replied. "That's scary. Was anyone hurt?"

"Not that I know of."

"Do you have an alarm system?"

"Yes, but so did the people whose house got hit. They had left a window open downstairs."

"Kind of defeats the purpose of having an alarm," Daisy said.

"Yeah," Mark John said curtly. He shook his head in disgust. Daisy knew the conversation was over and she left the office. She walked by Jude's office on the way to her own.

Jude smirked and pushed her chair back. "I'll go see him now. You were longer than I expected."

"He wasn't in his office so I had to wait for him," Daisy said. "He has a bad headache," she warned.

"I just want to ask him a couple quick questions. I won't bother him," Jude said.

Daisy returned to the conference room and sat down.

# NEWSLETTER SIGN-UP

Please visit https://www.amymreade.com/newsletter to receive monthly news, updates, promotions, contests, recipes, and more.

# PRAISE FOR AMY M. READE

*The House on Candlewick Lane*: "As in most gothic novels, the actual house on Candlewick Lane is creepy and filled with dark passages and rooms. You feel the evil emanate from the structure and from the people who live there ... I loved the rich descriptions of Edinburgh. You definitely feel like you are walking the streets next to Greer, searching for Ellie. You can feel the rain and the cold, and a couple times, I swear I could smell the scents of the local cuisine." From Colleen Chesebro, reviewer

*Highland Peril*: "This is escapism at its best, as it is a compelling mystery that whisks readers away to a land as beautiful as it is rich with intrigue." From Cynthia Chow, Kings River Life

*Murder in Thistlecross*: "Amy Reade's series has a touch of gothic suspense, always fun, and this particular entry has the extra added attraction of the old Clue board game (later a movie that was equally delightful) wherein the various suspects move around the castle and the sleuth has to figure out who killed who, how and where." From Buried Under Books

*The Worst Noel*: "You'll feel like you've spent an exciting holiday vacation in beautiful Juniper Junction, Colorado, with characters you immediately adore." From Goodreads review

*Dead, White, and Blue*: "Dead, White, and Blue, the second in the Juniper Junction Holiday mystery series, by Amy M. Reade has everything I look for in a mystery novel and more. Of course, an intriguing plot and a unique and realistic setting are important elements in a novel and the author did a great job with both.

But characters I can relate to and come to care about are the most crucial ingredients to me and this series has them." From Amazon review

*Be My Valencrime:* "What I like about an Amy Reade cozy mystery is that the author's writing is easy reading, the characters are all likable (except perhaps the characters who might be the murderer) and the setting is lovely. But Reade goes beyond these cozy attributes and gives real-life problems to her main character, Lilly, a single mom of teenagers as well as the daughter of an aging mom who is showing signs of dementia." From Goodreads review

*Trudy's Diary:* "The dual narratives of present day Daisy Carruthers and nineteenth century Trudy kept me turning pages and guessing about outcomes until the very end." From Goodreads review

# ABOUT THE AUTHOR

Amy M. Reade is a recovering attorney who discovered, quite by accident, a passion for fiction writing. She writes in the Gothic, contemporary, historical, and cozy mystery subgenres and when she's not writing, she loves to read, cook, and travel.

Amy is the *USA Today* and *Wall Street Journal* bestselling author of *Secrets of Hallstead House, The Ghosts of Peppernell Manor, House of the Hanging Jade,* the Malice series, the Juniper Junction Holiday Mystery series, the Libraries of the World Mystery series, and the Cape May Historical Mystery Collection.

You can visit Amy on all her social media platforms by visiting https://linktr.ee/amymreadeauthor.

Made in the USA
Middletown, DE
12 June 2020

97820485R00163